THE TRAIL AT HAND

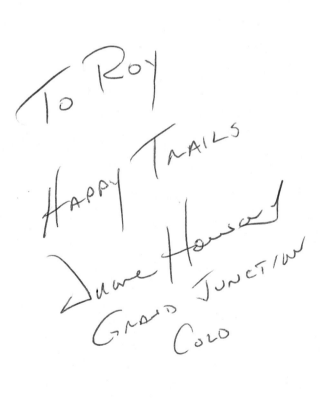

To Roy

Happy Trails

Duane Howard
Grand Junction
Colo

THE TRAIL AT HAND

▼

Duane Howard

Writers Club Press
San Jose New York Lincoln Shanghai

The Trail At Hand

Writers Club Press
an imprint of iUniverse.com, Inc.

For information address:
iUniverse.com, Inc.
5220 S 16th, Ste. 200
Lincoln, NE 68512
www.iuniverse.com

ISBN: 0-595-18751-X

Printed in the United States of America

DEDICATION

To Peggy Gore and Bill Ellis who gave much time and effort to this story by reading and making helpful suggestions.

To Fort Umcompahgre and the City of Delta, Colorado (the site of the first trading post in western Colorado) who so graciously provided the cover photograph.

And to my wife, Joyce, whose contributions are bountiful.

CONTENTS

FOREWORD

A man cannot glimpse all of his journey, only the trail at hand, the few steps before him and the few steps behind.

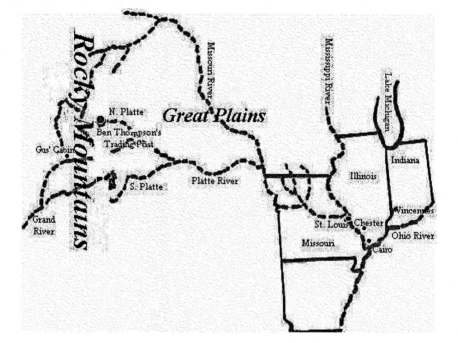

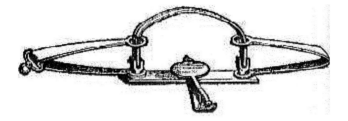

Chapter I

Packing out

Zack paused to sniff in the breeze as he approached the opening in the pines leading to the alpine meadow. He dismounted several yards back, knowing the meadow was ahead, and figured to make sure he was alone before stepping out into the open. For two days he worked at losing that bunch of horse stealing Crows and he continued to be cautious, not wanting to let them stumble on him if he could help it.

A recent wind felled pine served as a perfect screen to view the meadow below. This particular meadow was like a big finger to a much larger meadow off to his right. He made a slow visual scan in that direction, the

most likely direction to see his adversaries, if they were still looking for
him. He detected no movement. He then scanned the meadow directly in
front, again no movement. The sun warmed him, on this south slope that
was dry and free of snow, unlike the opposite slope where snow lingered in
the dark shadows. The meadow was a half-mile long and a quarter mile
wide with a narrow ribbon of a stream running down its length, disappearing into the dense pines. Zack's destination was a group of large boulders
that looked like huge out of place sentries, guarding the far side.

Satisfied there were no unusual activities in the meadow he backed quietly from the shielding pine. A scurrying sound in the pine needles caught
his attention and he slowly eased into a low hunkering position. A weasel,
still in his white winter coat, was stalking a mouse. The weasel was so
intent in his hunt that it was not until he completed his swift, savage
attack and was preparing to carry his prey away that he saw the hunkering
man. He briefly startled then darted along a rotting log, carrying the
mouse in his mouth. Upon reaching a safe distance he dropped the mouse
and reared up on his hind legs to get a better look at the intruder. His
bright, black eyes were a dramatic contrast to his snowy face, as he held
motionless. Having satisfied his curiosity he picked up the mouse and disappeared off the log.

Zack found himself smiling at the weasel's antics. He took another look
into the meadow. On the far side he saw some subtle movement in the far
tree line. A young mule deer cautiously ventured from the shadows toward
the stream. She drank from the stream and began to browse. Suddenly she
stiffened in alarm and bounded back into the trees. Zack came to a state of
readiness, drawing his rifle tighter, as he scanned for the danger. "Griz," he
said under his breath as he spotted a large bear ambling across the
meadow's outlet. When left undisturbed Grizzly Bears tend to mind their
own business, but can be curious critters and are known to walk right into
a camp just to see what it was all about. This one had traveling on his
mind and soon passed out of sight.

Zack eased his grip on his Hawken Rifle as the low, deep in the pit of his stomach, sinking feeling returned. The image of finding Gus all tore up by a bear filled his mind. He started to think again on that day, almost a month ago, when he heard the soft snort of his horse. Zack looked back to where Hunka and the mules were tied. The horse's color blended so well in the trees that at first Zack had difficulty making him out. That was one of the things Zack liked about his big horse. His color was that of a bull Elk and could blend into a variety of settings. Zack's unadorned buckskin clothing gave him the same advantage. Hunka softly snorted again and Zack knew he was getting restless. The better part of an hour had elapsed since he dismounted and scanned the meadow.

One last look and sniff convinced him the meadow was free of immediate danger. Still, out of habit, he moved with the quietness of an experienced mountain man toward his animals. The softness of the years of accumulated pine needles whispered beneath his moccasins as he walked up the slight incline between the pines. Stooping slightly to pass under a low branch, he caught the movement of a small gray squirrel feeding at the base of a tree. The squirrel quickly ascended the tree and skirted out of sight to the opposite side.

Hunka scraped in the pine needles with a hoof as Zack approached. Zack rubbed the horse's neck as he reached for the reins and softly said, "What's amatter ol' boy, getting restless?" Zack glanced at the mules, which appeared to be dozing. "We'll be moving now," he spoke as he stepped away from the horse, increasing the tension on the reins. The horse followed, heading for the spot to start traversing the hill down into the meadow. The slack rope tying the first mule to the saddle horn became taut, causing a slight startle reaction in the mule. His eyes widened and he raised his head as if he was going to resist the disturbance to his dozing, but stepped to follow the horse. A rope to the second mule was tied to a cross strap on the bundle secured above the canvas panniers. This mule reacted differently to the rope becoming taut. He appeared to continue his dozing as he followed.

Zack liked these mules he called One and Two. Both were young, strong, and had good endurance for packing a load. One was faster and more agile than Two, and Zack chose him to carry the panniers containing the things a man needs to survive and make a living at trapping. Two was Gus' mule and was loaded with three plews. Each plew contained sixty compressed pelts; mostly prime beaver with a few fox and otter thrown in. Each plew was assembled by compacting the pelts in a heavy log press, then tightly wrapped in deer raw hides. When the raw hides dried the pelts were even further compressed into manageable ninety-pound bundles.

The plews were tied to a pack frame made by Gus and his skill at woodworking was obvious with only a casual observation. He carved and fitted the oak frame to the mule's back, then covered the lower supports with tanned buffalo hide. When standing empty the frame resembled a bow-legged sawhorse. The joints were so well fitted and strong that Zack was sure that if Two ever fell on it something other than the frame would break. Buffalo hide straps secured the plews to the frame and a braided broad cinch and harness secured the frame to the mule. The plews were covered with a tanned Elk hide giving Two the appearance of a peculiar humped creature.

Zack picked his way through the trees and just before stepping out into the open he paused to scan the meadow again. Finding nothing amiss, he traversed the initial steep slope. The noon sun was warming the slope as he stepped into the green grass and wild flowers of the meadow floor. He felt a beginning of being revitalized by this familiar, peaceful meadow. Hunka tugged at the reins indicating a desire to graze. Zack tugged back saying, "At the stream."

In a short time they were standing near the narrow stream. Zack released the reins as Hunka lowered his head to nibble on the spring grass. Zack then stepped back to release the ropes to the mules. The mules were thirsty and were pulling against the knots in their efforts to get their heads down to the water. "Whoa," called Zack disapprovingly, causing the mules to pause so he could loosen the knots. He let the ropes go slack and the mules drank. Then, like Hunka, they began to graze. Zack moved a few steps up stream and knelt at the stream's edge. He scooped the snowmelt water in a cupped hand and drank. During his third scoop he noticed Two was doing more shifting of weight than grazing, indicating a desire to be relieved of his load. He went to the mule, calmed him with a forehead rub and said, "I'll get those plews off you in a bit." Zack reached for the lead rope and tied it to the panniers on One. He mounted Hunka while holding the rope to One and headed directly for the large boulders.

Zachary Clayton rode easy in the saddle and when mounted on the big, dark tan horse became one with the horse. Over time each had learned to communicate with the other, forming a confederation of purpose. Hunka was more than just transportation, he was a partner. And this was even more true since Gus had been killed. Man and horse served the other well. The caravan moved in an orderly line under the direction of the tall, powerful man who knew how to maintain the discipline needed to live and work in this mountain wilderness.

While dismounting Zack surveyed the familiar campsite and seeing nothing to indicate it had been occupied since his last stop here began to remove Hunka's saddle. The sun glinted off the copper butt plate on the rifle in the saddle holster. Zack had yet to fire Gus' .45 caliber N.Niles rifle. He preferred his .58 caliber Hawken and never understood why Gus chose the lighter round. The first time Zack heard Gus respond to a "Why?" from another trapper, Gus simply said, "A man makes do with what comes his way." Gus was not a man to waste words nor a shot. Zack figured to fire the rifle when he felt it was safe to rifle hunt again.

Stepping back to set the saddle down Zack looked at the big horse. He was a strong, intelligent animal, even in color and disposition. Zack acquired him from a Dakotah warrior named Pesla two years earlier. Pesla called the horse Catka, which meant Left Hand, for the horse's ability to turn very sharply to the left and rapidly return to a full gallop. Pesla painted a red hand on the left shoulder that had long since worn off. The stallion carried Pesla on raids and had proven himself worthy of being a favorite warhorse.

The Dakotahs were always at odds with the Kangi. The Kangi, more commonly known by the trappers as Crows, were skillful horse thieves and often targeted the Dakotah camps for the fine horses they raised. Zack preferred to call them "skulking horse stealers" for their sneaking way of patiently scouting a camp and slipping in at night to steal horses. Pesla trained the stallion for war and, not wanting to lose him in a Kangi raid, trained him to give an alarm of rough snorting at the approach of a thief. The price for the horse was one smooth bore trade musket and shooting lessons. Pesla was the first of his camp to own a firearm and, although would never be any more than just a fair shot with the cheap musket, was the envy of his fellow warriors. The stallion adjusted well to the leather saddle and heavier rider. A month or so following the trade Zack named him Hunka, Dakotah for a relative of choice. The bond that formed between them reminded Zack of the Dakotah custom of adopting another as a relative, a sign of respect and regard.

With practiced steps, Zack unloaded the mules and led all three animals back to the stream. He paused at a small pool for another drink and caught his reflection in the still water. He studied the reflected full bearded face under a wide brimmed dull brown hat. His beard was dark brown with lighter brown hair hanging loosely from under the hat. Removing the hat, to further study the image, his hair fell across his forehead into his eyes. His thought of, *I'll get Gus to trim me up,* was complete before he caught himself. Gus was dead.

Zack dipped his hands into the water and vigorously washed his face. The cold water caught his breath but he kept washing until his hair was matted onto his forehead and water dripped from his beard. Rising, he took a deep breath and sorrowfully exhaled. He stepped away from the pool to relieve himself. Shifting the Harper Ferry pistol aside in the wide leather belt he fumbled for the single deer antler button holding the fly closed. He drew another quick breath in response to his cold fingers and turned his back to the breeze.

Leaving the animals to graze he returned to the campsite. At first he looked for signs of his last stay here, none were obvious. He had buried the ashes, turned and scattered the blacken firestones, scattered the animal droppings and raked the area with a branch. The natural elements completed the erasure over time. Zack had camped here on three previous occasions and felt an exclusive ownership for this pristine meadow. To himself he called it, *My meadow.* He looked to the tree line behind the boulders trying to peer beyond the curtain-like darkness. A hundred men could be hiding in the black timber but men in this country did not ordinarily travel through the maze of fallen logs and dense upper foliage. In his more immediate surroundings Zack was dwarfed by the largest of the boulders, which loomed over him four times his height. Scattered about were five smaller boulders, a result of ancient natural forces, and were placed as to offer strategic positions should he ever have to defend himself here.

Zack arranged the plews and panniers in the order they were to be loaded. Then he found the thin horsehair ropes to stake out the animals later. He loosened the bedroll from behind the saddle and carefully unrolled it. He kept a short hunting bow and arrows in the bedroll. He laid them aside and positioned the bedroll next to the saddle and plews. He decided it would be safe to have cooking fire and soon gathered an armload of tree limbs. He scrapped out a shallow depression in the soil and surrounded it with double-fist-sized stones. Most of the stones were fire blackened on one side and he was careful to again face the blackened sides inward.

Zack had eaten only venison jerky and pemmican for two days in cold camps and was ready for a hot meal. He had to leave a venison haunch behind when those skulking horse stealers jumped him in his camp three days ago. Even though he felt safe to have a small cooking fire he decided it was too soon to rifle hunt. He could set some snares for small game or he could bow hunt. He decided to bow hunt. As he strung the bow he said to himself, *wanassa*, Dakotah for "it's time to make meat." The bow and arrows had been traded from a Dakotah weapon maker for a dozen iron arrowheads. The bow was three and one half feet long, made of Ash wood and had a sinew bowstring. Each of the six arrows had a razor sharp iron arrowhead. He chose two arrows; the most he could shoot in an ambush hunt.

Zack gathered Gus' rifle and pistol to hide them in a deep crack in a large boulder. He hated to leave his animals and goods unguarded but he wanted to hunt and if trouble did come he could return in short order. He checked the powder pans on his rifle and pistol. From his possible bag he removed a leather strap and fitted it to his rifle, which he then slung across his back. Picking up the bow and arrows, he was ready to hunt.

He followed the tree line up the meadow looking for a game trail. The spot where that deer had earlier entered the meadow would be a good place to look for sign. He had not gone far when he saw fresh tracks of an Elk cow and calf. They probably grazed earlier in the day and were bedded down in the black timber. He found the tracks of several deer in the shadowed snow and followed them into the pines. Just a few feet off the game trail he came to a large pine, which had fallen against a larger pine forming an inclining bridge to some sturdy branches, fifteen feet high. Testing his weight with each step he walked up the incline and at the apex quietly got into a sitting position on one of the branches. From this high point he could peer back into the dark forest and turning in the other direction could see the sun shining on the meadow grass. It was now a matter of waiting. The pungent and earthy odors of pines and rotting wood filled the still air. A few distant calls of Jays filtered through the trees as Zack tuned his hearing to the forest.

Zack's thoughts turned to Gus. He felt obligated to get Gus' share of the pelts to a family member. Gus never spoke of a wife or children, only of brothers and not much about them. Zack searched his memory for clues of Gus' origins, which were few. Gus did not talk much about his past. *Where did he come from? Where did he learn woodworking?*

Engrossed in his thoughts, Zack did not hear the soft sound of hooves on the forest floor below. When he saw movement a doe was within his designated ambush site. Zack's breathing shifted into very quiet, shallow breaths as he drew the bowstring and arrow into firing position. As he took aim the doe caught his scent, her ears raised in alarm and just as her muscles started to spring into escaping danger Zack let the arrow fly. The escape maneuver was just beginning when the arrow hit her. The razor sharp head cut its way into a lung. The doe tried to continue her escape but her leap was impaired and she was heading toward a tangle of exposed roots on an uprooted pine. She collided with the root mass, knocking pieces of soil loose as she tried to get her legs placed for a more directed leap. Zack notched the second arrow as her back legs sought firm footing in the soft soil. He was at a full draw when she tried to leap over the root mass. She was weakening from the arrow wound and did not clear it. Just as she landed Zack released the second arrow. The iron arrowhead struck her behind an ear and came to a sudden stop in her skull. The arrow shaft splintered with a resounding crack. The sound startled Zack and if he had not grabbed a branch he would have fallen from his high perch.

Zack gingerly picked his way down the pine bridge as the doe was death twitching. He pulled her from the root tangle when the twitching stopped. In the Dakotah fashion he thanked the doe for her meat. With some difficulty he knife pried the arrowhead from her skull and broke away the remains of the shattered shaft. He extracted the first arrow from her chest and found it to be intact as he cleaned the blood from it with a hand full of soil. With swift, sure strokes he completed rough butchering and carried the hindquarters up the pine bridge to hang. Pumas and wolverines were the only animals he knew of who might try to climb for this meat cache but it would be safe from bears, wolves and coyotes.

Returning to his butchering he piled the backstraps, deboned front quarters, heart, liver, and a portion of the small intestine on the hide and

tied it into a bundle. After burying the shattered arrow shaft he loaded the
bundle on his shoulder and set out for camp. He kept just inside the tree
line to minimize his movements being seen. He exited the trees just above
the big boulder. Hunka and the mules were grazing peacefully where he
had left them. Hunka looked up to the movement and, after recognizing
Zack, returned to grazing.

Zack cut a sturdy forked branch from a bush and tasted the wood at
the cut. Feeling satisfied the wood bore a neutral taste he cut two more
branches for forked skewers. Then in camp, with a few flint and steel
strokes he soon had a wisp of smoke rising from a wad of punk. It burst
into flame with some gentle puffs and he placed it beneath a small
mound of twigs in the fire pit. He was ready with pieces of kindling and
larger pieces of firewood. When the fire burned down to hot coals he
placed the forked meat over the heat by leaning the branches against the
firestones and weighing down the ends with other stones assembled for
that purpose.

He filled a small iron kettle at the stream and balanced it on the firestones. He arranged the ingredients for the rest of his meal and proceeded
to mix seasoned flour, rendered bear fat and water. There were not many
biscuits left in his flour sack, as was true for all his trading post supplies,
and he was careful to avoid spillage. Zack was ardent about biscuit making
and secretly delighted in the compliments offered by those who tried
them. With nimble hands he patted out three pieces of dough and placed
them in a greased iron skillet. He placed a tin plate, which fitted the skillet like a lid, over the biscuits and worked the bottom of the skillet into
the coals. With his knife and a branch he lifted out larger coals and placed
them on the plate. Then he added some coarsely ground coffee beans to
the steaming kettle. After turning the meat to allow for even roasting he
added more coals to the tin plate. The sun was almost down to the tops of
the tall pines when his meal was ready.

The tall pines obscured the sun as Zack dipped his cup into the slow
boiling coffee. Between short puffs of breath he sipped the steaming brew

from a blue metal cup. The venison steaks and biscuits filled his belly and now he was savoring the coffee. Carrying his cup he rose and walked out of the shelter of the boulders to scan the meadow. This time it was not as a vigilant man, rather as a man who felt a sense of peace for the first time for almost a month. He let his mind drift, enjoying the moment.

He returned to the fire and placed small pieces of wood close to the kettle. The wood crackled as it ignited, sending up gray puffs of smoke that quickly dispersed in the alpine air. Setting his cup down, he noted the light would be fading soon so he began to prepare for the night. He brought in the horse and mules and staked them out so he could quickly load them during the night if such became necessary. When his camp was arranged to his liking he decided to check his cache.

During his first trip to this meadow Zack cached some survival items as a precaution. They were bundled in a buckskin pouch. With some effort he rolled a larger than a horse's head sized rock a half turn so it rested against the wall of the largest boulder. Then standing on the rock he stretched his six foot frame toward a jagged hole in the boulder wall. His hand barely reached the bundle. He gripped the bundle and brought it down to his lap as he sat on the rock. He examined each item in turn: a knife, six iron arrowheads, a braided horsehair rope, a pair of moccasins and a piece of gray flint. He scrapped the rust from the knife and arrowheads by rubbing them on the rock. Then he applied a coat of bear lard to them. When he was finished he placed all the items into the pouch and returned it to its hidden recess. He also rolled the rock to its original position. The light had faded to the point that he couldn't make out the details of the tree line. He returned to the fire and his coffee. Well fed, and now very tired, he moved to his bedroll. Placing his weapons in easy reach, he pulled the blanket to his chin and drifted to sleep.

CHAPTER 2

THE CROWS

Five days ago Zack closed up Gus' cabin on the Yampa River. He bear greased and buried Gus' wood working tools in the corral, hung Gus' saddle in the rafters of the cabin and secured the shutters from the inside. Gus built this log cabin over the course of a couple of summers and it was the best built structure of its kind Zack had ever seen. It was built into a low hill with a south facing door and had a thick sod roof. The logs were well fitted and required only a small amount of chinking to seal out the winter wind. Gus had packed in metal hinges for the door and shutters. The stone fireplace was raised on the back wall with built in iron hooks from which pots and meat could be suspended. On the left wall a small low door opened into a firewood shed and was constructed of split pine. The door and shed could be used as an escape route if necessary. Completing the structure, a lodge pole pine corral fence connected to the wood shed. A pole lean-to was built at the end of the corral to shelter the horses and mules. The stack of hay, behind the lean-to, was gone. It was a warm, comfortable cabin and Zack hated to leave but it was May and time to head east, across the mountains.

Zack pulled the door closed and stacked stones to seal it. He also placed a flat piece of shale stone over the chimney opening. This is how it was when he and Gus arrived last fall, so he would leave it the same. As he fitted the stones, Zack planned his route to the North Platte River and to Ben Thompson's trading post. He figured the trip would take close to a month. Maybe more if he stopped to visit the Mahto, the Grizzly Bear Clan of the Dakotahs he wintered with two years ago. They would have moved out of their winter camp and hunting buffalo in the foothills, east of the mountains. If he came across them he would stop to visit and trade. He still had a few trade goods left and perhaps they had some good pelts.

They were a proud, hospitable people and he learned some of their customs and ways. He also learned about the horse stealing Crows from the Mahto and on one occasion joined a raid on a Crow camp. The brief skirmish, with only a few injuries, was rewarded with the capture of more than thirty horses. It was not the pitched battle Zack thought it would be. He was somewhat relieved by the Mahto's desire to only hit and run. Once the horses were herded away from the camp, leaving the Crows on foot, the Mahto were satisfied to retreat back to their own territory. The prize of the horses and the many touches on the enemy in ritual combat was cause for a celebration in the Mahto village. Zack was not a student of warfare but thought if there must be a war then what happened on the raid was a good, civilized way of fighting one.

Hunka and the mules waited impatiently for him to complete his tasks. They had been loaded and ready to go for almost an hour as Zack put the finishing touches on closing the cabin. They appeared anxious to get on the trail again

Zack traveled for one uneventful day but in the midmorning of the second day he was cutting through a grove of heavily budding quaking Aspens when he abruptly drew Hunka to a halt. Before him was a set of fresh horse tracks. He dismounted to study the tracks. Set in a patch of soft, wind swept soil at the edge of the grove was a clear, complete set of horse tracks. They were only a few hours old and were made by a horse carrying a rider who was traveling light. The impressions made by Zack's animals were deeper when compared. The rider had ridden through the quakies at a walk, probably hunting. But who or what was he hunting?

Remounting, Zack decided to follow the tracks to see if he could learn more. The tracks took him across a large meadow and in the middle the tracks were joined by another set of similar tracks. Then the two sets led him to a stream that tumbled out of a ravine at the edge of the meadow. The riders had stopped for water and left clear moccasin prints: Crows! There was no mistaking the smooth soles and pigeon toed walk.

What are they doing here, this far from their hunting grounds, this high, this early in the year? Zack puzzled. He could only conclude that they were hunting trappers. Nothing else made sense. Perhaps they knew he and Gus had trapped and wintered in this area. Maybe these two were only scouts for a larger party. They could be young bucks out to make a name for themselves by returning to their village with a load of goods and horses stolen from a trapper. After following the tracks for another mile Zack figured they were heading for the river to the southeast. It would be a likely area to catch a trapper just finishing a spring hunt or packing out. There were a few beaver left in that area but not in the numbers since Zack and Gus trapped it in the late fall.

Zack decided to continue his journey to the northeast and only changed his original plan by staying out of the open as much as possible. It would be slow going but safer. He rode at a steady pace for the rest of the day, not fast enough to excessively tire the animals but fast enough to put some distance between him and those skulking horse stealers. He rode until almost dark before he began to look for a place for a night camp. He knew this would be a fireless night. He exited a shallow creek, after riding in it for about a mile, onto a gravel bank. He hoped to minimize leaving a trail to follow, for he knew the Crows were excellent trackers, and he took advantage of the creek and gravel.

After riding another mile, he dismounted and scouted a stand of pines perched on a bluff overlooking a meadow. The steep ridge behind was thick with fallen timber and looked impenetrable for a man on horseback. The pines offered good cover and he could defend himself among them. If he had time to run from danger, he would be going down hill, into the meadow with plenty of room to try to elude a pursuer. With just enough light remaining Zack unloaded the animals and hobbled them. He chewed on a piece of jerky as he further studied his surroundings and planned how he would load in the dark before first light. He hung a venison hindquarter in a tree just in case a hungry four-legged critter came calling for it during the night. Wrapping himself in a blanket, Zack settled back against a log to mentally rehearse a rapid departure from this cold camp. By this time it was dark, a no-moon, deep-in-the-pines kind of darkness and all was quiet. Zack drifted asleep with his rifle across his lap. At sometime during the night he awakened with a start to the sounds of animal droppings hitting the ground. He had his rifle up and ready before he realized what the sound was.

Zack loaded the mules and saddled Hunka in the twilight. By full light they were in another stream with Zack letting Hunka pick the route between the high banks. They traveled this way for better than an hour until the high banks gave way to easy inclines lined with quakies and willow brush. When he was looking for a place to exit the water Zack was suddenly startled by a bull Elk, who must have been napping in the willows. The bull became aware of the wading sounds approaching him and cleared the stream in a single leap just a few yards in front of Zack. Reflexively his Hawken came up to the sudden movement. The sudden movement also startled Hunka who reared. Zack was able to stay mounted and pulled on the reins to regain control. The sound of the bull crashing through the willows rapidly faded while the travelers regained their composure.

After a sharp curve the stream became wider, more shallow and opened up so Zack could see more of the distant terrain. Leaving the stream he chose an area to let the animals graze and rest while he climbed a knoll to view more of the landscape. Thus far his sense of direction had him heading for the meadow in which he had previously camped. He would know better by sighting familiar landmarks as his journey continued.

Later in the day he came upon the largest beaver pond he had ever seen. The characteristic pointed stumps dotted the area with some of them appearing freshly chewed. He avoided the open beaver cut by staying in the trees. He began to note the landmarks thinking this might be an area to return to someday. The pond contained three large beaver lodges and he could see a beaver towing a leafed branch toward one. On the far side a small flock of black and white ducks were paddling about and softly whistling to one another.

Zack rode toward the dam end of the pond, heading for a stand of pines. Another beaver was pulling a branch into the water from the bank when he heard the approaching hooves. The beaver left the branch, entered the water, and gave the surface a loud slap with his tail before he dived for the bottom. The sound drew Zack's attention in that direction where he noticed a forked stick protruding from the water about three feet from the bank. This was a typical placement for a beaver trap. He dismounted and walked toward the stick, looking for tracks as he went. The trap was set and visible in the cold, clear water but lacked a castor stick lure. An experienced trapper would have dipped the end of a flexible stick into his vial of castoreum then positioned the stick so that the odor would attract a beaver to it and above the trap. The forked stick did not look freshly cut; in fact, it looked like it had been there since last fall. Zack hunkered on the bank to study on the deserted beaver trap. He decided the trap had been forgotten or something happened to the trapper. Zack waded in and extracted the trap. He hung it from a limb figuring the man who left it might pass this way again. It was the decent thing to do.

The trail continued to climb toward the break between the two mountains looming ahead. He wished he could be at the pass before dark but the animals needed to rest before the incline became steeper. Zack dismounted at the edge of a clearing and led them into the grass. As they grazed he checked the loads on the mules. While reaching to tighten the cinch on Hunka he got the distinct feeling he was being watched. He fought an urge to run for cover as he pretended to further check the loads while in fact he was scanning the trees. If the watcher was a four-legged critter he might not see it. If the watcher was another trapper he would call out. If the watcher was a skulking horse stealer no sign nor sound would be noticed. There were no movements in the trees and no call rang out. Zack had learned to trust this feeling, a sense of ominous apprehension. It brought him to a state of high alertness but it also produced urges that may not be the best course of action. He hated to wait, waiting for something to happen, but waiting was just what he needed to do. He decided to pick up his pace.

The increased pace and the steep grade were tiring the animals. Zack knew if it came to running from a pursuer he would lose the race. He studied the trail behind him, without obviously doing so, and saw no signs of being followed. The feeling of being watched persisted. Since he couldn't out run them, and since hiding probably would not fool them, the only remaining logical option was to set up an ambush. If Crows were following and were unaware that he was ready to be raided he would have the element of surprise on his side. He began to look for a place to camp and to set up an ambush.

Zack choose a small stand of quakies to set up his night camp. He unloaded the animals, staked them out to graze, started a fire and hung the venison haunch he was packing. He cut off two thick steaks and roasted them when he had a good bed of coals. While he ate he studied the details of the surrounding terrain. A large grove of Aspens occupied the mountainside to the east and appeared to continue over the ridge. He figured to cross the meadow during the night, making his way through the trees and over the ridge.

As the sun set Zack brought the animals in from grazing and tied them to a picket line. He kept the fire burning brightly, long past his usual habit of letting it die down as darkness fell. He figured if a large band of Crows were out there, waiting, they would have made an appearance by now. So it must be two men, three at the most, waiting for the right moment to slip into his camp. Even three Crows would hesitate from a straight on attack on a single, well-armed trapper. They would take the prudent, well-tried action of sneaking into a camp using darkness and stealth.

The sky was clear and moonless as Zack quietly began preparing for the expected intruders. He quietly loaded the mules, saddled Hunka, and tied them together for the trail. He placed the venison haunch on top of some arm-sized limbs next to the fire. In the dim firelight the pile could be mistaken for a sleeping man. Then he took a position of lying down along a rotting log just at the head of the animals. He was ready with a tomahawk in his right hand, his Hawken in his left and two pistols in his belt. He tuned his hearing to the night sounds. Coyotes yipped in the distance, a night breeze fluttered dry leaves and small pops and cracks emitted from the fire pit.

After a time the animals drifted into sleep as he maintained his wary vigil. Just when he was about to quietly shift his weight for more comfort, Hunka snorted. Zack's heart began to race, interfering with his ability to listen for the intruder. He focused on quiet, shallow breathing. In the minute it took to calm himself he also became more alert. The horse and mules were only dark silhouettes against the star filled sky. Hunka snorted again and a mule shifted his weight. Through these familiar sounds Zack began to hear at least two men slowly crawling into his camp. For several agonizing minutes he tried to sound locate the closest man. He then heard a horse stealer sliding on his belly, on the opposite side of the log, toward the animals. As quiet as the Crow tried to be his anxious breathing gave him away. Zack sat up slowly, calculated where the man's head ought to be on the rising dark form, and let go with a powerful swing of the tomahawk. The Crow was reaching for a lead rope and looking in the direction of the glowing embers when the blade hit him on the top of his head. The only sound he made was air escaping from his lungs. Zack brought his rifle to his right hand and came to a noiseless crouch. He left the tomahawk in the intruder's head for fear extraction would make too much noise. The horse and mules shifted uneasily because of the close activity and odors. Zack took advantage of the noise to come to a better attack position.

Not sensing his partner was dead the second Crow, also crawling, continued with his task of grabbing a lead rope. He was not aware that Zack had him located. Zack swung his rifle in a downward stroke. The heavy octagon barrel struck the man on his left shoulder with bone breaking force. The Crow collapsed with a deep groan, which agitated the mules and they began to protectively stomp. The Crow could not escape the heavy hooves and was stomped and kicked into unconsciousness.

Unknown to Zack a third Crow horse stealer, who intended to at least disable the sleeping trapper, had just discovered the venison haunch and limbs. He correctly assumed, since the trapper was not asleep where he ought to be, the ruckus he was hearing by the animals was the result of his companions encountering the trapper. He incorrectly assumed the trapper to be distracted, or maybe even injured, and made a running attack in the direction where he suspected the trapper to be.

Zack heard him coming and saw the rushing dark form but not in time to evade the attack. Zack was knocked to his back, losing his rifle in the fall. The Crow had his knife in his hand and slashed. Zack rolled and sensed the knife slice through the air. He reached for a pistol but they had become entangled in his belt during the fall. Rather than take the time to extract one he reached for his knife. The Crow heard Zack roll and dived in that direction. Zack instinctually grabbed for him and managed to get a grip on his wrist. The Crow's instincts were also good, in anticipating the trapper to counterattack with a fist or weapon, and reached to intercept the blow. Zack had his knife out and was stabbing toward the Crow's ribs. The knife penetrated through the palm of the Crow's hand. He screamed in surprise and pain and tried to pull his hand away.

Zack continued with his momentum and the two rolled on the ground. Zack pulled his knife free while keeping his grip on the Crow's wrist. He was preparing for another knife lunge when the Crow broke free and got to his feet. He rushed at Zack who also was getting to his feet. Anticipating the rush Zack delivered a vicious kick to the Crow's right knee. The Crow collapsed, but as injured as he was he began to roll. Zack kicked at the sounds of the man rolling in the dry leaves and missed. The Crow rolled again and got to his feet. He began hopping, as fast as he could, away from the fight. Zack heard him trying to get away and yelled out after him, "Huka hey, Huka hey," an obscene Dakotah war cry. The pace of the hopping increased as Zack shuffled his feet in the dry leaves and again yelled the war cry. This was followed by sounds of the man falling, rolling and then more hopping. Zack decided not to pursue his wounded adversary in the dark. The Crow must have expected to be pursued and knowing his injuries put him at a distinct disadvantage began to sing his death song.

In the darkness Zack located his rifle and was searching for his tomahawk when the sounds of a Crow death song filtered through the trees. Zack extracted the tomahawk from the head of his first victim and almost stumbled over the second as he reached for Hunka's reins. The horse and mules had backed away from the commotion and were beginning to calm. Zack grabbed the reins and led his animals through the trees. Once in the open he mounted Hunka and kicked the horse into a hard gallop.

Even though they had to pick their way through the trees, in the dark, they made good time. The run up the incline exhausted Hunka and the mules. Zack urged them on until they made it to the ridge. He stopped to rest them on the ridge. He knew he had a good lead on any pursuers who might try to find his tracks in the dark. The Crow he had crippled might be able to ride but it would take him a long time to limp to his horse. If there were others in the party they would have stayed with the horses some distance away. The Crow who had been on the receiving end of the kicking hooves would probably die from his wounds. If not, he'd be badly crippled for the rest of his life.

Zack did not abide with scalping. He had witnessed the grizzly custom but had no desire to claim such a trophy for himself. Others, more inclined to scalping, may have lingered to complete the battle by lifting a scalp but Zack was more interested in putting some distance between himself and the skulking horse stealers. He regretted having to kill a Crow horse stealer, not because of any humane reason, after all he had only defended himself, and as far as he was concerned it was kill or be killed.

He knew the Crows to be a vengeful people and because of this incident would attack the first white men they came across. Accepting the ways of the mountains and the tribes was part of this perilous life, however he tried to live by some principles of civilized decency. Scalping was not decent.

A cloudy twilight began to creep through the trees while Zack was leading his caravan off the ridge. The wind picked up, warning of a coming spring storm. As many mountain storms will do this one was clinging to a peak where snow was falling while wind blown rain fell in the surrounding lower elevations. As the sun rose a stream of sunlight poured through a break in the clouds, illuminating the trail ahead. It did not last long. A gathering thunderhead closed the break and dropped into the valley. The cloud rolled toward the travelers, booming and flashing as it moved. Zack saw it coming and knew he did not have time to seek shelter. So he pulled his heavy wool coat from a pannier and put it on. He also took a grease soaked piece of buffalo hide from his possible bag and fitted it over the frizzen of his rifle. The thick cloud descended upon him obscuring the surrounding landscape. He lowered his head to the wind driven rain and continued on the incline toward the pass. In a short time he was wet and cold. The rain turned to heavy, wet snow as the caravan climbed in elevation. The storm continued to move and just as suddenly as it appeared it disappeared over a distant ridge. The snow was beginning to melt in the afternoon sun when they reached the pass.

Zack continued to hide his tracks as best as he could by wading in streams, crossing rocky areas and at one area mixed his tracks with a herd of Elk tracks. From each high point he studied his back trail and each time saw no pursuers. This evidence, however, did not let him decrease his caution nor slow the pace. He knew that only time and distance would protect him from the skilled skulking horse stealers.

CHAPTER 3

THE MAHTO

Zack stayed in his meadow for three days. He returned for the venison hindquarters he hung in the tree and busied himself with resupplying his jerky stock. He also treated himself to boudins from the section of small intestines. He mixed the half digested grass inside the intestine with chopped meat, chopped liver, kidney fat, wild onions, sage, spring grass and salt. Then he stuffed the mixture back into the casing and tied off the ends. He wrapped the three-foot long sausage around a green limb and slowly roasted it over a bed of hot coals. The process was rather time consuming but the feast was well worth it. The savory sausage reminded him of the meals his mother made during his childhood in St. Louis. He liked a varied fare when available and kept alert for edible plants to add to meat. Boudins were his favorite way of mixing vegetation and meat.

In anticipation of leaving his meadow he began to work at erasing his signs and packing his goods. Hunka and the mules were well fed, rested and ready to get back on the trail. When all was ready he reflected upon his stay. For the most part his was a life of loneliness and danger. *It could be Gus packing out my possibles,* he thought. At the same time the serenity of the meadow and the mountains provided something that he could not foresee leaving. It was a risky business, the trapping of beaver, but it was also a life of freedom. He still ached with thoughts of missing Gus and was beginning to realize there was more to the feeling than that. Something was missing; something besides grief was beginning to nag at his being.

He kept a steady pace and routine, making his way to the Cache la Poudre River. The flow of the river provided the direction out of the shining mountains to the foothills. The river exited the mountains through a valley ringed with tall, slender pines. Zack came across an area where he saw freshly cut stumps and signs of trees having been stripped of limbs and bark. It was obvious a plains Indian work party had harvested the trees for lodge poles and hauled them away. Five horses were used to drag the poles by lashing them across their backs in the manner of a travois. Zack estimated the party consisted of fifteen mounted men but could not precisely identify the tribe. The Great Plains tribes usually traded for lodge poles but it was not uncommon for them to go to the mountains for the purpose of replacing worn poles. Since the tracks were heading the same direction Zack was going he followed them.

Zack left the trail periodically to scan the country ahead from high rises. More than once he found the tracks of a flank scout who used the same rises. He urged Hunka and the mules to a faster pace having decided to try to catch up enough to identify the party from a distance.

After several hours he dismounted and walked to a rise expecting to see the lodge pole party in the distance. He saw more than he was expecting. Between himself and the distant lodge pole party a band of Crows was setting a raid in motion. They had quietly killed the flank scout without raising an alarm and were divided into two groups. The lodge pole party had stopped in the shade of a small grove of Cottonwood trees to rest. Ten mounted skulking horse stealers were hidden in a ravine with a concealed scout watching the lodge pole party. He was also watching the progress of his companions who had dismounted, undetected, and were sneaking up on picketed horses through a gully leading to the Cottonwoods.

The mounted group of Crows waited, with their backs to Zack and almost directly below him, for a signal to start their attack. Their plan of initiating a mounted attack once the horses were cut free was obvious. Zack returned to Hunka to get Gus' rifle and pistol. In less than a minute he worked his way over the rise to a group of small boulders. The unsuspecting Crows continued to wait for the signal to attack when he was in position.

Zack decided to side with the yet unidentified lodge pole party. His decision was not wholly based on his contempt for the Crows. He also disapproved of the constant warfare between the tribes and thought their manner of surprise raids particularly unjust. The raids often resulted in the loss of life, property and the taking of captives for slaves. The Crows were counting on the element of surprise for this raid and he could spoil that plan without putting himself in much danger.

Zack picked up a fist sized stone and threw it at the assembled Crows below him. The stone hit a horse in the rump and the horse reared, dislodging the rider. The rider was carrying a cocked trade musket that fired when he hit the ground. Zack filled his lungs and yelled, "HUKA HEY, HUKA HEY." The shot and call sent the lodge pole party running for their horses and they were soon mounted. From a distance they looked like a pack of angry hornets boiling out of a nest looking for a fight. They gave chase to the Crows who were caught on foot in the gully and were trying to get to their horses. Another mounted group from the lodge pole party was riding in the direction of the shot.

The mounted horse stealers were trying to get their horses under control and in the confusion were banging into one another. Zack brought his rifle up to his shoulder and aimed at a Crow who had a musket. The man saw Zack and brought his musket up to aim. Zack fired first. The lead ball hit the man high in the left chest, and in doing so, the musket was pulled in that direction and fired directly into the adjacent warrior. Both fell from their horses, which greatly unnerved those trying to get out of the ravine. Zack brought Gus' rifle to readiness as the Crows were trying to kick their mounts out of the ravine, away from him, only to face mounted warriors racing in their direction. By this time Zack was able to make out the attacking group as Dakotahs. The howls of both groups filled the air as the gap closed. Another shot sounded and Zack saw a Crow fall. The man who fired the shot was Pesla, the Mahto warrior from whom Zack acquired Hunka. The Crows were more in the mood of escaping rather than engaging in a pitched battle. They outnumbered their adversaries but somehow bad medicine turned their plan against them and they were being routed.

The running battle was moving away from Zack so he decided to load his rifle and await the warriors of the Mahto Clan. He walked back to Hunka and returned Gus' rifle to the saddle holster. He mounted Hunka and saw Pesla riding in his direction. Pesla rode up and in a rapid stream of words greeted Zack. Zack had learned a few well-chosen phrases of the Dakotah language but relied mostly on sign language. Zack gave the sign for a friendly greeting. Pesla kept talking in an excited, rapid manner. Zack was picking out some words: *Kangi*, Crow; *takpe*, kill; and *pila maye*, thank you. Pesla signed for Zack to join him at the Cottonwoods and rode off to look for more Crows.

When Zack got to the Cottonwoods the Mahto warriors were returning, some carrying bloody scalps, others carrying booty, and leading captured horses. One led a horse draped with their dead scout. Pesla came toward Zack leading a large black stallion and addressing Zack as *Istahota*, Gray Eyes, pushed the reins into his hand. Zack caught the words *toka*, enemy; *octancan*, leader; and *sunktanka*, horse. The gathered warriors raised their voices with *hoye, hoye, hoye*, expressing their approval for giving the dead Crow leader's horse to Zack. The Mahto celebrated their victory by waving the scalps and booty in the air and by telling of their roles in the fight before settling into the task of returning to their village with the lodge poles.

They traveled for three days, out of the foothills and onto the plains. A messenger told the camp crier of their impending arrival and he in turn brought the whole village out to greet the party as they came in sight. Men, women and children crowded around Zack crying *Istahota* and touching him and his animals. As with all the plains tribes, the Mahto were a superstitious, spiritual people. They believed that by touching Zack they would be blessed with his skill and courage. Pesla led Zack to the center of the village and they came to a stop before the chief of this band, who stood in front of his tipi.

Huste, greeted Zack with, *Istahota, hiye aheye hibu mitawasicum he omakiyake,* the messenger tells me of the sudden return of Gray Eyes.

Zack signed a greeting and shook hands with Huste while saying, *o wayake was'te otancan,* calling Huste a handsome leader.

Huste was truly complimented by this greeting and with a grin said, "Hello Zack."

Returning the grin Zack said, "You remembered, good." Both had taught each other a few words of their respective languages during previous visits, which helped with communication, but both relied on sign language more than words.

Huste was a barrel chested man, a head shorter than Zack and at least twenty years older. He wore a single eagle feather in his graying hair and was dressed in his best ceremonial shirt. He had the look and bearing of a Dakotah leader.

With considerable dramatic flair Pesla told the story of the encounter with the Crows to Huste and the gathered Mahto. At various points in the story, the crowd cheered. As expected, the women began to wail at the end of the story when he reported the death of the scout. Members of the scout's family darkened their faces with ashes and began the ritual of mourning.

Huste signaled Zack and Pesla to enter his tipi. Patiently Zack sat through the ceremony of honoring a guest and watched Pesla respond to Huste's questions. They smoked the ceremonial pipe prior to Pesla departing. Zack was ready to introduce the topic of trading when he heard a squaw just outside the tipi calling, *weh, weh, weh* to a dog. Of the Mahto customs he disliked one was the serving of dog meat to respected guests. A squaw was getting a dog in reach of her club.

After the meal of boiled dog, which Zack was able to eat without grimacing, he told Huste of his plan to visit for only a short time. He wanted to be on his way in the morning. Zack timed his announcement with the presentation of a gift to Huste, who had just begun to voice his argument for Zack to stay longer. Skillfully Zack changed the subject to trading and listed the pelts he wanted: *capa*, beaver; *sungila*, fox; and *pte*, buffalo. In a few minutes they were outside and the announcement of trading spread through the village. It wasn't long before pelts were being laid out before Zack. The trading for knives, glass beads, and pieces of cloth soon com-

menced with Zack selecting the best pelts. In a short time he ran out of
trade goods, but had enough furs for a small bale.

  With the trading completed, Huste invited Zack to join him in the
initi, sweat lodge. A low, rounded hut had been constructed, close to the
creek, with tree limbs and covered with tanned hides. Huste and Zack
stripped off their clothing and crawled into the dark hut. Zack's eyes had
not yet adjusted to the darkness when a woman pushed several heated
rocks into a shallow pit with a stick. Huste unhooked a water bag, made
from a buffalo bladder, from the wall and poured water onto the rocks.
The initi was soon filled with steam and both men were covered with
sweat. When they exited the steamy hut Huste's two wives were there to
brush them with willow branches. Huste signaled them to stop and was
handed a fresh breechcloth. Instead of following Huste's example Zack
waded into the stream and began to wash himself in the cold water. He
reacted to the cold water with deep breaths. He dunked his head and vigorously scrubbed his face and hair. Emerging from the stream he pressed
his dripping beard and hair. The long winter of wearing heavy clothes left
him very pale of skin and while he stood dripping on the bank Huste was
laughing. He joked with his wives about Zack looking like a skinned bear.
Both women were giggling as one handed him a new breechcloth.

  Back at Huste's tipi Zack saw his clothes drying from a recent washing
and his belongings neatly stacked. Also, neatly stacked were new clothes;
buckskin pants, elk shirt and buffalo moccasins. Zack patted the pile of
clothing and said, *pila maye* to Huste's sign for a gift. Huste pointing at a
slim, round-faced woman, finely attired in a decorative tanned dress and
said, *winu*. In contrast to his obese wives this woman was young and doe
like. Huste explained she was a *Palani*, a Arikaree captive, he had adopted
to replace his, *wiyanna*, dead girl child. He also explained that she was a
widow. Her husband was killed during a buffalo hunt just prior to her
capture. She was still being addressed as Winu, which literally translated

into captive woman, indicating she had not yet earned a Mahto name. Being true to the Mahto custom she did not speak and kept her eyes to the ground.

The evening passed with more eating and Huste telling of events since Zack's last visit. As far as Zack could tell the Mahto had not been visited by other *wasicun*, white man. Zack feared the time when more white men would come to this country, suspecting history would repeat itself. Just as the tribes east of the Mississippi had been robbed, cheated and dispossessed, so it eventually would happen here. The trappers and traders would be followed by men who hungered for land and a clash of values would result. He had no idea when it would happen, but he knew it would, and could not be stopped.

Just before dark Zack checked on his animals. True to Mahto hospitality, he found his horses and mules well tended and grazing peacefully. He noted two Mahto riders slowly circling the herd. Their patrolling would alert the village if horse stealers tried raiding the herd. They also kept individual animals from wandering off.

Zack followed the stream as he returned to the village. Several women and children were bathing just off a sand bar. The naked children were splashing and laughing, their copper colored skin shinning from the water. Zack saw Winu several yards down stream bathing alone. He watched as she rubbed herself lightly with sand and rinsed by submerging and splashing. In the dimming light she stepped from the water, drying herself with a tanned hide towel. Zack felt a stirring in his groin as he watched her brush the water from her full breasts and rounded hips. She saw him watching her and smiled a barely perceptible smile. Without further sign of being aware of him she slipped her dress over her head, picked up her moccasins and walked toward the tipis. As her form faded in the twilight he felt a longing; a longing for a woman and more, a longing for a home.

Huste's tipi was eighteen feet tall and fifteen feet in diameter. Ten poles supported the conical buffalo hide covering and at the peak a flap could be adjusted to let smoke escape. The tipi was cool in the summer, but never really warm in the winter. A fire pit, in the center, was faced by a backrest for the man of the tipi. To the right another backrest, for a male guest, also faced the fire pit. Baskets and parfleches sat to both sides of the entrance. Sleeping robes were laid out in the evening around the fire pit and since it was spring a fire would not be needed for heat. Huste slept with his two wives on the left and Winu to the rear, opposite the entrance. Sleeping robes for Zack were laid out on the right.

Huste sat smoking his pipe and staring into the dark fire pit. Zack joined him and sat in silence. In the dimness Zack was aware of the women having retired to their sleeping robes. Huste soon joined his wives and Zack found his robes a minute later. As he was relaxing and bordering on sleep, his attention was drawn from Huste's low snoring to quiet movement in the tipi. Almost silently Winu slipped into the robes with Zack. Her hand slid gently across his bare chest, and coming closer, she whispered some words as her lips brushed his ear. Zack did not understand the words, but the language of her naked body was having the effect she desired. In a graceful, fluid movement she was astride him and he inhaled deeply as she guided him into her. She began with short, grinding strokes that gradually increased in speed and length. Zack became oblivious to everything except the mounting tension within. She sensed his tension and flexed her pelvic muscles to grip him tighter. He burst in waves of throbbing pleasure.

They remained in this position for several quiet minutes enjoying the release. Then from within a dream like state, Zack felt her begin again and she repeated the pleasuring. He was only vaguely aware of her returning to her sleeping robes.

*   *   *

Zack awoke to the sounds of the stirring village. Propping himself up he noted he was alone in the tipi. He pondered on the pleasuring with Winu and wondered if her behavior was a gift from Huste or from her own initiative. He was not sure about proper behavior between a guest and an adopted daughter. If he thanked his host for something that should not have happened the consequences could be severe. He decided not to mention the evening's pleasures unless Huste made reference to it. He dressed and exited the tipi.

Huste was seated at the cooking fire eating from a buffalo horn bowl. He motioned for Zack to join him and dipped another bowl into a kettle of bubbling, nondescript stew. Zack noticed a group of riders galloping away from the camp and moving behind them was a strung out, slower group of women leading horses with a travois mounted on their backs. Huste spoke and Zack understood him to say, *wanasapi*, buffalo hunt. He invited Zack to join the hunt.

Zack declined and watched Winu and one of Huste's wives leading a horse at the end of the caravan. The two women were engaged in conversation when suddenly the older women side stepped and grabbed Winu around the waist from behind. Winu did not struggle. The older woman called out to Huste with a short sentence and released Winu. Huste acknowledged her and the women continued toward the hunt. A smile of satisfaction crossed Huste's face. Zack was puzzled by the exchange, but did not inquire to its meaning.

A buffalo herd had been spotted by a scout and the hunting and butchering parties were heading in that direction. A buffalo hunt was a well-coordinated, efficient method of supplying meat for the whole village. The mounted hunters would drive their spears or arrows into the running animals as they rode along side. The mortally wounded buffalo would start dropping out of the herd and be scattered in the direction the herd went. The butchering began as each group of women came upon a downed animal. The hunters would return to help with loading the meat, and before long, the first load would be headed back to the village.

Zack reminded Huste that he would be departing and Huste offered to help load his animals. The village was close to being empty with most of the Mahto off to the hunt. A small security force patrolled around the village and the usual men patrolled the horse herd. Otherwise, all that remained in village was the elderly and small children.

As they walked toward the horses Zack noticed three boys with sticks were herding a group of mares around Hunka. The boys nimbly kept the mares milling around the stallion urging each to pass close to him. One mare communicated receptivity and Hunka mounted her. Zack and Huste slowed their walk to better watch the copulation. Zack knew the Mahto and other plains tribes practiced selective breeding in their herds and welcomed a stallion with desirable traits. Simultaneously, another group of boys presented mares to the Crow leader's black stallion, which also mounted a mare.

Hoye, hoye approved Huste to the sight of copulating horses. He then said something that at first puzzled Zack, but in the context of the breeding horses made sense. Huste indicated Zack had also contributed desirable traits that would benefit the Mahto. At one level Zack knew he had been used like a stud, at another level the pleasures he enjoyed with Winu was worth it. The Mahto worked hard at surviving and if a child from this union with Winu came to be, he hoped the child could contribute to their efforts. This also relieved him of worrying about violating a relationship rule of the Mahto. *Pretty foxy of the old chief,* he thought, *using me and my horses that way.*

With Huste's help loading of the mules went quickly. Zack saddled Hunka and tied the black stallion's lead rope to the pack frame on Two. He thanked Huste for the hospitality and promised to return with more trade goods. They shook hands, Zack mounted, and turned his caravan to head north.

CHAPTER 4

THE TRADING POST

Zack rode North for six days keeping to draws, low areas and places of cover as much as possible. There still were dangers to be alert for but this area was frequented by Indians more friendly to trappers. As he drew closer to the trading post he saw a collection of low log buildings with an adjacent, large corral. A crude parapet consisting of rocks, soil and logs surrounded the largest of the buildings. Outside this defensive barrier was a rude group of small cabins, canvas tents and a few tipis. A flatboat was being constructed on a gently sloping bank of the nearby river. The sounds of a small town began to greet Zack. There was the clanging of a smithy's anvil at work, the drawing of a pit saw, and of men and animals moving about the post. There was much more activity than when Zack and Gus left here late in the previous summer.

Zack tied Hunka to the hitching post in front and ducked as he entered the low porch. Adjusting to the dimmer light Zack paused and heard Ben say, "Zack, I plum took ya fer a red Injun".

Ben was a short, stocky man with a neatly trimmed gray beard, which made him look older than his forty-five years. In contrast to Zack he was dressed entirely in manufactured clothing, which seemed out of place in this wilderness outpost. He did, however, have a pistol tucked in a wide black belt. Three years ago he quit trapping and built this trading post, saying the wading in the cold streams gave him rheumatism.

"How ya doin' ol' hoss?" Ben inquired,
"Tolerable, just tolerable," Zack replied.
"Whar's Gus, tending the animals?"
"Gus's gone under."
"Waugh," said Ben sorrowfully, "Red niggers?"
"Griz," Zack replied.
"Waugh," Ben repeated. Both men knowingly avoided further talk of Gus' death. The many hazards of this life made sudden, violent death all too common and one of the ways they coped with such was through only brief acknowledgments of the tragedies. They were well aware of the risks but that did not diminish their sorrow for the loss of a friend. Changing the subject Ben said, "See any red niggers?"
"A few," Zack replied.
"Eny trouble?"

"Not much."

Noticing the new buckskins Zack was wearing Ben asked, "Ya packin' a squaw?" Knowing Ben was referring to the new clothing he got at the Mahto camp Zack said, "Nope, traded for'um." Both knew trappers who had either married or traded for an Indian woman to do menial work and to share the sleeping robes. These trappers were usually better dressed for the wilderness in the functional clothing made by their squaws.

"Got plews?" Ben asked.

Gesturing toward the door Zack said, "Three, plus loose on the mules."

Ben spoke harshly to two Indian women who were hunkered behind a pile of buffalo hides. They scurried out the door. "Squaws will get 'em," Ben said as he and Zack followed. Zack watched the squaws unloading the mule and turning to Ben asked, "What tribe?" for he had not understood the words that directed them to their task.

"Flatheads," Ben replied, "got 'em in a trade. Takes a powerful lot of doin' to keep 'em workin'." The squaws unloaded the bales, stacking them on the porch. "Mister Allen can get a count and the squaws will bale 'em up again," Ben informed.

"Mister Allen?" inquired Zack.

"I guess ya ain't heard," said Ben, "I got me a clerk, he keeps my books and he'll give ya a fair count. Once he's counted and sorted the peltries the squaws will press 'em back into bales with my new iron press. Price is up on prime beaver. I can give you four dollars a pound."

"Done!" replied Zack being pleased with the price.

Back inside Ben offered whiskey from a ceramic jug with "Wanna pull?" Zack shook his head no and asked, "Got coffee?" Without responding and leaving Zack sitting at the roughly hewn table and chairs Ben left and returned with two steaming mugs. As he handed a mug to Zack he said, "Vittles be a comin' iffen you're hungry?"

"I could eat," replied Zack. With their business concluded Ben was ready to tell of the news and Zack was ready to listen.

Joining Zack at the table Ben sipped noisily on the coffee and said, "I reckon ya ain't heard of the big doin's in these parts. I heard it after ya packed out'a here last summer."

"What doin's?" asked Zack.

"Lisa," referring to Manuel Lisa, "sold out to Ashley and Henry. Them two pilgrims brung a brigade, 'bout a hundred greenhorns, up the Missouri to trap. Scattered 'em from the Musselshell to the Green. Figure 'bout half to go under. Franko, Curly Bob and Windy signed on as guides. With them coons out front that outfit may stand a chance."

"Waugh," responded Zack with some surprise.

"And that ain't all," Ben continued, "They mean to supply the brigade by packin' goods to Henry's Fork on the Green." Ben went on to describe how company and free trappers could meet at a rendezvous on the Green River and exchange their pelts for goods. The furs then would be caravanned to the Yellowstone River to take a float trip to the Missouri River, then to St. Louis.

Zack was amazed at the enormity of such an enterprise and asked, "you see any of 'em?"

"Yep," Ben replied, "Their supplies passed through here. I bought some goods from 'em, besides what was comin' to me up the Platte. That's how I got Mister Allen. He got to feeling poorly and they left 'em here. All that dust got 'em off his feed. It chokes up his breath."

Zack continued to sip the coffee figuring Ben would have more to tell but was not prepared for what came next.

"Heard your brother threw in with Ashley and Henry by brokering for goods and furs in St. Louie."

"My brother?" reacted Zack, not having thought of him in months.

"Yup," Ben went on, "In fact I got a letter from 'em here for ya." He rose and thumbed through a box on the counter, pulled out an envelope, and handed it to Zack. The paper had lost some of its crispness through its means of travel. Rough hands left smudge marks but there in bold script was written *Zachary Scott Clayton, Esq.* Zack could not remember the last time he saw his full name in writing.

Ben, not knowing Zack could read, said, "This ol' hoss might be able to make out a few words for ya."

Tucking the letter in his shirt Zack said, "Thanks Ben, I'll read it later."

Ben was thinking that Zack was too embarrassed to reveal that he could not read and suggested, "Mister Allen would be a good'in to decipher the hard words."

"Thanks Ben," Zack repeated, "I'll do that," knowing he just wanted to read the letter later and in private.

Wanting to put reading the letter to rest and having some questions about Gus, Zack asked, "Did Gus ever speak of his folks?"

Ben thought for a time, "He came to the mountains first time with Colter," referring to John Colter who first came to the mountains with Lewis and Clark in 1804, "Ran away from home so he said. He were a talker in them days, got quiet three-four years back. Have no idée what made 'em quiet. Peers I recollect he talked 'bout comin' from Cairo. His pa was a carpenter, you see'd what he could do with wood."

Zack agreed as to Gus' wood working skills and asked, "His folks still in Cairo?"

"Don't rightly know," replied Ben. "Did he talk to you 'bout 'em?"

"Nope, not much. He mentioned brothers from time to time. He was a quiet man 'sept when it came to horse stealers, then he cussed and told of choppin' the skulkin' varmints."

"Yep, that were Gus", acknowledged Ben, "he were pizen on Crows, scalped a passel of 'em up on the Bitterroot I heard. I'm not sure zactly what got into his craw 'bout 'em, but he sent a bunch to hell."

Acknowledging with, "Waugh," Zack paused to watch the squaws bringing in steaming plate of steaks, spicy beans and biscuits. Zack and Ben attacked the plates.

"I didn't know squaws knew how to cook like this," Zack said as he dripped a biscuit with some honey.

"They didn't till I learned 'em," replied Ben, "I told 'em 'bout your biscuits, but they can't make 'em as good."

Thus far Zack had not revealed to anyone that his sack of biscuit fixins was a mixture of flour, finely ground corn meal, baking powder, baking soda, sugar, salt, and pepper. "Maybe they'll get it someday," he said.

"I hope so," said Ben with a mouth full of steak. "Your biscuits sure do shine."

With the meal finished both leaned back and belched. Ben lit up a pipe and said, "Can ya stay fer awhile?"

"I was just fixin to ask if I could put up here fer awhile," replied Zack.

"Ol' Hoss you can put up as long as you like. I'll put the squaws to tendin' your animals and settin' out your sleeping robes. You want one of 'em for some night poke?" Having gotten close enough to the squaws to see their grime and to smell their stink Zack declined. Without the structure and customs of their tribe the squaws had become lazy and remiss in their hygiene, which may have also protected them from unwanted attention. Zack knew most of the tribes practiced a unique brand of duplicity and these women certainly could be doing just that, biding their time until they found a way out of their enslavement.

The horses and mules were turned into the corral and Zack's belongings were stacked in one of the small cabins. The cabin lacked the workmanship of Gus' cabin and it was a mess from previous occupants. Zack thought to give it a try; after all he could always go back to sleeping outside, especially if the cabin was lice or flea infested. With Ben busy at the trading post the time for private letter reading had come. Zack broke open the wax seal and withdrew the paper. The letter was in the same script as was his name and was dated April 2, 1824, a little over a year old.

Dear Brother, I write to you hoping you will get this letter. I have gone into business with Wm. Ashley & And. Henry of the Missouri Fur Company. We plan to provision our brigade at a rendezvous in the mountains and have a need for a man, such as yourself, to guide. I am empowered to offer you a handsome fee if you want the position and will return to St. Louis.

Now for some sad news. Pa died Feb. last. I sold some of his properties at a tidy profit. I have deposited your share in an acct. for you. The city is growing rapidly and the livery stable is sought after by several buyers.

I have married and built a house not far from Pa's old house. I invite you to visit us and remind you that you always have a home here.

Your Brother,

James Todd Clayton

Zack read the letter several times. He did not expect to hear that his father was dead. The sadness of this news slowly sank in and renewed grieving for Gus. Both men played significant roles in Zack's life, now they were gone. He ached, a double ache, and swore to himself to make a return to St. Louis.

During the past few times he thought of St. Louis and his father he expected he would always be there. His thoughts drifted to the livery stable where he worked with his father. As a boy Zack liked doing the day-to-day chores and remembered rushing home to change his school clothes so he could go to the livery stable. Unless he was very busy, his father would greet him with, "What did you learn in school today, Zachary?" And Zack always tried to remember at least one interesting thing to tell him. James was another story. He did not care for menial labor nor the livery stable and was creative in finding ways to get out of chores. Zack doubted James had changed. *So James is married. He did not say what her name is* Zack thought. *And a new house; he must be doing well to have a wife and a new house.*

James was two years older than Zack and five years ago had convinced their father to let both of them to sign on with the Missouri Fur Company. James had excelled in school, spoke French and had a gift for selling. He talked Manuel Lisa into giving him a job as a trader, and once that was done, got a job for Zack as a clerk. James stayed in the mountains only that first year, returning to St. Louis with the furs. Zack had yet to return to St. Louis and heard that James was working with their father and running a distillery. This letter was their first direct communication since their parting on the upper Missouri River.

Zack pondered on the job offer and wondered if it was still good. If it was, then he could get paid for a trip back to the mountains. In some ways it was a tempting offer. Zack folded the letter and returned it to his shirt. Deeply engrossed in thoughts of his father, brother and Gus he did not hear Ben approaching until his boots hit the doorway.

"Say ol' Hoss. I got a buyer fer Gus' rifle iffen ya amind to sell it. It be a white man," Ben announced.

Zack had not considered selling any of Gus' belongings and at first felt inclined to refuse. He then remembered his desire to give Gus' share of the pelts to his family and thought he might as well throw in what he could get for the firearms and possibles. Wanting to know what was due him for the furs Zack asked, "What's the count on the furs?"

"Nine hundred and six dollars, after what ya owe," replied Ben, "and I can throw in thirty fer the rifle."

"And the pistol?"

"Another five."

"Seven," Zack countered.

"Done," said Ben. "Do ya want it in cash or goods?"

"Both," said Zack. "I'va mind to go to St. Louie and want to talk to ya 'bout it. Will ya take that black stallion fer tending my animals and possibles til I return?"

"Done," said Ben. "When do ya figure to get back?"

"Next summer, maybe sooner. That flatboat goin' to St. Louie?"

"Yep. Figure to have my plews loaded in a day or two. Wanna ride?"

"Yup. What's the toll?"

"Hell ol Hoss, I'll fix it so thar's no toll fer the man who helps get my plews to St. Louie."

"I'm obliged to ya Ben and I want to leave two hundred dollars with ya fer goods fer when I return. I'm gonna try to find Gus' folks and give his share to 'em."

"That's mighty Christian of ya Zack. Surely is. I'll write ya a draft on my St. Louie bank."

"Waugh," said Zack accepting the terms.

Alone again, Zack cleaned Gus' rifle and pistol. He sorted through the items that go with the firearms and inspected them for function. The powder horn was about half full and there were at least a dozen lead balls in the possible bag. The bullet mold looked in good working order. In a leather pouch he found a bar of lead, extra flints, needles, awls, and two folding knives. Working to separate those items he would take to Ben and those items he would add to his own gear he noticed a fist sized buckskin bag he had yet to examine. It seemed surprisingly heavy for its size. Yellow pebbles spilled into Zack's hand when he opened it. *Gold! Where did Gus get this kind of gold?* Zack puzzled. Then thinking of Gus' unusual activities concluded, *So that's what he was doin' with that extra pokin' about, lookin' for gold.* Zack had observed Gus from time to time putting gravel in a wide flat pan and washing it, but never thought much of it. Gus used that pan for lots of things. Then there was that small pickaxe that he took into caves. It was not among Gus' possessions. Zack did not recall looking for it when he found Gus' body. *He must'a been lookin' for gold when he went into that cave. Lookin' for gold is what got him killed,* Zack surmised. Gus went into that cave to pick around, as he had done on ledges and other caves, when he encountered the sow bear. Gus had obviously pressed some of the gold with his bullet mold, as there were several smooth, shiny, yellow balls. The remaining pieces were nuggets, just as he must have found them. Zack returned the gold to the bag and placed it in his possible bag.

After Zack took the firearms and accoutrements to Ben he went for a walk around the trading post compound. A blacksmith was busy with a forge, his muscular arms and leather apron bearing witness to his trade. Zack watched for a few minutes as the smithy shaped and fitted a handle to a kettle. Moving on he noted two men operating a pit saw. The pile of sawdust and stack of lumber indicated a good amount of labor had taken place. Another man was carrying pieces of lumber toward the flat boat. Zack did not recognize any of these men. *Ben,* he thought, *must be doing well to have all this activity at his place.* The flat boat had been launched into the water by way of log rollers and now floated a few feet off the bank. A lumber gangplank and mooring ropes secured it to the bank. Two men were placing a long pole sweep rudder to the roof of a small onboard cabin. The flat boat was forty feet long and twelve feet wide. Zack decided not to take a closer look; after all he would be spending the next several weeks aboard this crude, but functional craft.

After another meal and discussion with Ben, Zack spent some time with Hunka and the mules. Ben would see that they were properly cared for. Zack was already starting to miss them and as he brushed Hunka became lost in thoughts of Gus, the letter, and his anticipated journey to St. Louis.

CHAPTER 5

GUS

Zack trapped for two seasons as an employee of the Missouri Fur Company. The third season he wintered with the Mahto and became a free trapper. He liked the idea of being able to sell his furs where he could get the best price and the competition among fur buyers was increasing up and down the tributaries of the Missouri River. At the end of his second season as a free trapper he came limping into Ben's trading post with only his animals, firearms and a few possibles. A Blackfoot raiding party jumped him while he was packing out of the Salmon River country. After a brief but furious fight he had to abandon his plews and half his traps. He killed three warriors in the struggle and suffered a knife wound in the thigh. Only after a week of running and hiding did he elude the Blackfoot band.

By pure luck Zack met up with Windy Fergeson who was packing out from the Green River. They rode together across South Pass toward the North Platte River. Zack had some credit built up with Ben Thompson and figured it would cover new traps and supplies. If it didn't he'd ask Ben for a stake.

Several free trappers were gathered at Ben's trading post to sell their pelts and buy supplies. With more than the usual mouths to feed the supply of meat was running low. Ben asked Windy to organize a hunt. Windy was the oldest and most experienced of the gathered trappers and assumed command of the volunteer hunting party. He got his name from his tales of hunting a Grizzly Bear in the Wind River country; at least that is how he told it. From anyone who spent much time around him, it was said he got his name for the copious amount of gas he passed. He was a big, fearsome looking man when dressed in his Grizzly Bear coat. Even his cap was the scalp of a bear and with his dark brown beard he looked like Ol' Griz himself.

Zack was not well acquainted with the four other men who volunteered for the hunt. John "Gus" Gusterson was the same height as Zack but appeared heavier and more muscular. He was a quiet man who was dressed in unadorned Elk hide clothing, well-worn and grease stained, which he obtained in a trade. He was armed with a rifle, pistol, tomahawk and a large knife, as were the other trappers. Unlike the other trappers, who favored large caliber rifles, Gus carried a .45 caliber N.Kiles plains rifle.

Franko St. Vrain was a joker. He liked nothing better than to swap stories and play practical jokes. He was noted for his trading skills and his command of several Indian languages. He was a short, stocky man who kept his beard neatly trimmed in the fashion of his French and Spanish ancestors. He tended to wear colorful clothing and wore a gray hat with the tail feathers of a Great Blue Heron fastened in the band. His partner, Robert "Curly Bob" Parks, was as tough as they come. He had survived several wounds and injuries in the course of his life as a trader and trapper. The most dramatic was being captured and tortured by the Arikarees. He had been tied to a tree and beaten as part of his trade goods being pirated by a band of Ree young bucks. Fortunately Franko came riding in on the scene. As he approached it became clear the Rees were up to no good and he figured they would soon be turning on him. He shot two Rees and managed to get Curly Bob cut loose. Curly Bob took out two more with a captured war club. The Rees were confounded by their sudden change in fortune and lit out, taking most of Curly Bob's possessions with them. Franko and Curly Bob fled in the opposite direction and had been partners ever since.

The sixth member of the hunting party was Luke McBride, a greenhorn to the Rocky Mountains. Luke came up river with the canoes that delivered supplies to Ben. He was a thin, wiry young man who appeared younger than his stated twenty years. He was raised in the hills of Tennessee and had come west to make his mark and fortune. He carried a new rifle and wore home made linsey-woolsey clothing. He purchased the necessary equipment for trapping from Ben and let it be known that he was looking to join up with any group that would have him. No one voiced an objection when he volunteered for the hunt, so Windy included him.

They rode east for a few miles, paralleling the Platte River, then turned south along one of the feeder streams. They fanned out to scout for buffalo with Zack and Gus crossing the stream toward a high hill. Luke and Windy rode along the stream while Franko and Curly Bob rode off to the southwest. Seeing nothing from the hill Zack and Gus continued southeast and out of sight of the other hunters. Zack was taking a liking to this quiet, confident man even though little was exchanged between them.

They had not gone far when they heard a distant shot, followed by a second shot from the same direction. They turned their horses in that direction. They were just topping a rise when they saw a small herd of buffalo running directly toward them. In the same instant Zack and Gus kicked their horses into a gallop, straining the lead ropes to the mules. The herd leader, seeing this new threat, veered to the right. Zack and Gus turned to intercept them and soon were running beside the herd. Zack picked out a young cow in the cloud of dust and with a well-placed shot brought her down. A few seconds later Gus did the same and the herd thundered away. Both drew up short of the downed cows to watch the final death kicks from the safety of their horses. Both also reloaded their rifles and scanned in all direction before dismounting. Each noted these behaviors in the other with approval. After cutting a bleeding stroke in the neck of his cow Zack remounted and rode to where Gus was doing the same. Like a team that had done this many times before they butchered the cows into hump roasts, backstraps and deboned hindquarters. They had a limit on how much meat they could pack and only took the choice cuts. It was late in the afternoon when the meat was rolled up in the hides and loaded on the mules.

It wasn't long before they were on a rise that overlooked their fellow hunters. They crossed the stream in the area where Luke was struggling to skin an old bull while Windy held a rear leg in assistance. Franko and Curly Bob were sitting on the ground in the shade of their horses watching the scene. Zack and Gus stopped to dismount close to the relaxed pair. As they dismounted Franko teasingly said, "How ya coons like this camp ol' Windy picked? Real close to water ain't it?"

Windy dropped the leg he was holding and stepped toward the bull's liver, which he had placed, on a rock. He cut a thin slice of the raw liver and popped it into his mouth. Then as if he was not speaking to anyone in particular said, "Mother Fergeson's chile likes ta camp whar thar's meat."

Luke kept to the task of skinning and was pretending not to be affected by Franko's teasing, which had been going on for some time and now was being rehashed for Zack and Gus. Franko picked a grass stem and seemed to be casually chewing on it as he said, "Windy, ol' hoss, I read the sign that ya jumped those buffs way back yonder."

Windy grunted an agreement.

"Then how's it this old bull got all the way down here? Ya gettin' shaky in yer aimin'?" baited Franko.

"Could be," responded Windy, not wanting to give Franko any more information to add to the tease. Zack and Gus were becoming amused with Franko's antics but also were feeling sorry for Luke who was not progressing well with the skinning. They drew their knives and joined him at the carcass. As the skinning progressed they noted that the bull had been shot twice, once through the intestines and the second through a lung. Franko had read the same sign and figured Luke to having gut shot the bull. For some reason Windy was not revealing it.

Franko rose and walked to the liver. He sliced off a piece and suspended it on his knife tip as he returned to sit beside his partner. He gestured the slice to Curly Bob who said, "Don't mind if I do," as he cut a piece for himself.

Then with a devilish grin Franko continued the tease, "T'was right kindly of Windy fer not puttin' a hole in this here liver." Windy had returned to assist with the butchering and did not respond.

Luke was growing irritated with the teasing, especially with the implication that Windy had gut shot the bull. He walked up to Franko, who slowly rose as he approached, and said, "Mister Saint Vrain, I gut shot this old bull and Mister Fergeson brought him down on the run."

Franko feigning surprise replied, "Well now pilgrim, are ya saying ol' Windy there brought this here bull down on the run from way back yonder?"

"Yes sir, I am," responded Luke.

Walking toward Windy and dramatically gesturing apologetically Franko said, "Well now ol' hoss it peers I took ya wrong, yer ol' aimin' eye ain't all that shaky after all."

Windy knew he was not the primary target for the teasing and figured there was probably more to come. He had hoped to provide a buffalo hunting lesson to Luke but when the small herd was spotted Luke took off after them before Windy could direct him toward a cow. There was more than one way to learn a lesson and Luke was getting one through Franko's teasing. Windy paused from his butchering to gesture apology accepted to Franko.

Turning back to Luke, Franko's expression became serious and while looking the greenhorn straight in the eyes said, "Pilgrim, ya gotta learn to shoot better. I like my meat once shot."

Seeing the change in Franko, Luke sheepishly responded, "Yes sir."

"And another thing," Franko continued, "we like fat cow over tough bull."

"Yes sir," Luke repeated.

"And another thing," Franko sounding even more serious said, "Did ya reload yer rifle?"

With some embarrassment Luke replied, "No sir, I must have forgot in all the commotion." Realizing that Franko was passing on a serious lesson Luke stepped to his rifle, which was propped on the bull's head and began loading. Franko and Curly Bob joined the butchering.

When Luke rejoined the butchering the bull's hide had been removed and the meat was being stacked on it. Franko had played out the gut shot bull teasing and was preparing his next move on Luke. He cut off a chunk of liver and offered each man in turn a thin slice, saving Luke for last. He noticed that Luke had grimaced when first observing Windy eating a slice. Each man in turn popped the slices in their mouths and kept on working. Luke saw what was coming and so did the others He had almost gagged when he saw the men eating the warm, raw liver and now was faced with eating a slice or finding a reason not to. Since he could not think of a reason to refuse a slice he popped it into his mouth with a grimace. He was so preoccupied with the feel and taste of the liver that he did not notice the men had stopped working and were watching him. He chewed and tried not to gag. He blushed when the men started to laugh but managed to get the liver down.

Between laughs Franko patted him on the shoulder and encouragingly said, "You'll get it Pilgrim."

The sun was setting when Gus got a fire started under some large Cottonwood trees just a few yards upstream from the butchered bull. With everyone pitching in it wasn't long before steaks and boudins were roasting, biscuits were baking and coffee was boiling. Each man sliced off pieces of meat as it was cooked and helped himself to biscuits and coffee. Each in turn praised Zack's biscuits.

The moon was rising as Gus and Zack sat by the remains of the dying fire. Gus smoked his pipe in slow draws, letting the smoke escape lazily through his nostrils. The other men had retired to their sleeping robes, mixing their sleeping sounds with those of the night prairie. In a low voice, catching Zack by surprise, Gus said, "I hear red niggers got yer plews?"

"Waugh," affirmed Zack, "Blackfeet jumped me up on the Salmon. Took a cut in the leg but got out'a there with my animals and possibles." Gus nodded an acknowledgment as he drew on his pipe again. Zack continued, "Joined up with Windy the rest of the way to Ben's."

After a long pause Gus asked, "Gonna go back to the Salmon?"

Zack studied on the question and answered honestly, "I haven't rightly made up my mind but don't figure to go that far north for a spell. How about you? Where do you figure to trap?"

Gus was stirring a stick around in the embers in an effort to get it to ignite. The tip of the stick flamed and he brought it up to relight his pipe. Then with a slow exhale of smoke he answered, "Got a cabin up in Middle Park. Figure to go there."

Gus built the cabin with a wife in mind. He had the urge to settle down but did not want to leave the mountains, so the next logical step was to build a cabin and find a wife. He was considering searching for a wife among the Utes who had a reputation for gentleness and knowing how to live in the mountains. He had traded in some of their villages and figured to look further into their ways. If he saw a woman he liked he would have to know how to court her.

Gus was a man who wanted to live in peace but he was also a man who was trying to escape. He ran away from home to escape his father who cruelly turned on him. He was also trying to escape from the memories of his former partner's death. Gus' hatred for the Crows began when he found the scalped, tortured body of Charlie Ware. As an older, experienced trapper, Charlie Ware took Gus under his wing during Gus' first trip to the mountains with Manuel Lisa's brigade. Charlie was a skillful trapper, resourceful in surviving in the mountains and patient as a teacher.

While trapping the streams of the Musselshell River, Gus and Charlie agreed to meet up stream on a particular creek. When Charlie did not show up Gus went looking for him. He found Charlie's tracks and followed them. He found Charlie tied to a tree. He barely recognized his mentor, whose body was still warm. Gus buried Charlie and set upon a trail of revenge. He did not have far to go. The Crows who had murdered Charlie camped in a Spruce thicket only two hours away from their gruesome deed. They had become noisy and careless due to having found three bottles of whiskey in the bottom of a canvass pannier. As Gus crept up on them they were drunkenly feeding a large fire and bragging to one another about their deeds.

The first to meet his maker was a man who left the group to urinate. Gus practically decapitated him with a stroke from his heavy knife. The events of the next minutes occurred in a blurring rush. Gus walked into the firelight and shot the closest Crow with his pistol. He then butt stroked the next two with his rifle. One of them fell into the fire. The fifth one was trying to escape when Gus shot him in the back. He mutilated the bodies in a frenzy, then he killed their horses.

Three days later he rode into the brigade's base camp leading Charlie's horse and mules. "This be what's left of Charlie Ware." was all he would say of the incident. Although Gus continued to trap, he trapped alone.

And when the opportunity arose, which he planned to be as often as possible, he killed Crows.

Gus wanted to talk to Zack. There was something about Zack that made him ring true, a straightforward honesty that Gus found appealing. Gus wanted to reduce his self-imposed loneliness and to throw off the feelings for revenge. He wanted to talk about his desire to settle down and his notion of supporting a wife by trapping and prospecting for gold. But he was a prisoner of opposing forces; a desire for peaceful living and a desire for vengeance. He wanted to be with Zack and the other men of the hunting party, while at the same time feared that they too could become victims in the wilderness. To Gus closeness and friendship meant death and he would rather be alone than go through another Charlie Ware.

"Ain't that kinda high to winter in?" asked Zack, knowing some about Middle Park.

"Not bad on the Yampa," replied Gus, "Beaver shines and it's not crowded, like up on the Green or Mussleshell." He was about to add the area was far enough south of the Crow's traditional hunting grounds that one would not ordinarily run into them. But he bit hard on his pipe stem to keep back the words.

Zack stretched and yawned, signaling a need to retire to his bedroll. As he stood, bringing his rifle with him, he looked over at the sleeping men and then scanned in the direction of the horses. Everything seemed peaceful but he would feel more comfortable about going to sleep if he scouted the perimeter of the campsite. Gus felt the same degree of caution and said, "You go ahead and bed down. I'll poke around some before I turn in."

The hunters arrived back to the trading post early in the afternoon. Two more free trappers had arrived and Ben was happy to get the fresh meat. He was more than just a businessman to the gathering trappers. He thought of himself as one of them and wanted to be a good host. Franko, now with a new and bigger audience, took the opportunity to retell the story of the gut shot bull. The story became more exaggerated with each telling to the point where he had Luke beating the bull between the horns with his rifle while Windy had a grip on the tail trying to hamstring the beast. Luke was rapidly fitting in and joined the tale with his own version of events. Windy laughed to each exaggerated version and Gus found himself grinning and enjoying the antics.

In small groups, free trappers were riding in to sell their furs and to buy supplies. Also coming to trade their winter furs were bands of Dakotah and Shoshone. Ben ran out of trade whiskey within three weeks. The trappers were making up for their months of isolation and hardships by hardy drinking and playing. Between bouts of drinking the trappers staged contests of wrestling, shooting, tomahawk throwing and horse racing. And there were many trappers who were trying to entice sexual favors from the Indian women with beads and ribbon.

Zack did not care for the feeling of the fiery liquor fuzzing his senses and he had not seen a squaw he found attractive. He did participate in some of the contests and won a horse race. But for the most part he tended his animals and worked at getting himself ready for the next trapping season.

Zack obtained the essential supplies from Ben but did not have enough credit to get trade goods. Ben staked him for his remaining needs. Zack hauled his supplies to a camp he set up for himself, close to the river and away from most of the commotion. Gus was similarly inclined and joined Zack in the small grove of Cottonwoods, up stream from the trading post. Over the course of the next two weeks they went on another buffalo hunt and hauled firewood for Ben.

Zack spent the better part of an afternoon mixing his seasoned flour and getting it poured into three leather bags. He gave the same care to packaging beans, dried apple slices, and coffee. He noticed Gus was packing in a similar manner. That evening they shared a meal in their camp. In his usual manner of smoking his pipe in the evening Gus sat quietly staring into the low flames. In spite of their having spent considerable time together neither man spoke more than was absolutely necessary. Each man, however, had observed that their ways and habits were strikingly similar. It was obvious to anyone who saw them that Gus was more of a loner than Zack and no one was surprised that they would get along.

Zack was convinced that if there was ever a man who would make a good partner it was Gus but he also accepted that Gus was very private. If Gus wanted a partner he would ask, otherwise he'd more than likely want to trap alone.

Gus was thinking close to the same about Zack and knew Zack was likely to be asked by more than one group to join them for the next season. It was obvious Zack was liked and trusted by the other trappers. Gus had seen the ease in which Zack gleaned and gave information about terrain, beaver concentrations and Indians

"Wanna hook up with me and trap Middle Park?" spoke Gus as he continued his stare into the fire. Zack was leaning back against a pannier and as he moved forward to stir the fire said, "Yup, I'd like that."

"Good," responded Gus, "We'd oughta head out in the next day or so."

Zack returned to leaning on the pannier and said, "I'll be ready."

*   *   *

In early August the trappers were departing the trading post for the mountains. Luke McBride joined up with a group heading for the Powder River country. Zack and Gus rode out with Windy, Franko and Curly Bob. After two day of riding along the North Platte River they parted when Windy, Franko and Curly Bob turned north for the Bighorn Mountains. "Keep yer powder dry," and "Watch yer top knot." was exchanged in the good-byes.

Gus led the way as they followed the North Platte River. The river turned south when they left it to travel westward. They had plenty of time to get to Gus' cabin before the fall trapping season. When they established a night camp near a stream Gus would scout the gravel bars to pan for gold. He also made short detours to pick at rocky outcroppings and caves. He knew Zack noticed these unusual behaviors for a trapper and appreciated that if he had any curiosity about it he kept to himself. Gus was not ready to reveal his purpose.

Zack was mildly curious about Gus' panning and poking around but thought it was just an eccentric trait. He had no argument with it and as far as he was concerned as long as they made good time, Gus could pan and poke around as much as he wanted.

Late one afternoon Zack shot a yearling Elk calf so they set up their night camp early to cook and enjoy the tender meat. Thick, white clouds rolled into the alpine meadow just as they finished the butchering. By the time they got their fire going a light rain was falling. They set up their camp under the leafy boughs of a large Aspen tree at the edge of the meadow. The tree was chosen to give them some protection from the rain and to disperse the smoke from their campfire. Later the evening turned noisy with the growling and yapping of wolves and coyotes that discovered the remains of the calf carcass. Zack and Gus were the quietest creatures in the meadow and were glad when the noise stopped in time for them to retire to their bedrolls.

An hour before dawn the clouds were breaking up and the light of a full moon sought its way through the breaks. The sliding edges of lunar illumination brushed the meadow as the clouds lazily drifted to the east.

In his sleep Zack became aware of movement in the camp. As he awakened he opened his eyes slightly while his hand moved quietly toward his pistol. As his alertness increased he saw Gus moving toward him. When close enough to make out in the dim moonlight he signaled to be quiet by placing his index finger to his lips. Gus turned and began to silently crawl out of the camp. Zack quietly sat up and listened. The patches of moonlight revealed a light fog rising from the dew laden meadow grasses.

Zack rose to his knees, strapped on his belt and positioned his pistol and knife. He picked up his rifle as he rose. Hunka snorted roughly and Zack heard muffled sound of men rolling in the grass. He stalked toward Hunka while trying to make out the direction of the rolling sounds. He stepped past the picketed animals and suddenly saw a dark figure rise out of the tall grass to come rushing at him. Zack side stepped and slashed with the Hawken shoulder stock. With a hollow crunch, the dark figure took the blow to the forehead and crumbled at Zack's feet. Zack froze to listen; all was quiet again. A ray of moonlight revealed a human trail through the dewy grass. Zack saw Gus' dark form rise from the grass about fifty feet away. They signaled to one another. Gus came to a crouch and moved away. With slow, quiet steps Zack began to follow the man sign. It led to a peninsula of trees on the opposite side of the meadow. Through the fog he began to hear muffled sounds of restless horses. Guiding on the sounds he found a lone, mounted skulking horse stealer holding the reins of three horses. In the fog the Crow mistook Zack for a returning companion and did not realize his mistake until Zack grabbed him, pulling from his horse. Before the horse stealer could defend himself Zack delivered a upper cutting butt stroke with his rifle to the man's chin. With the sound of breaking jawbone the man's head snapped back. Zack stood quietly looking for signs of life. When there were none, he tied the horses to a tree and began to retrace his steps.

The moonlight was ebbing to twilight when Zack saw the light from the campfire. He increased his pace knowing Gus was building up the fire. He changed course for a more direct route to the camp. In doing so he came across the scalped body of one of the horse stealers. Gus looked up as Zack entered the camp site and quietly said, "Coffee's on."

Zack stood on the opposite side of the fire pit to Gus and reported, "I got two. Tied up four horses back yonder," gesturing in the direction from which he'd come. "Saw one comin' in. Where's the fourth?"

Hunkered at the fire Gus pointed over his shoulder with his thumb. Zack walked in that direction and within a few yards found a scalped Crow tied to a tree. The faint rising of his chest indicated he was still alive. Zack returned to the fire and Gus asked, "Is that skulking nigger still alive?"

"Barely," responded Zack.

Then after a pause to feed the fire Gus questioned, "Any trouble?"

"None to speak of. You?" Zack queried.

"Some," replied Gus as he gestured toward a blood stain behind his left shoulder. Gus stood up and pulled off his shirt. Zack examined a shallow stab wound.

"Need tobaccie?" asked Gus, as he held up a short twisted tobacco rope.

"Small piece," Zack replied, as he broke off an inch and stuffed it into the wound. Gus winced to the tobacco plug being poked into the wound. Then he sat to pour the coffee. He handed a cup to Zack.

Zack sat on the opposite side of the fire sipping the coffee watching Gus fumbling around in his possible bag. Gus removed a curved needle; threaded with twine and proceeded to sew up the hole in his shirt He sipped coffee between stitches. When he was finished, he returned the needle to his possible bag. During this time Zack busied himself with getting a skewered Elk roast over the fire. The roast had cooked the evening before and he positioned it to heat.

Gus, still shirtless, drew his knife and began to hone the edge on a stone. In a low, contemptuous voice he said, "Iffen that red nigger still be alive when we finish eatin' I'm gonna skin 'em."

Zack did not approve of scalping and torture. He was uncertain of how to present it to Gus but he knew he had to. He decided he would give himself some time to think about it by going to get the Crows' horses. During the round trip he decided he must be direct with Gus but it worried him on how Gus would take it. Gus obviously hated Crows and it seemed to Zack that the hatred was about more than their horse stealing ways.

Zack tied the horses up near the other animals and joined Gus at the fire. Gus had put on his shirt and was slicing off a piece of roast. They ate in silence. When Zack was finished eating he looked Gus in the face and said, "Gus, I don't abide by scalpin' and torturin'. It ain't decent for a white man."

Gus was startled by this pronouncement. His hatred for the Crows had dulled his sense of decency. Up to this point he had not been presented with a moral code different from what had evolved through his desire for revenge. Zack's statement caused him to think back, beyond the murder of Charlie Ware, to a time he felt civilized and believed in honor and decency. Flashes of moral teaching, especially from his mother, filled his mind: *do unto others.... thou shalt not.... forgive those who have trespassed.* He knew his hatred for the Crows was distracting but had not discovered a way to free himself from its grip. Zack did not know it but he caused Gus to decide to return to a more civilized way of thinking. Gus had grown to value the younger man's skill and courage, grown to value his companionship and now appreciated his moral code. Gus blinked, like a man who had just entertained a profound idea, and said, "You be right, Zack." Gus rose with his knife in his hand with the intention of cutting the horse stealer loose. The horse stealer was dead. Returning to the fire he announced, "Skulkin' nigger's gone beaver."

They gathered and bundled the Crow's weapons, including a well worn, poorly maintained trade musket and dragged the bodies off into the trees. In a short time they were back on the trail leading the captured horses. Gesturing toward the horses Gus said, "The Utes are usually eager to trade fer horses. I figure we can get some prime peltries fer 'em."

Zack was not familiar with the Utes and asked, "Where do they range?"

"South of here by five days or more," responded Gus. "They hunt the high country in the summer. We can trade with 'em and by the time we head back north beaver should be startin' a winter coat." Gus went on to describe what he knew of the Utes. This was the most Zack had heard him say since they met and kept the conversation going by asking questions about the Utes and their habits.

Gus knew a few Ute words and between his and Zack's ability with sign language they traded with a band of Utes south of the White River. Unlike most Ute villages this band was horse poor and was eager to trade for the Crow horses and weapons. They had several prime beaver pelts and an assortment of other desirable furs. Gus traded the Crow musket to the chief of the band and was surprised to learn that the chief had more than a passing familiarity with firearms. At one time he had served as a guide for traders who reached the Grand River from Santa Fe. The chief had hoarded a small supply of gunpowder in hopes of one day being able to obtain a gun. While Zack was busy with bundling the furs the chief displayed his collection of yellow stones. He planned to use the soft metal as musket balls. After a cursory examination, Gus realized the yellow stones were gold. He traded molded lead balls, gun powder, two knives and a hand axe for the gold nuggets. Gus did not reveal his trading for the nuggets to Zack. Prior to departing, Gus noted the village contained several young, unattached women. He figured this band might be a place to start when he was ready to look for a wife.

As they scouted their way to the Yampa River, they noted the beaver had yet to develop their winter coats, so they blazed some trees in the areas to which they would return. They arrived at Gus' cabin with enough time to prepare for the coming winter. The secluded cabin was ideally constructed for wintering in the mountains but it would take much work to prepare for surviving, especially if the winter was severe. The cabin sat at the end of a long narrow meadow, protected by tall trees. It was sparsely furnished with a table and two chairs, which Gus had handcrafted. From dawn to dark they gathered firewood, cut the tall grass for hay, jerked meat and made pemmican. The preparations for winter were complete when the first yellowing appeared in the higher Aspens.

They started the fall trapping season by being gone from the cabin three to four days at a time. Each would set their traps in the beaver ponds and the closer tributaries of the river. After collecting a rolled stack of fresh beaver pelts they returned to the cabin to scrape the pelts on the graining block and stretch them on willow hoops. After drying, the pelts were stacked in the corner of the cabin. This pattern of trapping continued until the middle of December when the snow and cold prohibited venturing too far from the cabin. There were some mild, sunny days in late January in which they trapped and hunted for fresh meat. Gus constructed funnel shaped fish traps from willow branches, which he placed in the river. They checked the traps when returning from hunting. Brook Trout and Whitefish were a welcomed change to their repetitious fare of antelope and deer.

In late March they were able to return to more distant trapping sites although had to wear snowshoes to get to some of the streams and ponds. By the middle of April it was obvious, by the growing stack of beaver pelts, that they were having a good season. Using the log press Gus constructed, they began compressing the dried pelts into bales.

Toward the end of April Zack returned to the cabin after being gone for two days. He dressed and stretched four beaver pelts while he waited for Gus. Gus had departed at the same time in another direction. Zack figured they were probably up to the limit in pelts they could pack out and planned to discuss setting a departure date with Gus. He waited for three days and Gus did not appear. On the morning of the fourth day, Zack set out to search for his missing partner.

Zack found Gus' body after two days of searching. It did not take an expert reader of sign to tell what happened to him. Gus had inadvertently come up on a sow Grizzly Bear, just awakening from hibernation, while exploring a cave. He managed to mortally wound the bear with his pistol and, while being mauled, thrust his knife into her throat. She killed Gus in a frenzy of pain and did the same to his horse, which had been securely tied just outside the cave entrance. She died next to the horse, leaving her cub to starve to death in the cave.

Zack covered Gus with a pile of stones after he gathered all of Gus' possessions he could find. Each stone he placed was like leaving part of himself. Over the months of living and trapping together he and Gus had become friends.

It was only after a stern talk with himself that Zack was able to begin preparations to pack out. For several days after returning to the cabin he sat in stunned grief. He began to stir from his isolation when Hunka appeared at the door of the cabin and snorted to gain Zack's attention. Then he became aware of his having neglected the horse and mules and set about to tend to them. He cooked himself a hot meal and thought through the tasks for packing out. Never had he felt a loss such as losing Gus. He was grieving and felt enormously lonely. Deep within him he knew he needed to get to Ben's. He hoped he might run across other trappers during the trip but if not there would surely be someone he knew at Ben's. He needed to be around his own kind.

CHAPTER 6

THE FLATBOAT

Ben was a man who had accurately assessed the potential of locating a trading post where he did and so far it was paying well. He had a very profitable load of furs soon to be on their way to St. Louis and was staying competitive with the rendezvous system organized by The American Fur Company. The greatest danger to his enterprise was the lack of a predictable flow of supplies from St. Louis. Up to now he had been lucky and he knew if he wanted to stay competitive he must have a better system of resupplying. He was working on an idea and invited Zack for a meal to make an offer to him.

Ben started the offer in a seemingly causal manner, "What ya figure to do after ya finish with Gus' kin?"

Zack pondered the question and replied, "I have some business to settle with my brother. He made me an offer to throw in with him to guide fer the caravans. I don't have the details on it so I'll just have to see what it's about. But I figure, like I said, to be comin' back this'a way fer a few more seasons of trappin' and maybe a bit more tradin'. Gus showed me the way to the Utes and they be prime fer a heap of tradin'."

Ben had known Zack for some time and knew that Zack could be counted on to get a job done. There wasn't another man he trusted more. He also knew that Zack was respected enough that any number of offers could be presented to him. Knowing that he decided to make a strong pitch. "Ol' Hoss," he said, "you be a man I can trust and count on. I want ya to throw in with me."

The offer took Zack by surprise and he replied, "Whatcha got in mind Ben?"

Ben described wanting Zack to be his purchasing agent in St. Louis and to be responsible for seeing the supplies got delivered to the trading post. He went on to describe that he could have Mr. Allen draw up a letter of credit at his bank and a letter of introduction to the Berthold Mercantile Company. He was nearly finished with a list of needed supplies, which was going to St. Louis with the flatboat and offered to show it to Zack. "Mister Allen," he reported, "tells me this be a good way to get a good price on goods and delivery. And that's figuring a fee fer you fer buyin' and packin' to my place."

Zack asked a few questions as he pondered the offer. On the surface, Ben's offer was more appealing than the one from James. Zack would be the master of the outfit in Ben's offer. To work for James and the American Fur Company presented the possibility of many masters. Both offers would get him back to the mountains from St. Louis. Ben's offer was well timed in that Zack had been thinking that very day about what was he going to do now that Gus was gone. He needed a purpose; a sense of direction beyond trying to find Gus' kinfolk and Ben was filling that need.

Zack stood and with his hand extended for a handshake said, "Done! When do I leave?"

Ben gripped Zack's hand and with a big smile replied, "Tomorrow. That'll give us time to go over the papers and get ya introduced to Cap'n Mac. We'll go over to the flatboat to meet 'em. He's a right good pilgrim fer a flatlander."

Patrick McCracken, or Cap'n Mac as he was known to his crew, was a short, broad man with the appearance of great strength. His rust red hair was trimmed and combed beneath a gray knitted cap. His beard, also neatly trimmed, matched his hair. He wore a plaid shirt with the sleeves rolled up and two pistols were firmly secured in a wide belt. While navigating the river he commanded the crew of five from atop the boathouse while he manned the long sweep rudder.

Patrick McCracken learned his trade on the Ohio and Mississippi Rivers. As a young man he crewed on several flatboat trips to New Orleans, where after the cargo was sold, the boat was disassembled and sold for lumber. Twice he walked the Natchez Trace back home to Pennsylvania. He earned the reputation of being an honest, dependable boatman before he started to build his own boats and seeking out cargo contracts. When the steamboats on the Ohio River captured the better cargo contracts he went west to ply his trade in new waters. In November he and his crew brought a load of supplies to Ben in twin-hulled cargo canoes. While building a flatboat they wintered with Ben. The flatboat would take them and a load of furs back to St. Louis.

Cap'n Mac was supervising the loading of the last of the supplies to get them to St. Louis when Ben and Zack boarded the flatboat. With an introduction and a handshake Cap'n Mac approved the well-armed trapper as a passenger. He reported the flatboat as ready to depart in the morning.

*   *   *

The first rays of the rising sun streaked the thin, white clouds in the eastern sky when Zack boarded the flatboat. With the command "shove off," the craft was pushed away from the bank toward the current. Zack gave a quick wave and "Watch yer top knot," to Ben who stood on the bank to watch his furs start their journey to St. Louis.

"Watch your'n," Ben called back. He watched the flatboat until it disappeared around the bend in the river.

The flatboat crew quickly fell into the rhythm of poling the heavily laden, clumsy craft while it was expertly maneuvered by their captain. Zack easily adapted to the routine of the rivermen, however soon found it boring. He volunteered to take a turn at poling, with Cap'n Mac's approval, and before long was being assigned a poling station to give a crewman some rest. The days were spent poling all day with only a short rest at midday. Toward evening Cap'n Mac would select a site to tie up for the night. He preferred banks bare of brush or, when available, a river island. The evening was spent preparing a meal, eating and sleeping. A low-rise platform, in front of the boathouse, served as the onboard cooking fire. A heavy iron grill resting on flat stones had been constructed to fit the platform. The meals were monotonous servings of beans and stewed jerky. Before long Zack wished he had brought along a sack of seasoned flour. After sleeping among the bales the crew started again at dawn.

On the sixth morning of the journey Zack rose as usual and was puzzled by the inactivity of the crew. They were not rising and attending to their duties. Two men continued to sleep while the other three appeared to be taking the day off. One man was leisurely washing a shirt in the river. Cap'n Mac was sitting on a fur bale sipping coffee. Seeing Zack's puzzlement he said, "It's Sunday."

"Sunday?" queried Zack.

"Aye, Sunday, a day of rest," responded the captain, "I pay no mind to preaching and church doings on the river but I give my crew some rest every Sunday morning when I can." After another sip of coffee he continued, "We have a feller who will read from the good book later if you a mind to listen."

"Ain't heard readin' from the Bible since I can't remember when," responded Zack

After a leisurely morning meal a tall, thin man named Enos Bates read the story of Sampson. Zack enjoyed his deep, rich voice and the feeling he put into the story. The story of strength and deceit somehow seemed appropriate in the wilderness, under the expansive spring sky. After the reading Zack asked Cap'n Mac if he could go hunting. He had a desire for fresh meat as a change to the routine meals. Cap'n Mac told him he had two hours to hunt. In a few minutes Zack was standing on a knoll overlooking the river. Off in the distance he saw a small group of antelope grazing. It took Zack almost an hour to stalk to rifle range. From the cover of a thick sage bush he removed the patch cloth from his possible bag and tied it to his ramrod. Keeping low he pushed the ramrod vertically into the soil an arms length away from the bush. The patch cloth fluttered in the breeze. Moving to the opposite side of the bush he assumed a sitting firing position. The curious pronghorns were taking some steps in his direction when he was ready to shoot. When they approached to within one hundred yards he fired. Within seconds, living up to their reputation as the fleetest animals on the prairie, the antelope were gone. Except for one. Zack retrieved his ramrod and reloaded.

Zack decided to prepare the antelope for transportation with minimal preparation. He cut off the head, lower legs and disemboweled it. He was able to carry it over his shoulders with having lessened the weight. He chose a more direct route back to the river and guided on a huge boulder, which stood out as the only significant landmark in the surrounding wind waving prairie grass. At the boulder he paused to read the signs of a long abandoned camp, only a few ashes were left of someone's fire. A steep gully, full of brush, lay behind the boulder and at its edge Zack studied the brush for a trail.

He took a few steps on a narrow game trail when he heard thunder. He stopped to scan the cloudless sky and was puzzled by the sound. The thundering sound was increasing, not only as a sound but also as a vibration through the earth and into his moccasins. He scanned the horizon and saw a boiling cloud of dust rising from the direction he had just come from. The dust was preceded by a black mass of stampeding buffalo moving rapidly in his direction. He did not have much time to decide what to do and dropped the antelope. He ran back to the boulder and placed himself up against it. Within seconds the leading animals thundered past the boulder and with them came a thick cloud of dust. The herd parted to pass around the boulder and the opening closed as they ran into the gully. Zack fought back the urge to run as he pressed his face into the boulder. For several minutes the roar of stampeding animals continued until the last of them passed the boulder into the gully. Zack choked and coughed from the thick dust. Cautiously he stepped from the boulder and brushed a thick blanket of dust from his hat and clothes. The dust cloud was becoming more distant in the direction he was going. He walked to the spot where he dropped the antelope and found only scant evidence of it remained. The mass of pounding hooves had crushed and scattered his meat as they had also crushed and scattered the brush. The gully itself was transformed by the herd. The walls had been dug out and the loose soil shifted to fill in the gully to almost a shallow depression. The crush of buffalo had stripped and pounded the land, reshaping the terrain and destroying the vegetation. Only the boulder was unchanged.

Moving toward the river Zack marveled at how the land he recently walked across had changed. It was as if a giant razor had shaved the prairie. In a small grove of Cottonwood trees, closer to the river, he found a dead buffalo calf impaled on a large splinter. He soon had it prepared for carrying and set out for the river. From the high knoll where he started his hunt he saw the flatboat about a half-mile down river from where he left it. From the appearance of the landscape the buffalo had stampeded to the river then turned up stream. Three men were walking on the bank and Zack hailed them. They stopped and waited for Zack to join them.

"It's good to see you alive Zack," exclaimed Cap'n Mac, "I was afeared you was caught in that stampede."

Zack told him about finding safety behind the boulder and asked, "Whatcha doin' out here?"

"Looking for Enos," replied Cap'n Mac, "He went for a walk shortly after you left. We saw the stampede coming and poled down river a piece for fear they was gonna come right on board."

Zack dropped the calf and joined the search. It wasn't long before one of the men found a small piece of cloth. In a few more yards pieces of a boot were found. Just ahead of the search party a gust of wind stirred the dust and with it pages of a Bible tumbled on the ground and swirled in the air funneling into a dust devil. A stronger gust lifted the pages higher and like autumn leaves blew them toward the river. "Your man's gone beaver," concluded Zack as he watched the flying pages, "We'll only find more pieces."

"Aye, I'm afeared you be right," replied the Captain.

"Here's more, Cap'n," shouted one of the men who continued to move forward and he waved a piece of a belt with the buckle still attached. Signaling with his arm and raising his voice Cap'n Mac shouted, "Come on back."

In most circumstances a meal of fresh veal steaks would be very welcomed but the sudden death of a crew member created an atmosphere of gloom. The usually jovial crew ate in silence. Although Zack did not know Enos Bates well, he could identify with the men who did. He knew what it was like to lose a friend. They were all reminded that this harsh, often cruel, land had them at its mercy.

Cap'n Mac changed the poling routine by putting himself into a poling station. While he took a turn at poling the men who wanted experience with steering the flatboat took the sweep rudder. Zack took some turns at the rudder. Cap'n Mac resumed his position at the rudder when they entered the Missouri River. The Missouri River was notorious for its currents, snags and floating debris and he wanted to be on the rudder in order to be able to steer clear of the hazards. In just a few miles down stream he gave the command to prepare to tie up to a crude wharf. He steered the flatboat into position while one of his crew jumped to the wharf with a rope. The flatboat was quickly secured to the wharf. The path from the wharf opened into a wide trail, which lead to a collection of rude cabins that faced a common street. Cap'n Mac led the way into this crude settlement with his destination being the largest of the buildings.

Zack noted a stench in the air as they got close to the cabins, the stench of where man has lingered to long without taking proper care of his waste. Several dogs began to bark at the strangers and the people of the settlement looked to see who was coming.

Cap'n Mac pushed through the door of the store that also served as a saloon. Zack joined the rivermen at a table. A fat, dirty woman served them mugs of warm ale. As they drank their ale one of the crew tried to get friendly with the woman and while making sexual remarks patted her on her huge buttocks. She ignored his remarks and hands. She was more interested in some other patrons in this dingy saloon and waddled off to tend to them. The fat woman returned to the table of rivermen to serve more ale but Cap'n Mac dropped some coins on the table as he downed the last sip in his mug signaling it was time to depart. The men finished their mugs and pushed away from the table. Cap'n Mac handed some coins to one of the crew and told him to buy any sort of food that would add some variety to their meals during the remaining trip. He expressed a desire for a pie or any fruit. The four crew men left together to fill the request.

Once outside Cap'n Mac remarked, "A foul place, but a welcome stop for a crew that has worked hard." Zack nodded in agreement as they leisurely walked toward the river. While walking Cap'n Mac asked, "Zack, where are you going to be staying in St. Louis?"

Remembering his brother's letter Zack replied, "I reckon I'll put up with my brother."

"Who's your brother?" questioned Cap'n Mac, "Maybe I know him."

"James Clayton," Zack responded.

"James Clayton of the Missouri Fur Company?" inquired Cap'n Mac.

It seemed strange to Zack to have his brother described in that manner but he replied, "Waugh, that be him. You know him Cap'n?"

"Can't say I know him," Cap'n Mac hesitated, "I know of him and saw him once at the wharf when I started the trip to Ben's. How long has it been since you seen him?"

"Four, maybe five seasons," and sensing the hesitation in Cap'n Mac's voice Zack asked, "Why do ya ask?"

With a pause to carefully choose his words, Cap'n Mac said, "Maybe he's changed some since you seen him last. He's become a big man in the fur business since your Pa died."

Puzzled by Cap'n Mac's vagueness and wanting more information Zack asked, "Changed, how has he changed?" Zack stopped walking in order to better focus on the conversation and when Cap'n Mac stopped a voice coming from the direction of the settlement called his name.

"Cap'n Mac, Cap'n Mac." It was the crew hurrying to catch up. They displayed two loaves of freshly baked bread and a jar of apple butter to him and said, "Couldn't find a pie but we bought this off a lady who was in the store. Store didn't have what we wanted so she said for us to come to her place." Cap'n Mac examined their buy, nodded his approval and told them to go on ahead to the flat boat.

When they were far enough away to be out of hearing Cap'n Mac turned back to Zack and said, "James Clayton has over bid just enough on furs to drive some of the smaller outfits out of business and there's talk he has pirated more than one plew. Now I can't say he has pirated any furs from me or anyone I know but the stories sound more than just grumbling."

So far Cap'n Mac had not impressed Zack as a malicious man, in fact just the opposite. Zack regarded him as a decent, respectful man. It was not surprising that James could be mixed up in some shady deals but pirating was a bit too much. Feeling a need to come to his brother's defense Zack said, "I've heard of pirating on the Missouri but I figure my brother keeps himself in St. Louie. He never took a shine to the trail."

"Aye, and you be right, from what I hear," responded Cap'n Mac, "but that don't stop him from doing business with river pirates. I hear a big, mean cuss named Snow Logan leads the pirates."

"Never heard of 'em," remarked Zack.

Cap'n Mac continued, "Big feller with snow white hair. Some say his hair turned white when he about drowned down on the Ohio. They say he's as tough as old Mike Fink."

Zack recognized Mike Fink's name who was becoming a legend on the Missouri River and said, "I seen Mike fight once back in St. Louie. Licked four bullwhackers all at once."

"Aye, that be Mike," replied Cap'n Mac, "Like me he's moving furs, only on the upper Missouri or so I hear. Steamboats taking most of the trade on the Mississippi to where a flatboat can't make a decent living."

Wanting to get back to the topic of his brother Zack asked, "How does Snow Logan figure with my brother?"

Up to this point Cap'n Mac was impressed that Zack was not disturbed by the remarks he made about James Clayton. As they resumed their walking he said, "Well, I hear Snow was pirating furs and wanting to sell them short of hauling them to Pittsburgh himself. Your brother was buying furs from his livery stable, before he threw in with the Missouri Fur Company, and he bought furs from Snow."

They stopped at the entrance to the wharf while Zack pondered this information. Just a few yards away they noticed two rough looking men push a canoe into the water and began to energetically paddle down stream. Zack was distracted from his thoughts about James by the activity and said, "Those coons 'peer to be in a powerful hurry. Know 'em?"

"Seen them around," answered Cap'n Mac, "A couple of no account river rats named Pettis. They take odd jobs on the river, short hauls and such. Never crewed for me." The canoe was disappearing around a bend as Cap'n Mac boarded the flatboat and climbed to his position on the boathouse. Zack got into position at his poling station, waiting for the command to shove off.

From atop the boathouse Cap'n Mac called to one of the crew, "Mister Cooper, before we shove off hand me up that swivel gun."

"Aye, Cap'n," the man responded and sitting down his pole moved toward the boathouse door. He stepped in and reaching beyond the stored food, lifted the heavy flintlock gun to his chest. Then facing up toward Cap'n Mac he lifted the gun toward the roof. Cap'n Mac grabbed the gun and placed the swivel rod to drop into a pedestal that was positioned so he could reach it while manning the rudder. The swivel gun was a two-inch, smooth bore, short barrel musket especially designed for boats and ships. It was loaded with a half dozen lead rifle balls. Cap'n Mac gave the order to shove off and the crew poled into the swift current. The water was too deep to continue poling so the crew secured their poles to let the river do the work.

All the talk about river pirates made Cap'n Mac decide to prepare his defense for a possible encounter during the miles remaining to St. Louis. The swivel gun had been placed in the boathouse the day before during a heavy rainstorm but with a growing apprehension Cap'n Mac wanted it immediately available to him. The crew, including Zack, was in a mood to just sit back while the flatboat drifted with the current. Zack was thinking about James and the disquieting report when Cap'n Mac called out, "Keep a sharp eye for trouble."

"Aye, Cap'n," someone said as the crew took lookout positions, one on the bow and one on each side. The man in the bow called out, "Tree ahead, Cap'n."

"I see it," came a response. It was not uncommon to encounter large floating tree trunks on the Missouri River and Cap'n Mac steered to avoid it.

They were making good speed as Cap'n Mac steered the flatboat to take full advantage of the swift current. He was steering to avoid another tree in the water and the course was toward an area where dense brush covered the bank. Suddenly from the direction of the bank came a yell, "HELP, HELP."

The crewman in the bow pointed in that direction and as a man waded in the water called, "Man in the water ahead."

"I see him," acknowledged Cap'n Mac. The man was wading in waist deep water and waving his arms as he continued to call for help. With the command of "To the poles," the crew took up their poles and stood in readiness for the next command. As they approached within one hundred yards of the man Cap'n Mac ordered "Set poles."

The crew and the poles strained to accomplish this abrupt braking maneuver. With just enough volume in his voice for the crew to hear Cap'n Mac said, "Be ready to pull away on my order. This could be a trap."

"Aye, Cap'n" the men responded in quiet unison.

In the next breath Cap'n Mac shouted, "WHAT BE THE TROU-BLE?" in the direction of the man in the water.

The man stopped waving and cupping his hands to his mouth called back, "PIRATES JUMPED ME. TOOK MY FURS."

The gap between the flatboat and the man was slowly closing. "HOW LONG AGO?" called Cap'n Mac.

"TWO DAYS. THEY TOOK MY WOMAN," came back a reply.

Suddenly Cap'n Mac shouted, "QUICK POLE!" and steered to return to the middle of the river. The crew responded instantly, straining their poles on the river bottom. Zack saw something move in the brush. A shot rang out. The round hit Cap'n Mac in the right thigh and he saved him-self from falling off the roof by holding onto the rudder pole. The man in the water furiously swam toward the bank. Zack dropped his pole and grabbed his rifle. He aimed and fired at the muzzle flash of a second shot from the brush. His shot caused a pained howl. That man's round harm-lessly hit the wall of the boathouse.

"GET 'em!" was shouted in the brush and two more shots rang out. One round hit the side of the flatboat and the other hit the pole of a laboring crewman. The pole splintered causing the man to drop behind a bale for cover. Keeping low Zack reloaded his rifle then cautiously raised his head above the gunnel. He saw a canoe pulling out from some overhanging leafy limbs and was being paddled to come up behind the flatboat. Another shot from the bank hit the edge of the boathouse roof. The pirates were trying to disable the man steering the flatboat.

Cap'n Mac returned fire with the swivel gun. The rifle balls spread out, ripping through the brush. They did not hit anyone but their effect caused the pirates to seek more cover. Zack raised his rifle to aim at the men in the canoe. The man who was riding in front raised a rifle to aim at the back of Cap'n Mac. The canoe was getting close enough that Zack recognized the Pettis brothers as he fired. Zack's round struck Luke Pettis in the chest, knocking him out of his seat and into his brother's lap.

Cap'n Mac saw Zack shoot and realized that something was happening behind the flatboat. He turned, drawing a pistol and also fired at the canoe while Carl Pettis was struggling with the sudden shifting of weight in the canoe. Cap'n Mac's round penetrated the canoe wall striking Carl in the foot. He howled as the canoe capsized. Zack fired his pistol at the bank just to keep the pirates heads down while the flatboat was getting out of rifle range.

The flatboat was continuing to pull away in the current when Cap'n Mac called out, "Mister Cooper!" Then he collapsed, falling from the roof onto some fur bales and rolled off onto the deck. Mister Cooper quickly scrambled up on the boathouse roof to man the rudder while Zack and a crewman rushed to Cap'n Mac. They quickly examined the fallen Captain and saw blood on his trouser leg. Zack carefully cut the trouser material open and applied a kerchief to a bleeding rifle ball wound. They brought Cap'n Mac to a sitting position on the deck with his back to a bale and held a cup to his lips for a drink of water. Zack was handed a long scarf, which he used to tightly wrap the kerchief in place. "How bad is it?" gritted Cap'n Mack through his teeth.

"Ball took some hide and a little meat," Zack replied, "Peers it missed the bone. You'll be gimpy fer awhile."

Cap'n Mac ordered the crewmen to get to lookout posts. Zack set about gathering all the firearms and brought them back to where Cap'n Mac was sitting. "Hope ya don't mind if I get us reloaded." he asserted. Cap'n Mac nodded his approval. When Zack had all the small arms loaded he loaded the swivel gun and returned it to the pedestal.

"Did you see it was the Pettis boys in that canoe?" asked Cap'n Mac as Zack was checking the bandage for bleeding.

Satisfied the bleeding was slowing Zack sat back and replied, "Waugh, I got the one in front."

Seeking more information Cap'n Mac asked, "Anyone see either come up?"

Zack had not seen either man come to the surface but called out to the crew for their observations before he replied. They all answered by saying they did not see anyone in the water. "Nobody seen 'em, Cap'n," reported Zack.

After a pause Zack questioned, "How did ya know that coon was a pirate?"

Looking up from his leg and with a pained grimace Cap'n Mac answered, "I didn't know for sure. I know that pirates and Injuns used the same trick on the Ohio and I was just being careful."

"Waugh," acknowledged Zack.

Cap'n Mac took deep breath and called to above him, "How we doing, Mister Cooper?"

"On course, Cap'n," came down a reply.

Zack leaned closer to Cap'n Mac and said, "Cap'n, I want ya to put me on the bank."

Cap'n Mac's eyes widened, as he looked Zack in the face and asked, "Why?"

"Figure to scout those varmints," Zack replied with deadly seriousness, "I don't shine to skulkers. I wouldn't ask ya to wait fer me. I can walk to St. Louie from here iffen I have to."

Cap'n Mac thought of trying to dissuade Zack but with his pain and ebbing energy could not think of a reason to refuse him. He called upward, "Mister Cooper, head for the bank. We're putting his man ashore."

"Aye, Cap'n," was the reply as Mister Cooper made the rudder correction to change course.

Zack quickly packed for a several day journey and returned to Cap'n Mac's side. The flatboat was easing toward the bank while Cap'n Mac told Zack how to locate his house in St. Louis. Just as Zack was slipping over the forward gunnel into knee high water Cap'n Mac called out, "Any message for St. Louis, Zack?"

Wading toward the bank Zack answered over his shoulder, "No message, Cap'n."

Zack watched the flatboat back up and swing toward the center of the river. He knew Cap'n Mac's offer to carry a message to St. Louis meant carrying a message to James and he pondered on why he declined. He concluded the rule of being cautious about announcing one's whereabouts, learned in the mountains, also applied to St. Louis and to James. If James had changed, as Cap'n Mac indicated he had, then it just may be best to be cautious. As the flatboat was again drifting in the current, Zack started his trek up river.

The first man sign Zack came upon was where a man had crawled out of the river, leaving a wet impression on the bank. His footprints indicated he was limping heavily and Zack thought, *That Pettis fella must've made it.* There were no efforts to conceal the tracks, which made them easy to follow. Carl Pettis obviously was not expecting to be followed. Zack continued to be wary, however, knowing it could be a fatal mistake to under estimate even a wounded adversary. The next sign he found was where the first man in the ambush plan had waded into the water then returned to the brush. One by one Zack found signs of four other men who participated in the ambush. Most telling was where he found pieces of a rifle. His round must have struck a rifle, shattering the stock and hammer. There were a few drops of blood around the spot. The owner of the rifle should have at least some minor wounds from wood and metal splinters. Zack also found the area where the balls of the swivel gun ripped through the brush.

Zack located the pirates' camp behind a knoll. It appeared to have been hastily abandoned, fire ashes were still warm. Skewered above the ashes was a venison roast. Zack cut off a slice and ate it as he prowled the campsite. The only other item of value, left behind, was a thirty-foot piece of hemp rope that had been used for a picket line for a dozen horses. Zack followed the horses' tracks for a mile and saw where two sets of tracks left the others. He decided that since two horses were heading in the general direction of St. Louis he would follow them.

After two hours of following the tracks, Zack left the trail to walk up a hill so he could see farther ahead. The sun would be setting in an hour and he hoped he would be able to see some sign of the riders before it got dark. He could see no sign of the men he was pursuing. It took him another hour to walk to the next high point in the rolling hills and from that elevation scanned in the direction he figured the men to be going. He was about to descend to a grove of trees to set up a night camp when he saw a thin wisp of white smoke coming from beyond the next hill. He figured he had just enough light left to get over the hill. If the smoke was coming from the camp of the men he was after, he'd have to try to slip in on them in the dark, or get into position to ambush them in the morning.

Zack quietly picked his way through the trees, guiding on a brightly burning fire. Every few feet he stopped to study what he could see in the ring of light. When he came to a big tree that stood on the edge of the camp he carefully slipped behind it. From his close vantage point he was able to make out enough details of the dim camp. One man appeared to have retired to his bedroll while the other sat on the ground starring into the fire. While Zack watched the man fed small limbs to the fire. There wasn't enough light to tell how well the men were armed. Two horses were tied up just beyond the campfire light.

While Zack was trying to figure out if these were the men he was following the man at the fire rose and limped toward the big tree. Zack recognized

him as a Pettis. *But why is he coming this way?* Zack wondered with some
alarm. The question was quickly answered as Carl Pettis manipulated his
trousers to urinate. He stopped to aim his stream at the base of the tree
when Zack stepped from behind the tree with his rifle leveled at Carl's belly.
"Just keep pissin' and don't make a sound," whispered Zack. Carl made a
startled, "Ugh!" Zack cocked the rifle as the muzzle came up to Carl's face.
"I said not a sound," growled Zack, "Now get down on yer belly!" Carl
Pettis was dumfounded by the sudden, threatening figure and immediately
complied with the order. Zack tied the man's hands behind his back with
the picket rope. Then removing the man's bandanna from around his neck
poked it into his mouth. When that was done he whispered close to Carl's
ear, "You lay real quiet ol' coon or I'll skin ya alive!" Carl was effectively
immobilized by the rope and by fear.

In the next minute the sleeping man was awakened by something hard
and cold pressing against his nose. His eyes snapped open with a start to see
a pistol in front of his face. He reached for his rifle and realized it was gone.
A cold chill raced through him and before he could react he heard, "Just lay
easy ol' coon. We got some talking to do. Pull yer kiver back real slow. One
quick move and ya be a dead coon!" Unlike Carl, this man did not comply
and reached for the pistol in his belt. Zack shot him in the chest.

Carl Pettis was forced to limp back to the fire and was roughly pushed
down to sit on the ground. With a wooden spoon Zack helped himself to
a skillet of beans next to the fire. He did not like the beans and poured a
cup of coffee. The coffee was barely warm so he sat the pot closer to the
fire. "Cold coffee and bad beans, can't say much fer yer camp ol' coon,"
Zack taunted.

Zack drew his knife and approached the terrified man. If ever fear
could be seen in a man's eyes Carl Pettis was the man. Zack removed the
gag while he rested the heavy knife point on Carl's chest. Zack had no
intention of causing physical harm but Carl did not know that.

"Now ol' coon, I want some answers. No lies iffen ya know what's good fer ya." Still dumfounded by the suddenness of his calamity all Carl could do was nod his head in acknowledgment.

"Who was ya with in that pirate ambush today?" interrogated Zack.

Fear and the bandanna gag left Carl's mouth dry and he paused to try and form some words. Zack increased the pressure of the knife point and Carl rushed a stream of names, "Snow, Jake, ah… Jeb, Luke, ah…Potter, ah, ah…Black Dog."

"Who's Snow," was the next question.

"Snow Logan, he'sss the bossss," trembled Carl.

Zack asked about each name. He learned that Jake was the man he had just shot and was the man whose job it was to lure the flatboat into the ambush. Luke was Carl's older brother whose body was floating somewhere in the Missouri River. Jeb and Potter Akins were cousins who had come west with Snow from Ohio. Black Dog was a half-breed Osage Indian.

"Where's Snow and the others now?" grilled Zack.

"Don't know fer sure, back to the store I reckon," quivered Carl.

"Who got shot?" Zack continued.

"Luke, Luke my brother got shot." Carl answered.

"Who else?" Zack pressed.

"Snow, Snow took a ball on his rifle. Got some splinters in 'em," Carl replied.

Through more questioning Zack learned that Carl and Jake were returning to Kentucky. They quit Show Logan's pirating gang because Snow blamed them for the ambush having gone afoul. And Carl, who saw his brother die, just had enough of the pirating life and wanted to go home. Then suddenly remembering his traveling companion, Carl asked, "Where's Jake?"

Using the knife as a pointer Zack signaled in the direction of the man lying dead in the bedroll. Seeing Jake's body was more than Carl could take all in one day. He hung his head and moaned, a deep hopeless moan from the depths of his soul.

With the blade of the knife raising Carl's chin, Zack continued the questioning, "Ever hear of James Clayton?"

Carl was almost too overcome with the day's events to answer, but the prodding of the knife forced a response, "Yeah, he be the man Snow sells furs and goods to." Carl did not know where the exchanges took place nor where the furs were stored, except he heard something about a warehouse. He had not been there.

Zack led the depleted man to a tree and loosely bound him to it, facing away from the camp. He took Jake's pistol but left the rifle, camp gear and supplies. He figured Carl would come around enough to work his way out of the loose knots and by that time would find his tormentor long gone. Zack drank some coffee, saddled the horses and headed for St. Louis. He figured to slow ride in the dark for an hour or so then get some sleep in a cold camp.

As he rode he felt no remorse for killing the two river pirates. One died in the heat of battle and the other in a duel of the quickest. But having captured Carl Pettis was another story. Zack had not faced a situation of having an adversary as a prisoner. It was not difficult for Zack to decide what to do with Carl once he had the information he wanted. He figured the man to have enough grit to limp to a settlement and was not left defenseless. Under the circumstances it was the decent thing to do.

CHAPTER 7

ST. LOUIS

St. Louis had not grown so eastern that the people on the streets would stop to stare at a man dressed like a trapper fresh from the mountains. Such a sight was not unusual. St. Louis had become an important center in the fur business and all manner of men associated with the fur trade were commonplace. To Zack, the city was much different than when he left it. What used to be a town with homes and businesses located near the waterfront was now a city, spread out where nothing but trees and brush used to be. He marveled at some of the grand houses in what used to be the edge of town. He rode by the house where he was born and raised and it appeared to be occupied. True to the letter James' house was located on a new street, not far from their family home. Riding slowly past a white-washed fence and gate with the name CLAYTON painted boldly on a cross member Zack decided to glean as much information as possible without stopping.

The house was a large, two-story wood framed structure with a spacious front porch. To the side of the house sat a stable. The double doors of the stable were open and within it sat a shiny black carriage. Between the house and the stable a Negro man was slow beating a rope suspended carpet. An older, heavyset Negro woman appeared at the door of a small house, to the rear of the stable. She scolded the man and he began beating the carpet more vigorously. A whitewashed picket fence surrounded the property. Roses and other flowering plants added bright colors to the grounds.

Three women were standing on the porch, two of which wore bonnets that matched their long dresses. The third woman was slightly taller than her companions and also wore a full-length dress. Zack heard a carriage coming up behind him, which turned into the short driveway leading to the house. The women stopped their conversation to look in the direction of the approaching carriage and Zack got a better look at them. The taller woman with dark hair, fixed in a bun on the back of her head, looked at Zack then back to the women. Zack figured her to be James' wife who was seeing guests to their carriage.

*   *   *

The large brick building of the Berthold Mercantile Company came into view as a familiar landmark from which Zack worked his way through the wagons and horses toward the waterfront. He found Cap'n

Mac's flatboat and noted it had been unloaded. Two hundreds yards away a steamboat was maneuvering to a new wharf and Zack paused to watch it.

With only one inquiry for further directions to the McCracken house Zack soon found himself tying up the horses in front. The house reminded him of the house he was raised in, small, snug and neat. He ducked to step under a low porch roof and rapped on the door. A round-faced woman in a white apron opened the door. "Scuse me ma'am, I'm lookin' fer Cap'n Mac," Zack politely inquired.

The woman was startled by the appearance of an armed, trail worn trapper and in her uneasiness stepped backwards. She stepped on the foot of a small boy who had followed her to the door. The boy howled and began to cry. She quickly picked him up and was ready to say something to Zack when a voice from within the house called out, "What in tarnation is going on?" Before she could respond Patrick McCracken crutch stepped into the room. He saw Zack standing at the door and with some exuberance said, "Zack! Come on in. I figured you'd show up sooner or later."

Cap'n Mac steadied himself on the single, crude crutch and extended his hand for a handshake. "It's good to see you Zack. You look fit," Cap'n Mac greeted.

"It's good to see ya too Cap'n. I didn't figure to see ya standing this soon," said Zack observing the crutch from the doorway.

"I'll be on my own power before I get used to this fool stick," replied Cap'n Mac as he waved the crutch while gingerly balanced on his one good leg. "Come on in and let's sit a spell. I want to hear how you made out," invited Cap'n Mac.

Removing his hat, Zack entered the house, which was filled with the aroma of baking bread. The woman retreated a few steps, still holding the crying boy. "Zack this is my wife, Lucy, and my son, Robert." Zack nodded in their direction. "Lucy, this is the fellow I was telling you about," as the introduction continued.

Lucy smiled and said, "Pleased to meet you Mister Clayton," acknowledging having learned his name from her husband.

Pointing to the boy Cap'n Mac said, "Robert turned three years old while we floated the Platte."

The boy stopped crying and Zack said, "Good to meet ya, Robert."

Robert turned his face into his mother's ample bosom. "Oh now, you can say hello to Mister Clayton," cajoled his mother. Robert shook his head no. Addressing Zack Lucy related, "He's a might shy with strangers."

"Waugh," replied Zack, communicating he understood, which produced a look of puzzlement on Lucy's face. Zack noted the puzzlement and realized that the slang of the trappers may not be understood by city dwellers. He was about to explain the meaning of the singular sound when Cap'n Mac said, "How about some vittles? We was just fixing to eat."

"Don't wanna be no trouble," replied Zack.

"No trouble, no trouble at all. Besides we got lots of talking to do," Cap'n Mac said affirming the invitation and in the next breath instructed his wife to set another place at the table.

The meal was unlike anything Zack had eaten since leaving St. Louis. There was roast beef and gravy, boiled potatoes, newly picked peas and fresh baked bread. Between bites, Cap'n Mac reported the final events of the trip, the delivery of the furs and the fuss his wife made about his wound.

Zack ate hungrily and made only brief acknowledgments to the report. He found himself watching Lucy helping Robert with his plate. The boy was more interested in staring at the stranger than eating. Zack was working on a large piece of mincemeat pie and coffee when Cap'n Mac asked about the pirates. Lucy began to clear the table and Zack felt a little uncomfortable about going into any details with Lucy in hearing distance. He minimized the story and only revealed that he learned Snow Logan was the leader of the attempted ambush. Sensing the discomfort Cap'n Mac did not ask for more details. Except for the initial few minutes of uncertainty Zack felt warmed and welcomed in the McCracken home.

Lucy reminded him of his own mother, who died when he was eight years old. Cap'n Mac also reported having dispatched Mister Cooper to report the death of Enos Bates to his family, along with his wages. He concluded the report with, "But his wages won't last long with that passel of kids."

Zack figured to keep one of the pirate's horses for himself to get around on but he didn't need two. He offered the horse to be delivered to the Bates family. Cap'n Mac accepted the offer. The talk of the grieving Bates family reminded Zack of his intention to find Gus' family and he asked about a place to board the horse while he was gone. Cap'n Mac did not have a stable nor ground to keep a horse and suggested a neighbor who did.

"Have you looked up your brother?" asked Cap'n Mac.

"Not yet," Zack replied, "There'll be time enough fer that later."

"Well the reason I ask is to say you're more than welcome to put up here, just like I said before," invited Cap'n Mac. Zack thanked him for the hospitality already extended and accepted the invitation.

Zack departed the McCracken house early in the morning to take care of business. He went to the bank and cashed the draft from Ben Thompson. Then he went to the Berthold Mercantile Company store and purchased a full set of clothes plus a newly designed belt with holsters sewn into it that would hold a brace of pistols. He also bought a small bag of stick candy. Zack carried the bundle of new clothes into a barbershop bearing a sign: BATHS- New water: 10 cents/ Used: 5 cents.

After almost two hours he emerged from the barbershop clipped of his mane, clean shaven, bathed and wearing new clothes. By the time he walked back to the McCracken house his feet hurt from the new boots. Lucy and Patrick McCracken were awed at his change in appearance. He had left a grizzled, trail worn trapper to return as a handsome, amiable gentleman.

Knowing some of the ways and words of the mountain men Cap'n Mac teased Zack, "Iffen I didn't know ya, I'd took fer a pilgrim." Zack grinned at this pun on the greeting often exchanged between trappers: "I'd took ya fer a Injun."

Lucy offered to wash up his leather clothing and took the bundle into the kitchen. To Robert a new stranger had entered his house and he tailed his mother from the room. Zack had Cap'n Mac tempt him back with a piece of stick candy. Robert remained close to his father while he sucked on the sweet treat. With his father's encouragement he did, however, thank Zack for the candy.

Still having some things to do Zack saddled his horse and noted the other one was missing. Cap'n Mac had it delivered to the Bates family for sale or use. Zack went by the neighbor's place that agreed to board the horse and Zack paid him in advance. He then went to the office where tickets for steamboat tickets were sold and bought a ticket for the next day to Cairo, Illinois. Having completed his business for the day he decided it was time to visit his brother.

Zack rode through the gate and dismounted at the hitching rail near the porch. As he dismounted he heard a pained cry of, "No mo', Masta. I be good," coming from behind the stable. Zack walked to the stable and as he turned the corner he saw a Negro man on the ground, protecting his face from a flailing buggy whip.

The man beating him was coughing into a handkerchief while wielding the whip. Out of the corner of his eye the man saw someone approaching. He turned toward the intruder and gruffly said, "What do you want?" Almost at the same moment James recognized his brother. He lowered the whip and handkerchief and exclaimed, "Zachary!" Before Zack could react James grabbed him in an embrace. A spasm of coughing terminated the embrace as James disengaged to cover his mouth.

Regaining his speech James said, "I was just teaching this Nigra some manners," and turning to the downed man ordered, "You get back to work, Toby. Don't let me catch you sassing Aunt Milly again!"

The man responded, "Yas suh, Masta." and crawled away.

Zack barely recognized his brother. He was dressed in the finery of a wealthy St. Louis gentleman, like some men he had noticed in the bank and store. James was thin and very pale. Waiting for another coughing spell to subside Zack asked, "How are ya, James?"

Wiping his mouth with the cloth James replied, "Could be better," and giving a sweeping arm gesture said, "You look well, brother."

"I am," responded Zack as James indicated they should walk toward the house.

They entered the rear door of the house and from the kitchen James called out, "Nancy, Nancy, guess who's here?"

A woman's voice called back, "I'm in the parlor, James." Following James, Zack maneuvered around a large, formal dining room table as he followed James toward the parlor. Nancy Clayton was seated on a settee being served a glass of sherry by a shapely, young mulatto woman. She remained seated as the men entered the room.

"Nancy, This is my brother Zachary." Nancy smiled and extended her hand to the visitor. Nancy Clayton was an attractive, cultured woman who knew how to be charming.

Zack felt awkward as he grasped her soft, white hand and said, "Pleased to meet you." Zack was becoming conscious of his usual rough manner of speaking and was struggling to return to a more civilized style. His struggle was not apparent to Nancy.

"Lilly, pour these two gentlemen some sherry," she directed to the waiting servant. Lilly poured the dark wine from a decanter into small matching wine glasses. "This is my afternoon repose," Nancy reported as she raised her wine glass, "and I'd be delighted if you gentlemen will join me." Lilly brought the wine to them on a silver tray. "That will be all, Lilly," ordered Nancy. As Lilly departed Nancy added, "Oh, Lilly, tell Aunt Milly we'll be having a guest for dinner and see that the guest room is prepared."

"Yes'um," came a quiet reply.

Then turning to Zack she continued, "That is if you have no other plans, Zachary?" Before he could respond she changed the subject to

James' success and his plan to build a bigger house for them. She expertly engaged Zack in conversation and before long had him telling of his "adventures," as she put it, in the mountains.

Zack was careful to avoid telling of his encounters with the river pirates. He told of his intention to travel to Cairo to locate the Gusterson family. James was suddenly overcome with a violent coughing spasm and excused himself from the room. Watching him leave, Nancy commented, "Poor dear, this is not one of his better days."

"What's wrong with him?" Zack asked.

In a mocking tone Nancy described many visits to local doctors, whom she declared to be incompetent. She practically spit out the word "consumption" as the diagnosis rendered, and followed with, such was the proof of their incompetence since consumption is a disease of city squalor, not genteel living. Her railings against the doctors were politely interrupted by the heavy set black woman who Zack saw scolding Toby the day before. Aunt Milly wanted Nancy's approval for the dinner menu. Zack rose to Nancy's excusing herself to go to the kitchen but before she left he said, "If I'm staying for dinner I'd better tend to my horse." Nancy told him to call for Toby who would take care of the horse.

Zack led his horse to the stable figuring to find Toby in the vicinity. He opened the closed double door just enough to step through. As his eyes were adjusting to the dimness he heard voices coming from behind a tack room door. The door was slightly ajar and light from a small window in the room streamed through the crack. He recognized James's cough and heard a female pleading voice, "Please Masta, not now." Zack peered through the crack to see James fondling Lilly's exposed breasts. Quietly Zack retraced his steps and as he exited the stable he almost collided with Toby.

Toby had been watching Zack's horse, trying to decide if he should tend to it or wait for instructions. Earlier he saw James and Lilly enter the stable. Toby was in turmoil about the two developing events that could bring his master's wrath down upon him. First, he had long standing instructions to guard his master's privacy when using the tack room, and secondly, he was to tend to a guest's horse if the visit was going to be any more than just a short stay.

He emerged from the outhouse adjusting his trousers and suspenders to see Zack stepping into the stable. He ran toward the stable and nearly ran into Zack while Zack was backing out the door. He nimbly avoided Zack and reached for the horse's reins.

Zack was startled by Toby's sudden approach and came to a defensive posture. When he saw who it was he relaxed and said, "Toby, I'm looking to have my horse tended to."

"Yas suh, Masta Zachary," Toby replied while catching his breath.

Zack had never been addressed in this manner and felt uncomfortable with the extreme subservience. He also felt uncomfortable about inadvertently spying on his brother.

Toby took the reins of the horse and said, "I tend to da horse, Masta Zachary." Zack followed to watch Toby remove the saddle while the horse was drinking from a trough.

Zack studied the working slave and noted him to have the strength of a lithe, wiry man. He appeared to be in his early twenties and was dressed in well-worn trousers, a white short sleeve shirt and was barefoot. His black skin was a dark contrast to the white shirt. When Toby began to curry the horse Zack tried engaging him in conversation and only got "Yas suh" and "No suh" for his efforts. Remembering how he enticed little Robert to be less shy Zack reach into his coat pocket for the sack of stick candy. He removed a stick and began to suck on it. He offered a stick to Toby. Hesitantly, Toby took the candy.

Toby sensed there was something different about Zack, a kindness and respectfulness that he had not known in a white man for a long time. Earlier he overheard Lilly telling Aunt Milly of the introduction in the parlor and his first inclination was to be wary of Zack. He could see now that Zack was different than James, just how different was yet to be seen.

Zack missed his coat pocket when he went to return the sack and it fell to the ground. He knelt down to retrieve it just as James rounded the corner of the stable. What James saw was Toby smiling, to the sweet taste in his mouth, while Zack was picking up something off the ground. James was infuriated by what he interpreted as a lack of servitude on Toby's part. He picked up a stick and advanced toward Toby saying, "How much whipping does it take to teach you some manners, boy?"

Zack stepped between James and Toby, blocking the advance, and said, "James, I was just teaching your Nigra how to properly tend to my horse."

That did not quite ring true to James but he decided for the time being to accept the explanation. But he wasn't through with Toby and while waving the stick at him ordered, "You mind my brother, you hear, boy? No sassing!"

"Yas suh, Masta James," returned a downtrodden reply.

When Zack and James reentered the house they found Nancy supervising Lilly who was setting the table. Seeing James, she said, "I don't know what's got into this girl lately. I have to go looking for her when I want to get something done."

Taking Nancy's arm James led her toward the parlor and promised, "I'll have a word with her later, dear."

Later, in the parlor, Zack inquired about their father's death and the status of his share of the estate. James was vague and evasive as he described having put Zack's share of the estate in a business venture with a high potential for profit. Zack was beginning to understand that there was no account from which he could draw funds when Lilly announced dinner was ready.

During dinner James freely indulged in wine and expounded on Missouri's statehood as a slave state. He reported a growing population of slave owners were becoming politically influential and he was among them. Up to this time Zack had very little experience with the institution of slavery, except for what he'd learned about slavery among the Indians. Before leaving for the mountains he could not recall knowing one slave owner. James was his first direct experience with the relationship between a white master and a Negro slave.

More than once Nancy changed the topic to one of lesser intensity but the more James drank the more he expounded. His political narrative, however, contained pieces of information about his own brief evolution as a slaveholder. When he married Nancy, Aunt Milly was given to them as a wedding gift. She was trained as a cook and household manager in Memphis, Tennessee by Nancy's wealthy uncle. He feared his favorite niece would be left without a competent servant in the frontier culture of St. Louis. James bought Toby shortly after moving into the new house and Lilly was purchased during a trip to New Orleans. From what he'd seen and heard this day Zack concluded his brother was caught up in personal power and status, to which the institution of slavery contributed.

James was barely able to walk when he excused himself from the table. Nancy and Zack sat in embarrassed silence as they listened to his unsteady progress on the stairs. After a heavy door upstairs slammed Nancy turned to Zack and said, "I hope you'll not be too hard on your brother for over indulging. He's been preoccupied with business. I know he'll apologize for his conduct in the morning." Then she began to talk about planning a social so Zack could be introduced to their friends and business associates.

Zack stated his intention to be on a steamboat in the morning. Nancy graciously accepted a delay in her plans for a social and extracted a promise from Zack to attend one when he returned to St. Louis.

Zack thanked Nancy for the dinner and informed her that he had several things to do to prepare for his journey. He rose from the table with the intention of leaving for the McCracken house. Nancy expressed disappointment that he was not staying the night and persuaded him to see the guest room by saying, "This way you'll know your way around when you return."

Zack acquiesced and followed her up the stairs. The sound of James' snoring was heard in the hall as Nancy turned into the guest room. Lilly, who had just finished lighting the lamps from the candle she was carrying, stepped back as Nancy entered. Zack followed and Lilly left the room with only the rustle of her skirt signaling her presence. The room was finely decorated with heavy dark wood furniture and colorful draperies. The oil lamp light softly reflected in the mirror over the fireplace. The headboard of the bed was ornately carved and highly polished. Zack was raised in a home of plain, simple furniture and in recent years, with few exceptions, made his bed on the ground. He could not recall ever having seen a bedroom such as this. In itself it was almost as big as Gus' cabin.

After he had taken in the richness of the room he turned to speak to Nancy and in doing so just about bumped into her. Nancy had positioned herself to take advantage of such an opportunity. She feigned being startled and reached around Zack's waist to steady herself. As she pulled herself to him her ribs collided with the pistol in his new belt.

With a slight recoil she said, "What's this," as her hands slid across his abdomen to the pistol. While using the pistol to lift herself she placed her lips close to Zack's ear. Her scent of soap and flower perfume became very evident to Zack. "There must be some way I can persuade you to delay your trip," she whispered.

Zack was taken by surprise and momentarily seduced by her closeness but just as quickly knew it was not right to be with his brothers wife like this.

Counter to what she expected he drew her closer with a force that uncomfortably trapped her hands between the pistol and his abdomen. She gasped and was about to protest the excessive pressure as Zack whispered, "You're my brother's wife and I'll not be a party to your troubles with him." He increased the pressure.

Barely able to breathe in the trap of his arms Nancy grunted. "You're hurting me." She tried to struggle free.

Zack held tightly and said, "Do you understand me?" Nancy continued to struggle. Zack increased the pressure slightly and repeated, "Do you understand me?"

She responded with a pained "Yes."

Zack eased the pressure of his arms and Nancy brought her hands to her face. She began to sob. Intermingled with sobs she said, "You don't know… what its like… to have him lusting…after Lilly. He can't… be with me… without that…horrible coughing."

Zack tenderly enfolded her into his arms in a brotherly embrace while she sobbed uncontrollably. After a minute he picked her up and carried her to the bed. He laid her down and she curled up with her knees to her chest. Zack covered her with the fan folded quilt at the end of the bed, blew out the lamps and left the room.

Zack took a deep breath as he stood on the porch. The still, late evening air bore the scent of the flowers that surrounded the porch. He heard the sounds of a horse approaching and from the light shining through the windows saw Toby leading his horse toward the porch. Zack stepped out to meet him and as Toby was handing over the reins he said, "Thank you, Master Zachary."

Zack noted the lack of the subservient accent and asked, "Are you an educated man, Toby?"

"Yes sir," responded Toby, "My first Master taught all the children to read and speak properly. When he died his widow had to sell us."

Zack shook his head sadly, mounted his horse and urged it into a slow walk toward the gate. When he turned into the street he looked back and saw Toby waving in his direction. Zack returned it with a single, saluting wave and doubted Toby could see it in the darkness.

As he slowly rode through the dimly lit streets he reflected on the events of the past hours. He felt sad and cheated. Saddened by his brother's deteriorating condition and the disease that was ravaging him. Saddened by the desperate loneliness of Nancy and her struggle to maintain a facade of a prominent, blissful household. Saddened by slavery and how it tore at the very fabric of decency. He knew his brother was in league with river pirates and, from the recent events, capable of deceit and cruelty. He felt cheated out of a kindred relationship with his brother and possibly his inheritance.

CHAPTER 8

CAIRO

The wharf was alive with activity as cargo and passengers were loaded on the big stern wheel steamboat. Zack arrived at the wharf in a carriage hired by Patrick McCracken who insisted on delivering his friend to the steamboat. The carriage was to also serve his family for an outing. They had not been out since his arriving home with a wound in his leg. Robert sat on his father's lap holding onto the reins as if he was driving the carriage and enjoying every minute of it. Earlier in the day Robert begged his mother to let him go with Zack when Zack took the horse to be boarded. In spite of Lucy's apprehension she permitted Robert to take the short ride. She hoisted Robert up to sit between Zack and the saddle horn. The boy squealed in delight with the adventure of riding the horse. Zack was pleased that Robert warmed up to him and enjoyed the boy's enthusiasm.

Zack got down from the carriage and unloaded a stuffed coarse weaved sack and his rifle. Lucy also stepped down and Robert suddenly became fearful with the mistaken thought that his mother was going somewhere without him. She took the apprehensive boy from his father's lap. Zack shook hands with Patrick, who remained seated, and thanked him again for the hospitality. He turned to Lucy to say good-bye to her and Robert when Lucy hooked an arm around his neck and pulled him to her.

Zack's hands were full of the sack and rifle. In this sudden embrace she whispered, "Thank you for helping bring my man back to me." Robert had not recovered from the dreaded notion that his mother was going somewhere and clung to her during the embrace.

Zack responded, "You're welcome, Lucy," as she stepped back. Zack said good-bye to Robert and while shifting the weight in his hands turned toward the steamboat. Robert suddenly realized that it wasn't his mother who was leaving; it was his new found friend, his source of horse riding adventures. His face puckered as his eyes filled with tears and he held out his arms to Zack. Setting down his load Zack took the boy in a wrap around bear hug. After a few seconds he said, "You be a good boy, Robert. When I get back we'll go for another horse ride." Assured by the words but still uncertain about saying good-bye Robert clung to Zack's sleeve as he was handed back to his mother. Zack again filled his hands and turned toward the steamboat.

"Watch yer topknot," Patrick called after him.

The McCracken family watched Zack work his way through the crowd of gathered well-wishers around the gangway and lost sight of him as he stepped around the passengers at the railing. He reappeared again in an open spot on the railing on the next upper deck. The steam whistle sounded as the gangway was raised and the mooring lines were being cast off. Those on the wharf waved to the passengers and the passengers were waving back when the big stern paddle wheel moved the boat in reverse.

Zack explored the boat for about an hour before he found a bench with a view. This was his first ride on a steamboat and he found it exciting. He watched the other passengers strolling the deck. Except for his moccasins and a rifle in a fringed leather case he was dressed like most of the male passengers. He noted the difference in how fast the landscape was passing by compared to his recent flatboat ride. The steamboat passed smaller, drifting boats and exchanged steam whistle greetings with others of its kind.

Prior to Zack's departure Patrick McCracken gave him information about the facilities and services aboard a steamboat. Zack rose when he noticed the boat was slowing and walked toward the bow to look for the reason. Ahead lay the port of Cape Girardeau and the boat was being maneuvered to make a stop. Zack lingered at the rail to watch the unloading and loading of cargo and passengers. When the steamboat was underway again he decided to go to the saloon he located in his initial exploration.

Zack entered the saloon through a double door, which had panes of etched glass. Tables and chairs filled the large, richly decorated room. At two tables some men were playing cards. Most of the other tables were occupied by groups of two or three men engaged in conversations. Zack ordered a beer from the fat bartender who perspired and wheezed as he worked. After sipping on the beer, Zack helped himself to the small buffet of food set out on the bar. He was not particularly fond of beer but recalled having gone to a saloon on more that one occasion with his father to have a beer and to partake of the buffet. A customer who bought a drink was entitled to take some food. Zack filled a small plate with sliced meat, cheese, bread and pickled eggs. He retired to the end of the bar.

Zack was still thinking of his father when a man stepped up to the bar next to him and interrupted his reminiscing.

"Going far?"

"Cairo," Zack replied as he sized up the slightly built, smaller man wearing a new suit and a top hat made of beaver felt.

"Me too. I mean I'm going to Cairo also," and extending his hand introduced himself. "I'm Ned Shiller."

Shaking Ned's hand, Zack introduced himself, "Zachary Clayton, folks call me Zack."

Ned signaled to the bartender and ordered a beer. "Cairo home for you?" inquired Ned.

"No, I'm going to visit the family of a friend of mine," Zack replied.

"What's their name?" asked Ned, "I may know them. I've done a lot of business and met lots of people in Cairo."

"Gusterson," Zack replied.

"Gusterson…Gusterson," Ned repeated, "Can't recall ever meeting anyone named Gusterson. Although I do recall a furniture making shop a couple of years ago with the name Gusterson on it. Haven't noticed it the past couple of trips though. Did they run a shop in Cairo?"

"I really don't know," responded Zack, "The man I knew was John Gusterson and I aim to look up his folks to keep a promise." Zack began to think of Gus and wondered if he learned woodworking in the furniture shop Ned mentioned.

He was about to address a question to Ned about the shop when Ned spoke, "You going to be in Cairo long? The reason I ask is if you are I'll be needing some hands to help me in a week or so. You see I'm going to buy as many horses and oxen as I can find and will be needing some help to get them back to St. Louis. You look like a man that knows his way around horses."

"I've rode a few," responded Zack, "and I thank you for the offer but I'm not sure just how long I'll be in Cairo. Just as soon as I find Gus' folks I'll head back to St. Louis."

"Well, if you change your mind I'll be at the Skyles Hotel just off the waterfront. You can ask for me there. If you're looking for a place to stay it's better than most."

Ned was a talker and went on to describe working for his father-in-law, Miles Garrett, who was the largest supplier of horses and draft animals in the St. Louis area. Ned traveled to several ports on the Ohio and Mississippi Rivers to buy livestock. He mentioned the Missouri Fur Company had ordered twenty draft horses and twenty oxen to pull supply wagons in the spring. Zack was reminded of his brother's offer to guide for the Missouri Fur Company and wondered if it was these horses and oxen that would make the trip. Zack commented that he was not that familiar with oxen. Ned explained it was his first time to buy oxen and he did not know that much about them either but men who did were saying oxen had better endurance than draft horses. Also they were better about foraging. Zack had some difficulty imagining oxen pulled wagons on the prairie and through the mountains but thought, *I guess it's possible.*

Ned expressed curiosity about Zack rifle, brace of pistols and moccasins. He soon had Zack talking about beaver trapping and his life in the mountains. Zack was surprised by his lack of caution with this energetic, little man but just to be on the safe side he did not mention the river pirates nor Gus' gold. Finally Ned said he needed to find a certain Kentucky horse trader who was aboard and left the saloon to find him.

For a man who was used to sleeping on the ground Zack found sleeping beneath a bench on the lower deck most uncomfortable. He bought the lowest class ticket to conserve funds, which left him to seek a spot for the night on the main deck. There was not much competition for deck space and he chose to crawl under a bench. The vibration of the big steam engine could be felt through the boat's structure and getting to sleep was close to impossible.

It was late morning when the process of exchanging cargo and passengers was complete at the Cairo wharf. Zack stood on the wharf half expecting to see someone with a family resemblance to Gus. The crowd, which had assembled for the steamboat's arrival, dispersed in small groups. He found the Skyles Hotel by using the directions Ned provided. He checked in and found his room to be acceptable although not as warm and comfortable as the McCracken's spare room and certainly not as richly furnished as the guest room at his brother's house. This was his first time to stay at a hotel and he was glad it would only be for a few days.

The hotel was close to the waterfront and was permeated with a damp, musty odor. Zack changed into his boots, vowing to wear them a little each day until they were comfortable. Also new to Zack was a door key. He locked his rifle and few possessions in his room and set out to explore the town. On the way out he stopped at the hotel dining room. He found it to have a rather dark atmosphere and the odor of lard-fried fish. He decided to look for a cafe as he conducted his search for the Gusterson family.

Zack walked around the hotel in a wide circle noting the streets and other landmarks. He saw a brick building with a faded sign on the wall that read, *GUSTERSON & Sons: Woodworking & Furniture*. He inquired within and learned that the current owner did not know where to find the Gustersons and suggested that Zack talk to the town Marshal. Just up the street Zack noticed a cheerful looking cafe bearing a sign; BELL'S CAFE and decided he would try it later. He returned to the hotel after inquiring at two other businesses. He was tired from the poor night's sleep and decided to take a nap.

Zack woke from his nap feeling rested and hungry. With water from the matched set of ewer and basin he washed his hands and face then dried with a towel draped on the dresser. Out of curiosity he pulled the dresser away from the wall to examine the back. On the back of a rear leg, printed in black ink, was the name of the furniture maker: GUSTERSON & Sons. He replaced the dresser in its original position.

By the time Zack got to the cafe the sun was setting and the traffic of wagons and people on the street had decreased to very few. He was reaching for the cafe door when the door was violently swung open by a man being pushed through it. Zack staggered backwards and fell in the street with the man landing on top of him. Before he could dislodge the man two larger men rushed out of the cafe door and began to kick at the man they had pushed out of the cafe. In an effort to avoid further kicks, and with Zack's help, the man rolled and got to his feet. Zack got to his feet at the same time and was roughly pushed away.

"You keep out'a this farmer," the pusher growled and readied his hand for another push. Zack avoided the push and kicked him on the knee. The man went down with a howl. The second man saw the kick and turned his attention toward Zack. He drew a short club from a back pocket and charged. Zack avoided the club and drew his pistol. He counterattacked by using the pistol as a club and brought the barrel down hard on the extended club-wielding wrist. A bone-breaking crack was followed by a groan as the man dropped the club and grabbed his wrist with his other hand. The first man got to his feet and was limping to his companion's defense. He stopped when the pistol was leveled at his chest. The original victim in this melee took advantage of his attackers being occupied with Zack and made his escape by running down the street.

"This ain't no concern of yours," growled the man facing the pistol.

"Then I reckon I can be on my way, peaceable like," ventured Zack as he took a step backwards, keeping the pistol pointed at the man.

"My arm's broke!" groaned the man, which brought his limping partner to his side.

Zack noted how remarkably similar the men were to one another. Both wore heavy dark trousers and boots, wide leather belts, stained long sleeve shirts, and dark gray, wide brimmed hats. Both faces were covered with full, unkempt beards. They looked like a mirror image of one another. The limping man glanced at Zack, then to the patrons of the cafe who had gathered at the door. He decided to retreat. He tapped the other man with the back of his hand and signaled with his head to back away. They stepped backwards but before turning away to leave the limping man threatened, "You'll be seein' us again. We'll have yer ears fer this."

Zack watched them disappear around a corner. He heard his name being called, "Zack, Zack, Are you all right?" It was Ned Shiller.

Returning the pistol to its holster and dusting himself off Zack assured, "Yeah, just a bit dusty." He walked toward Ned who was making an opening through the cafe patrons. The eyes of the patrons followed him as he entered the cafe. Ned pointed him toward the table he had occupied prior to the disturbance. Two of the patrons were in a hurry to pay their bill and leave the cafe. They were concerned that the brawl, they had just witnessed, may not be over if the men who retreated returned.

When he got seated Zack asked, "You know those fellas?"

"No, never saw them before," replied Ned, "I just got seated when those two started a ruckus. They were saying something about not being paid enough for some work and when that other fellow said he wasn't paying them any more they grabbed him and pushed him out the door. As mean as they looked they might have killed that fellow if you hadn't come along."

"They came on me," declared Zack, "I was just minding my own business."

Ned continued to talk in an excited manner about the brawl until a man in a white half apron who came to take their food order interrupted him. Zack noticed that he and two women had reset the overturned chairs and straightened up the table where the brawl must have started. Zack and Ned ordered the beef stew the man recommended and sat back to await their meal. The stew was served by the younger of the two women. She wore a full white apron over a blue dress and had a pressed lace cap over her blonde hair. In spite of the hot, busy work she had a fresh scrubbed look about her and Zack noticed an odor of scented soap when she placed the bowls of stew on the table.

Between bites Ned continued. He told Zack that this was his favorite cafe, owned by Anthony Bell, and that he tended to avoid the food at the hotel. Zack was working on his second bowl of stew when he noticed the man in the apron pointing him out to a tall man wearing a dark suit, tall black, highly polished boots and a wide brimmed black hat. He walked toward the table and as he did he pushed the front of his coat aside to reveal a pistol tucked in a belt. Arriving at the table he faced Zack and said, "Mister Bell tells me you mixed it up with the Gusterson twins."

Turning to Zack, Ned blurted out, "Zack, that's the name…"

But before he could say more Zack interrupted by saying to the tall man, "Me and two fellas came to a understanding out there in the street, if that's what you're talking about." Zack rose from his chair and drawing himself up to his full height to face the dark suited man said, "And who might you be, Mister?"

"Town Marshall, Seth Thomas," was the reply. "I hear you laid out Billy and backed down Frank."

Ned tried to speak and Zack cut him off again while responding to the Marshal, "Well, Marshal, if that's those fellas' names then that's pretty close to what happened."

In an easy motion the Marshal moved an empty chair and sat down. He signaled Zack to do the same. Before long Ned was telling his account of the brawl. They were interrupted once by the young woman who asked the Marshal if he wanted to order. Marshal Thomas addressed her as Ann as he ordered coffee. Upon her return she brought his coffee and filled the other two cups. Zack watched her as she cleared the table and thought how pretty she was and how nimble and efficient she worked. She caught him studying her and returned his stare with a smile. Zack felt a slight rush of embarrassment. He shifted back to the conversation while tucking her smile in his memory.

Once Marshal Thomas was satisfied that Zack's encounter with Billy and Frank Gusterson was strictly by chance he offered a warning to be wary of them and to expect that they would try to get revenge. Seth Thomas had been town Marshal for eight years and was a confident, resourceful man. He liked his job and he liked the usually quiet river town in which he plied his trade. He developed a good first impression of Zack and liked how he handled himself.

Zack took the opportunity to reveal the purpose of his visit to Cairo and asked about the Gusterson family. Between sips of coffee Marshal Thomas told of John Gusterson, Sr. who ran a successful woodworking shop for several years. He lived in town with his wife and four sons. John, Jr. was the first born, then the twins and lastly Kenneth. Gusterson furniture sold well locally and was shipped to various ports on the Ohio and Mississippi Rivers. John, Jr. worked in the shop when he got old enough, followed by Billy and Frank.

The fortune of the Gusterson family changed dramatically when John, Sr. got brain fever in the spring of 1818. It took him several months to recover and in the meantime John, Jr. did the woodworking and ran the business. When John, Sr. returned to the shop he was a changed man. He would become enraged for no apparent reason and take a strap or club to whomever was in reach. John, Jr. endured his father during the winter but disappeared in the spring. Mrs. Gusterson had Marshal Thomas make some inquires but no word of his whereabouts ever came of it. John, Sr.'s behavior got worse and Marshal Thomas was called to the shop on several occasions to subdue loud accusations or to pull him off Billy or Frank. The production of furniture declined and people were afraid to go to the shop.

By the time John, Sr. died the business was close to ruin. Mrs. Gusterson sold the business and bought a small farm north of town where she lived with Kenneth. Billy and Frank drifted to odd jobs and had been in and out of trouble since their father's death. They developed a reputation for drinking and brawling in several river towns and the scene in the cafe was not uncommon for them. Besides being brawlers and bullies, Marshal Thomas suspected they might be involved in some robberies involving travelers but had no direct evidence on them.

In light of Marshal Thomas' report Zack said he wanted to meet Mrs. Gusterson and asked about her. Marshall Thomas told him that Mrs. Gusterson ran a small dairy farm and raised a few horses. He described her as doing fairly well and was aware that Billy and Frank had bullied her out of money on more than one occasion. She refused to press charges against them. He described Kenneth as a big, simple-minded nineteen year old who needed his mother to look after him. He could work the dairy under his mother's direction but probably would never be able to be more independent.

Marshal Thomas offered to accompany Zack to the Gusterson farm saying that the news of John, Jr.'s death would probably go easier if he was along. Zack accepted the offer and they agreed to meet in the morning. Ned rose with Marshal Thomas saying he had to get an early start in the morning and they left the cafe together.

Zack looked around and noticed he was the only patron left in the cafe. Anthony Bell and his daughter, Ann, were clearing the tables. Mister Bell approached Zack and asked, "Will there be anything else, Mister? We're getting ready to close."

"If you don't mind I'd like a piece of pie, Mister Bell," Zack requested. Seeing the slightly puzzled look on Mister Bell's face Zack said, "Mister Shiller told me your name." As he rose Zack extend his hand and introduced himself, "I'm Zachary Clayton, out of St. Louis."

Taking the extended hand Anthony Bell responded, "Pleased to meet you Mister Clayton," and in the next breath called over his shoulder, "Ann, bring Mister Clayton here a piece of pie and more coffee."

Anthony Bell was a friendly, jovial man who often joked and told stories with his patrons. He had a reputation for putting out a good meal and maintaining an atmosphere of congeniality and humor in his small cafe. Mostly he served the local folks but had a fair amount of traveler business. Somehow people traveling through heard about his cafe and were usually pleased with the meal and pleasant social surroundings. He was telling an amusing story to Zack when Ann returned with the pie. He introduced Zack to Ann as she set slices of pie in front of both men. She knew her father would enjoy some pleasant socializing after a busy, and somewhat harrowing evening. After pouring the coffee she returned to clearing the

tables. Zack enjoyed talking to the congenial cafe owner and was aware of
his pretty daughter as she worked.

A woman's voice called Anthony to the kitchen and he politely excused
himself. Zack rose to pay his bill. As he extended the coins in his hand he
said, "Miss Bell, that was a mighty fine meal and I want to say I enjoyed
meeting you." As the coins were transferred Zack found the courage to
add, "You're right pleasing to look at."

Their hands touched lightly with the coin exchange and Ann blushed.
"Thank you Mister Clayton," she managed to say, "I hope you don't have
any more trouble with those awful Gusterson brothers."

Just then Anthony Bell reappeared and called to Zack, "You come back,
Mister Clayton. We'd be proud to serve you again."

Heading for the door Zack replied, "Thank you, Mister Bell. I'll do
that."

Long after she went to bed, Ann Bell thought about the handsome
stranger who was somewhat a contradiction. His entrance into her life was
one of abrupt violence and his departure shy and gentle, a gentleness that
seemed incapable of his earlier altercation. She relived the light brief touch
in the cafe and wondered how it would feel to touch him more. She hoped
he'd return and drifted to sleep saying his name.

*   *   *

The odor of coffee greeted Zack when he stepped into Marshal
Thomas' office. They drank a cup of coffee and talked for several minutes.
Marshal Thomas said he saw Ned riding out of town as he was walking to
the office. They walked to the livery stable where Zack rented a horse.
Marshal Thomas saddled his horse while talking to the livery owner. The
gossiping livery owner reported Ned Shiller as having rented a horse the
day before with instructions to have it ready early in the morning. He also
tried to get the Marshal to talk about the brawl at the cafe. Seth Thomas
might use information from a gossip but he was not about to contribute

to it. The shops were just beginning to open when the riders headed their horses north. They set an unhurried pace on the dirt road and talked while they rode. Marshal Thomas provided more details about the Gusterson family and himself. Zack told more of his life as a trapper and how he came to know Gus.

When they rode into the barnyard Kenneth Gusterson was arranging milk cans in a wagon parked in the shade of a big Oak tree. Seeing the riders he jumped down from the wagon and hurriedly walked to the house. He disappeared through a rear door and almost immediately reappeared with his mother. As the riders were dismounting Mary Gusterson called out, "Seth, Seth Thomas, it's good to see you. What brings you out this way?" She drew closer adding, "Billy and Frank ain't in trouble again, are they?"

Deciding not to report their latest brawl Marshal Thomas replied, "No, Mary. It's other business that brings me out to see you." Gesturing toward Zack he added, "Mary, I want you to meet Zachary Clayton." Kenneth stepped up behind his mother as the introduction was made.

Zack could see a strong family resemblance, to each other and to Gus, in their faces. Kenneth dwarfed his petite mother and in height and weight was bigger than either visitor. Marshal Thomas continued the introduction, "Mister Clayton, This here is Mary Gusterson and her son Kenneth."

Removing his hat Zack said, "Pleased to meet you Misses Gusterson, Kenneth."

Mary Gusterson took Kenneth's hand and pushed it toward Zack saying, "Kenny, shake hands with Mister Clayton, just like I taught you."

Zack took his hand in a handshake and in a dull voice Kenneth said, "Good to meet'cha, Mister Clayton." as his big hand pumped Zack's arm.

His mother gently reminded him to be easy in a handshake and directed, "Now Marshal Thomas."

Kenneth gripped the Marshal's hand and with less vigorous shaking said, "Good ta meet'cha Marshal Thomas."

Seth patted the boy on the shoulder and greeted, "How you doing, Kenny? I swear you get bigger every time I see you. I don't know how your mother keeps you in britches. Just look at you, you barely fit in them now."

Kenneth broke into a wide grin and replied, "I'm fit, Marshal. How's you?"

Seth grinned back at the boy and responded, "I'm fine, Kenny. Just fine. Mighty polite of you to ask."

With a tease in her voice Mary Gusterson interrupted, "If you two are through jawing I'll serve up some breakfast, if you a mind? Kenny and me was fixin' to eat before we took the milk to town."

With the same kidding manner Seth Thomas returned the tease, "Well now, that is an offer a man can hardly refuse," and turning to Zack continued, "Mary here sets the best table in the county. A man would be a fool to turn down an invitation to her table."

Mary Gusterson giggled and while patting Seth on the arm said, "Seth Thomas, you always was a man that knew how to talk to a woman. Come on in."

It wasn't long before they were all seated at the table eating ham, eggs, biscuits with honey and big mugs of milk. In spite of the task ahead Zack and Seth ate with good appetites. They both marveled at the big, simple-minded Kenny who ate more than both of them. Seth Thomas and Mary Gusterson exchanged news about the area and people as they ate.

Finally Mary said, "You never did tell me what brings you out this way. I know it can't be just for my cooking. What you got on your mind Seth?" Seeing a serious look on his face, instead of his coming back with a light remark, she exclaimed, "It's one of my boys, isn't it? Something happened to one of my boys!"

Seth nodded to the affirmative and before he could speak Mary asked, "Is it Frank? Billy? Is he hurt bad?"

As he shook his head no Seth answered, "No it's not Frank or Billy. Mary, it's John Junior. He's dead." Mary Gusterson's hands went to her mouth and her eyes filled with tears. Seth continued, "Mister Clayton here was his partner in trapping beaver out west and came all this way to tell you what happened." She turned to Zack as Kenneth rose to stand behind his mother placing his big hands on her shoulders. She reached to grasp a hand while pulling a cloth from a pocket on her apron.

"That's right, Misses Gusterson," Zack started, "Me and Gus, I mean John Junior, were partners."

Mary was wiping her eyes and was barely able to ask, "How did he die?"

Zack glanced at Marshal Thomas who urged him to go on with the story. Taking a breath and turning to face Mary he answered, "This last spring he came on a bear when he wasn't ready for one. I wasn't there and had to study on the signs to figure it out. He must have killed the bear with his dying breath. His knife was stuck in that bear clean to the hilt. I don't figure he suffered much."

With tears running down her face Mary sobbed, "Was he a good man?"

"Yes Ma'am, he was," Zack replied, "He was the finest man I ever rode with. He was a man a fellow could depend on and I miss him very much."

Gaining some composure Mary said, "I thank you for your friendship to my boy, Mister Clayton and coming all this way."

Marshal Thomas touched Zack on the arm to get his attention and to signal he should continue with his mission. Addressing the next step he said, "Mary, Mister Clayton has more he wants to say."

Reaching into his coat pocket Zack brought the buckskin bag up to the table. He removed a roll of paper money and placed it in front of Mary as he announced, "This is Gus' share for the furs and what I got for his goods, rifle and such." Then Zack poured out the nuggets onto the table as he said, "I don't know where he got these. He had a habit of poking around in creeks and caves. I believe this is gold."

Marshal Thomas picked up a nugget and after examining it agreed, "I believe you're right, Zack. It looks like gold to me. You say you don't know where he got it?"

"No sir, I don't," Zack replied, "He could have traded for some or all of it from Injuns. As you can see some of the pieces are pressed into rifle balls. Injuns might have done that. They look for round stones and such to shoot since lead can be hard to come by for them."

Mary wiped her eyes and picked up a large nugget. "Have you taken a share of this gold, Mister Clayton?" she asked.

"No ma'am, I didn't have anything to do with getting it. It was all found by your son, so I brought it to you," Zack replied.

"Well I want you to have some," she insisted, "After all you and John were partners."

Zack tried to decline but Mary pressed him. She selected an odd looking kidney shaped nugget about the size of the end of a man's thumb and handed it to him saying, "At least take this one to serve as a memento of John Junior. I'm sure he would have wanted for you to have at least that much."

Zack tried handing it back to her but she refused and Marshal Thomas signaled for him to put it his pocket. With that done Mary Gusterson patted Kenneth on the hand and said to him, "Kenny do you understand what Mister Clayton has been talking about?"

Kenneth nodded and replied, "Yeah, Ma. He said Johnny's dead, just like Pa. And he were a good man."

Continuing to pat his hand she confirmed his understanding, "That's right son. A very good man, a man to be proud of."

After a pause Seth said, "Mary, I reckon you should take this money and gold to the bank today while you're in town." Mary acknowledged his suggestion with a nod.

Standing in the barnyard Mary Gusterson embraced the visitors and thanked them again for their kindness, "You don't know how much this means to me. After all these years of not knowing where he was or what he was doing. Thank you."

She invited Zack to return for supper the next evening saying by then she was sure she would have thought of some questions to ask of him about her son. Zack accepted the invitation. Mary directed Kenneth to say good-bye to the visitors and another round of handshakes transpired.

Marshal Thomas and Zack mounted their horses and while tipping their hats turned their horses toward the road. They turned to wave. Mary waved back as Kenneth was heading for the wagon to complete the loading.

Marshal Thomas and Zack rode most of the way back to Cairo in silence, both occupied with their own thoughts. Marshal Thomas was worried about Mary having a large sum of money at the farm knowing Billy and Frank could show up at any time to demand money for their drinking and carousing.

Zack was tired, bone tired, just like he'd worked hard all day. The energy drain of carrying the news to Mary Gusterson was more than he anticipated. He wondered if Gus would have made a trip home if he'd known his father had died. Zack liked Mary Gusterson and was glad about having made the trip to see her. Now that he'd fulfilled the pledge to visit Gus' family his business in Cairo was complete. Outside of going to supper at the Gusterson farm there was nothing to keep him here. Nothing, that is, but a desire to see Ann Bell again. Thoughts of her frequented his mind since their meeting in the cafe.

Even if both men had not been occupied with their thoughts, they would not have seen Billy and Frank Gusterson hiding in a patch of trees, watching the riders. From afar, the twins spotted the characteristically dressed Marshal and took to cover to watch him pass. From the distance between themselves and the riders they did not recognize Zack as the man who had bested them in the street in the previous evening. When the Marshal was out of site they turned their horses toward their mother's farm.

As the Marshal approached his office, he noticed a group of men standing outside. They gathered about him as he dismounted, all talking at once in an excited fashion. One man talked about two horses having been stolen. Another interrupted saying he had been assaulted and robbed. The

other men present came along to lend their support and to demand immediate action by the Marshal.

The men followed the Marshal into his office. Zack followed out of
curiosity. After a few minutes Marshal Thomas managed to draw out
calmer accounts from the injured parties. The horses were stolen sometime during the night from a corral used to hold animals while they
waited shipment on a riverboat. The horses were a matched pair and the
only animals in the corral at the time. The shipping clerk had a good
description of the horses and described the circumstances of finding them
missing.

Satisfied he had enough information about the missing horses Marshal
Thomas turned his attention to the man with a bandaged head and facial
bruises. He was a clothing salesman from New York who had too much to
drink in a waterfront saloon late in the previous evening. He recalled stag-
gering from the outhouse, where was beaten and robbed by two unknown
assailants. When he came to his wallet and watch were gone. The only
thing he could recall was that one of the assailants wore a splint on one
arm.

Marshal Thomas and Zack exchanged knowing glances without revealing the significance of the clue to the group. Marshal Thomas herded the
men out of his office with a promise to investigate. After they departed he
speculated to Zack, "I figure that salesman ran into the Gusterson twins.
It fits with what you told me about your ruckus with them."

The Marshal asked Zack to deliver the horses to the livery stable while
he visited the saloon and corral, which were within easy walking distance
from his office. Zack returned to the hotel after returning the horses. He
needed some time to rest and to think.

                    *   *   *

Late in the afternoon Zack got seated in the crowded cafe, abuzz with
talk of the stolen horses and the robbery. He was hoping to find Ann free

enough to spend some time talking with her but the hungry crowd kept her busy.

The diners hushed as Marshal Thomas entered the cafe and joined Zack. Anthony Bell took their orders and rushed off to attend to other patrons. Marshal Thomas told Zack that the result of his inquires strengthened his suspicions that the Gusterson twins committed the robbery. He had not learned anything that might lead to their whereabouts, and had nothing more on the missing horses.

Zack and Marshal Thomas left the café after completing their meal. Zack was thinking about returning later to talk to Ann when a saddled, riderless horse appeared in the street. Marshal Thomas stopped the horse and recognized it as belonging to the livery. Zack walked along as the Marshal led the horse to its owner. The livery owner confirmed the horse as his and in a teasing manner said, "That's might kind of you Marshal, delivering that horse for one of my customers."

Puzzled by the remark Marshal Thomas questioned its meaning and learned the horse had been rented to Ned Shiller. The livery owner thought the Marshal has met the tired horse buyer somewhere and volunteered to return the horse. Once it was understood how the Marshal came to be in possession of the horse, they all concluded that something must have happened to Ned. Marshal Thomas planned to make more inquires about the whereabouts of the Gusterson twins after his evening meal but also was worried about Ned. He asked Zack to try and back trail the horse and to provide help, if necessary. Zack agreed to the request and learned from the livery owner that Ned had said he was going to visit the farms north of Cairo looking for horses to buy.

Ann Bell was more than aware of Zack dining with Marshal Thomas and several times tried to approach their table on the pretense of pouring more coffee for them. On each try she was detoured by her father or a patron wanting something. When she was returning from the kitchen with plates of food she noticed their table was empty. As she served the patrons seated next to the big front window she saw Zack and the Marshal in the street with a horse. She watched them lead the horse away. She did not have time to dwell on the disappointment she felt.

Once again Zack found himself riding out of town, only this time it was at a quicker pace. He wanted to back trail the stray horse as far as possible in the remaining light. He was able to read the signs of a horse dragging the reins in the dusty road while riding until the light faded. In the twilight, he dismounted twice to examine the tracks in the road and felt confident he was still on the trail. The evening star appeared in the darkening sky and the lights from the farmhouses along the road began to appear. The night sounds of the farm animals joined the other night sounds as he kept to the road. These sights and sounds were somewhat assuring. If Ned was injured there were plenty of places to get help. It was not like the mountains where a man could go for weeks without seeing signs of other people.

Zack kept riding until it was too dark to go on. He was debating a plan of returning to Cairo, to get a fresh start in the morning, versus finding a place to rest for the night where he was when he noticed he was approaching the Gusterson farm. As he rode into the barnyard he could make out the dark form of the milk wagon with the horses still harnessed. The rear door of the house was open and the light of the kitchen lantern glowed into the darkness. Zack dismounted and as he approached the door his foot hit something soft. Reaching down he picked up a hat and held it up against the glow from the kitchen. The beaver felt hat looked like to one belonging to Ned. As he got closer to the door he saw that it was not just open, it was ripped from its hinges and rested against the doorframe. The broken door and mislaid hat signaled a warning. Zack backed out of the light to scan the area and listen. He did not hear nor see anything that indicated immediate danger. In a slow, deliberate stalking manner he circled the house. From one window he saw what appeared to be the shadow of Mary Gusterson pass across a thin lace curtain. Stepping up to the window he could make her out as she leaned over a bed. He quietly withdrew from the window and continued scouting the area around the house, barn and milkhouse.

When he was satisfied that there was nothing unusual in the area he returned to the kitchen door. He was stepping past the leaning door just as Mary Gusterson entered the room with a metal basin in her hands. She startled at Zack's sudden appearance and dropped the basin. She was about to scream when she recognized him and cried out, "Thank God, it's you Mister Clayton!" She reached down and picked up the basin as she said, "I'm so glad to see you. I'm going to need some help."

When Zack stepped toward her Kenneth, who heard the basin clatter on the floor, staggered into the doorway from within the house. Holding on to the doorframe for support he feebly called, "Ma?" Both of his eyes were close to being swollen shut and his face was bruised. Mary rushed to him and tried to support his sagging weight. In a few steps Zack joined her and they guided Kenneth to sit on the floor.

"Kenny, Kenny," Mary assured as she rubbed the boy's chest, "Mister Clayton is here to help us." As Zack supported the slumping Kenneth, Mary retrieved the basin and blood spotted towel. She added fresh water to the basin and rinsed the towel. She returned to Kenneth and wrapped the towel around his head. "I'm so glad to see you, Mister Clayton," she declared, "I've got two injured men here and I'm not in the best of shape myself."

That's when Zack noticed her dress was torn and she bore a bruise on her upper arm. "What happened here?" Zack asked.

Mary Gusterson did not answer the question until Kenneth was safely put to bed and having taken a fresh wet towel to Ned Shiller. Ned was lying on her bed and was more severely injured than Kenneth. He hovered in and out of consciousness as she bathed his battered face. Ned drifted into a fitful sleep. Mary led Zack back into the kitchen where they returned the table and chairs to their original positions. There she described the calamity that had come to pass.

Unsure of how to use raw gold as currency, Mary left the nuggets behind. She followed at least half of Seth Thomas' advice by taking the paper money to the bank. Mister Ellis, the bank manager, was not in his office for the day and Mary decided to wait to talk to him about the gold during a future trip to town. When she and Kenneth completed their deliveries they headed back to their farm.

Concealed in the trees, Billy and Frank Gusterson watched their mother and brother turn the horses and wagon toward Cairo. When they were sure the wagon was out of sight they rode to behind the barn and tied up their stolen horses. Once they were inside the house they began to search for money. Frank found the bag of gold nuggets and Billy found a jug of corn whiskey. Between drinks they discussed the gold. Both were familiar with gold coins but had not seen nuggets before. They became convinced that their mother had somehow come into a source for raw gold and decided to confront her when she returned. They concluded they were entitled to a rightful share of any and all property she held, especially gold.

Kenneth parked the wagon in the barnyard and, as usual, accompanied his mother to the house to get a drink prior to unhitching and caring for the horses. They discovered Billy and Frank in the kitchen. The twins wasted no time in bullying their mother about the gold. When she was not telling them what they wanted to hear Frank grabbed her by her upper arms and shook her. Kenneth tried to come to her aid and the whiskey sodden twins lost control. They beat Kenneth to stop his intrusion into their objective of learning where their mother got the gold. Frantically Mary told them of Zack's visit and why he brought the gold to her.

Billy and Frank were trying to absorb this information when Ned Shiller knocked on the door. He saw several horses in the farm's pasture and was stopping to inquire about buying some of them. Mary went to answer the door hoping to find someone who could help. Billy watched her open the door to a well dressed, prosperous looking man and jumped to a desperate conclusion. Up to now their mother had not filed charges against them. But they had not beaten their brother nor roughed her up during their previous episodes of bullying her out of money. Now a potential witness to their misdeeds was standing in the doorway.

Billy grabbed Ned, pulled him into the kitchen and delivered a fist to Ned's abdomen. In the struggle the kitchen door closed and Billy pushed Ned against it with such force that Ned crashed through it. Billy followed Ned out the door and began kicking him as he struggled to get up. Frank joined the assault and when Ned stopped moving the twins went through his pockets. They found some paper money and coins, which they put in their pockets. It soon became obvious to them that if they delayed a departure much longer the chances of their crimes being discovered increased. They had the gold and information about how their mother came by it. They also realized that if they stayed in the area much longer Marshal Thomas would find them. They argued loudly with one another as they walked to their horses.

Their mother heard them decide to leave the area by the river.

CHAPTER 9

ANN

Zack woke several times during the night to check on the sounds he heard. Each time he found Mary Gusterson at a bedside tending to bruises by changing the wet towels on Kenneth's and Ned's faces. During the hour before dawn Mary asked Zack to ride to her neighbors' farms to ask for help with the farm chores. Then she went to sleep beside Kenneth.

Within an hour of banging on the doors of Mary's neighbors they gathered at her farm to begin the routine chores of milking and feeding. When it was obvious that the Gusterson farm was in good hands, Zack searched for tracks that might lead him to the twins. They were only hours ahead of him but, whether by accident or design, they did not leave a trail he could follow. It was late morning when he gave up on trying to cross their trail and rode into Cairo to find Marshal Thomas.

Seth Thomas had been out most of the night looking for Billy and Frank Gusterson. He arrived at his office in the early morning darkness to get in a little sleep before setting out again. He was sleeping on a cot when Zack pounded on the door. Weariness showed on both men as they talked of recent events. Marshal Thomas had scoured the waterfront and the Gustersons' usual hangouts during the night and learned that Billy and Frank occasionally stayed in a shack that overlooked the river, south of town. Zack reported the assaults at the Gusterson farm, the conditions of Mary, Kenneth and Ned, and his failure to find a trail. Marshal Thomas asked a few questions and decided that he needed to act immediately on the information about the shack. It would take too much time to deputize a group of men to check out the shack and he did not want to risk doing it alone. He asked Zack to join him in a search of the area south of town and Zack agreed to accompany him. They planned to meet at the cafe after Zack went to the hotel for his rifle and Marshal Thomas went to dispatch the doctor out to the Gusterson farm.

Marshal Thomas tied up two horses in front of the cafe and was inside talking with Anthony Bell when Zack arrived. He placed an order for ham and biscuits to be prepared, along with filling two canteens of water, so he and Zack could eat as they rode. He signaled to Zack that a cup of coffee had been poured for him said, "Drink up. We'll ride out as soon as Miss Bell delivers my order."

Zack was sipping the coffee when Ann appeared with a sack and the canteens. Marshal Thomas rose to pay the bill. Ann set her load down on the table and asked Zack if there was anything he'd like to add to the order. Zack wanted to say, "One of your smiles," but in light of the seriousness of the situation and her father's close proximity he indicated he could not think of anything to add. Ann Bell made a point of handing the cloth sack and the canteens to Zack. She let her hands linger on his as she whispered, "You be careful, Zachary Clayton. I want to see you coming back here."

Zack was so taken aback by her boldness that he was only able to mumble an awkward response. He was saved from further embarrassment by Marshal Thomas urging, "Let's go, Zack!"

Between bites of the ham and biscuits, Marshal Thomas described the lay of the land as they rode south. He knew there were several cabins and shacks that overlooked the river and the Gusterson twins could be staying in any one of them. He figured to check them all.

One by one they checked the shacks by slowly stalking around them to see what they could see before Marshal Thomas called to the shack or knocked on the door. They found two shacks empty. Those that had occupants fell prey to the Marshal's questions. In a series of three shacks, fairly close together, a worn, dirty woman living in the first reported seeing two men who fit the description of the Gusterson twins. Over the past several days she saw them around the third shack with the most recent sighting being early in the morning. With extra alertness, Zack and the Marshal advanced on the shack. When they neither heard nor saw anything to indicate the twins were in the shack Marshal Thomas eased the door open with his pistol. The shack was empty.

Billy and Frank Gusterson had been hard at work since sleeping off the whiskey. They stole a rowboat shortly after selling the horses and beached it so they could load the provisions from the shack. They were pushing off from the bank while the Marshal exited the shack to tell Zack it was empty. Zack noticed the path leading to the river through the trees and brush. Then he heard the sound of a squeaky oarlock. He signaled the direction of the sound with a point of his finger. Making quiet steps, he started down the path with the Marshal following close behind.

Frank Gusterson was rowing away from the bank and saw something moving in the brush. He alerted his brother to the movement. Billy turned in the seat, cocked his pistol and waited. Zack stepped up on a log to try and see over a pile of mud caked, tangled driftwood just as Billy recognized the Marshal's black hat through a break in the foliage. Marshal Thomas stepped past Zack when Zack stepped up on the log. In the next second Billy saw Zack's hat rising above the driftwood. Billy fired at the hat.

The round hit a wrist-sized limb directly in front of Zack's face. The limb splintered, throwing dried mud and bits of wood in his eyes. Zack slipped off the log and fell backwards.

Marshal Thomas broke through the last of the brush to see Frank rowing with all his strength and Billy trying to reload the pistol. His splinted arm was slowing the task. Marshal Thomas called out, "BILLY, FRANK, PUT INTO THE BANK OR I'LL SHOOT!" Frank ignored him and rowed even faster into the fast flowing current. They were getting close to being out of effective pistol range and Marshal Thomas thought to have Zack put a round into the boat with his rifle. He suddenly became aware that Zack was not with him and quickly looked around while he called, "Zack, Zack, Where are you?" He heard a muffled voice behind him but could not make out the words. When Zack did not appear the Marshal gave up on trying to stop Billy and Frank and retraced his steps through the brush.

He found Zack sitting and rubbing his eyes with a bandanna. Marshal Thomas quickly realized that Zack would not be doing that unless something was drastically wrong. "Are you hit?" he asked.

"Took something in my eyes," Zack replied.

The Marshal restrained him from rubbing his eyes further and examined Zack's eyes. "Can you see?" the Marshal questioned.

"Not much," Zack responded.

"Close your eyes," the Marshal ordered and he tied the bandanna as a blindfold over Zack's eyes, "I'm going to get you to the doctor."

Marshal Thomas led Zack carefully through the brush back to the horses. Zack felt helpless and was thankful to be in hands of a man he could trust. His eyes irritated and burned as he fought the urge to rub them. They got mounted and set a brisk walking pace to town with the Marshal leading Zack's horse.

The sounds of the town indicated generally where he was going but without his vision Zack was not sure of the exact location. When they passed the blacksmith shop and the Marshal announced a turn toward the doctor's office, Zack knew exactly where he was.

Ann Bell was sweeping dirt and crumbs out of the cafe door when she saw Marshal Thomas and Zack riding on the opposite side of the street. It was obvious to her, with Zack having his eyes covered and resting his hands on the pommel while the Marshal was leading the horse, that something was wrong. She dropped the broom, raised her dress for running and made a dash for the riders.

Zack heard her coming and not knowing the source or the intention of the running feet instinctually hunkered down into a defensive posture. Then he heard her voice, " Zachary, what happened?" He started to relax when she reached his side but before he could respond another voice called out, "ANN!..ANN!" It was the voice of Anthony Bell who observed his daughter suddenly drop the broom and run into the street. He arrived at the cafe door to see her running toward two riders.

Anthony Bell had some concerns about his headstrong daughter and worried about her occasional unladylike behavior. Ann ignored his calls and began walking beside Zack's horse. Marshal Thomas saw Ann's dash across the street and slowed his horse's pace.

In a matter of fact manner Zack responded, "I got some dirt in my eyes and the Marshal is taking me to the doctor." The Marshal nodded an affirmative to Ann's pleading glance to him. Actually he was more apprehensive about Zack's eyes than he let on to Ann. He saw that her concern was more than just everyday concern for Zack and did not want to alarm her more with his uncertainty about the extent of the injury. He hoped he was wrong but he feared Zack's vision was in jeopardy.

When Marshal Thomas got the horses tied up in front of the doctor's office Anthony Bell caught up with his daughter. Puffing from the exertion he disapprovingly said, "Ann...what... are...you...doing?"

Ann switched to a more formal form of addressing Zack in hopes of decreasing her father's disapproval by saying, "Father, Mister Clayton is injured and I'm going to help him if I can." The Marshal guided Zack with dismounting and Ann stepped in to take Zack by the hand. With words and hand pressure she guided Zack through the gate, up the three stairs and to the doctor's door. Marshal Thomas and Anthony Bell followed a few steps behind.

Doctor Samuel Wilson was a round, soft looking man with a neatly trimmed blonde beard, which he had grown to make himself look older. This was his first practice and he had concerns that his youthful appearance did not inspire confidence in his patients. He really did not need to be concerned. The citizens of Cairo were pleased with him and his charming wife ever since they arrived. Cairo needed a doctor when they disembarked from a riverboat to inquire about setting up a practice. An ad hoc committee of citizens quickly formed to welcome them. Doctor Wilson was astonished by the committee's warmth and receptiveness, just what this uncertain man needed at this stage of his life. In spite of having graduated from a good eastern medical school, Samuel Wilson had not developed the personal confidence to practice medicine as the only doctor in town. In the year since he arrived he had made good progress but by his own estimation had not yet become the mature, older doctor he wanted to be. Fortunately for the citizens of Cairo, he tended to be conservative in his treatments.

The Wilson house was a combined home and doctor's office. The front rooms served as a waiting room, treatment-surgery room and a single bed hospital room. The Wilsons lived in the rear and second floor. Mrs. Wilson was a trained nurse and an active participant in the practice. They were in the hospital room, busy with an elderly man who had fallen in a store and was very confused when Ann led Zack through the door. The door mounted bell jingled and Mrs. Wilson left her husband, and the patient's wife, to see who had entered the waiting room. She quickly got the reason for the visit from Marshal Thomas and led Zack into the treatment room. She guided him onto a table to lie flat on his back and left to get her husband. Doctor Wilson administered a mild sedative to the elderly man and instructed his wife not to let him get out of bed. Mrs. Wilson told him of another patient waiting.

Doctor Wilson was somewhat surprised to see so many people in his treatment room but quickly got a report from the Marshal about Zack's injury. He carefully removed the bandanna and flushed Zack's eyes from a small pitcher of water. Then he took a magnifying glass and examined each eye closely. He stepped away from the examination to get a small vial from a cabinet while his wife dried Zack's face and eyes with a towel. Doctor Wilson instilled an ointment in Zack's eyes and covered both with soft cotton oval patches. He then wrapped the patches in place with a long white strip of cloth. While he did that, he gave Zack a long explanation of the anatomy of the eyes in relation to the injuries. He concluded, when asked, the injury did not seem threatening to vision but it would take several days of resting and keeping the eyes covered to know for sure.

It became obvious to everyone assembled that Zack would be unable to return to the hotel and a discussion developed of how to best manage the doctor's recommendations. Doctor Wilson was unable to offer his hospital room since it might be occupied for at least an overnight. Ann offered her bedroom but her father objected, being concerned about the propriety of such an arrangement. Zack found the discussion a bit frustrating in that everyone was talking about him as if he was not present. At the same time he realized he was in the hands of concerned people and had no reason to doubt that they only had his well being in mind. Finally the Marshal suggested

Zack could be taken care of by occupying the cot in his office. It was close to the cafe and the doctor's office. Everyone agreed, including Zack.

While Seth Thomas was still in the office Doctor Wilson reported having visited the Gusterson farm earlier in the day. He found Kenneth "a bit puny feeling" but up and about. He looked worse than he felt with all his facial bruising and was eating and able to do a little work. Mary Gusterson seemed no worse for wear and was appreciating all the help her neighbors were providing while she spent most of her time tending to Ned. She figured it was partly her fault that he got stomped. Ned was fully conscious but weak and very sore from all the heavy boot kicks he suffered. Doctor Wilson planned a return visit to them in a few days.

Marshal Thomas got Zack oriented to the cot and to the office while Anthony and Ann Bell watched. Anthony was finally able to get his daughter to return to the cafe by saying, "Well he's not going to get any rest if we stand all around here bothering him."

Before she left Ann promised to return later with a meal. As he and her father departed Marshal Thomas heard her bluntly say, "Well Father, you're just going have to find someone else to help you then. I'm coming back to help Mister Clayton."

Zack was getting comfortable on the cot when Seth Thomas pulled a chair up close to him. With a grin he chuckled and said, "Zack, it appears to me that girl has her cap set for you." Zack heard the words but was preoccupied with the dreaded notion of being blind, even temporarily. He wanted some assurances about his eyes not observations about Ann Bell.

"Did you see my eyes, Seth," he asked in an anxious, subdued manner, "How did they look?"

Seth did not completely hear the questions and leaning toward Zack asked him to repeat it. When he understood Zack's question he got serious and said, "Looked pretty mean to me, Zack but I'm no doctor."

Zack asked for a detailed description of his injury and a plain language account of what the doctor said. Seth explained his impressions as best as he could. When he finished Zack felt encouraged by the report and said,

"Well, since it sounds like I may be holed up here for awhile you'd better teach me how to find my way to the outhouse and back."

Seth agreed to the request and talked Zack through the landmarks on two trips. Zack made the third trip alone. When he returned to resting Seth announced he was going to get his part-time deputy to assist in the office.

When the Marshal returned he found Ann Bell feeding Zack so he left again to go to the cafe. While feeling somewhat uncomfortable and helpless about being fed Zack enjoyed the meal. The ham, butter beans, corn bread and sweet cider would have been enough to satisfy him in most circumstances but the addition of Ann's soft voice and sweet scent made the food even more appealing. Their conversation was casual as Ann inquired about Zack's life in the mountains, his brother, and his relationship to the Gustersons. She was about to ask him about his plans when Verle Rogers, the part-time deputy, entered the office. It was clear that he intended to be around for awhile when he started to sweep and clean up the office and the two jail cells. When Zack finished the meal Ann gathered the tray and returned to the cafe.

The pattern of Ann feeding, Doctor Wilson checking in daily and either Seth Thomas or Verle Rogers in attendance continued for the next four days. Twice, with the room maximally dimmed, Doctor Wilson removed the eye patches and Zack reported blurred vision, which improved between the two examinations. Doctor Wilson instilled more ointment and recommended the patches remain in place for at least two more days.

Also during these days the Marshal or Ann read newspapers to Zack. Cairo did not have a newspaper publisher but newspapers were available from several eastern cities by way of the steamboats. They were usually well worn by the time they got passed around from hand to hand among Cairo's citizens. One day Ann read about passengers in England who had ridden a coach powered by a steam engine that ran on two tracks. The article went on to say that American companies were forming to adopt this rail system of transportation. There were articles about slavery and the growing abolitionist movement in the northern states. Zack reflected on the slaves owned by his brother with a growing awareness of the nation-wide sentiments that divided the country. Mary and Kenneth Gusterson visited one day while resuming their milk deliveries and reported that Ned Shiller was mending.

Zack was finishing a meal, assisted by Ann, when Doctor Wilson arrived. Once the room was dimmed, Doctor Wilson removed the eye patches and waited for Zack to adjust to the light. As Doctor Wilson opened a shutter halfway Zack blinked and focused on Ann's face. Although he did not come to a clear image he could sense her concern and said, "I see the face of an angel." Doctor Wilson stepped between them as he prepared to examine Zack's eyes through a magnifying glass. Zack focused on him and continuing with a bit of a bravado in his voice remarked to the doctor, "Are you sure I'm not dead and have gone to heaven?"

Departing from his usual overly serious presentation Doctor Wilson looked at Ann and responded to Zack, "Well, no, I'm not completely sure. You certainly are looking at an angel, of that I'd be willing to testify." Doctor Wilson's response broke the tension of the moment. He adjusted his magnifying glass and in the half-light continued the examination. As further light was let into the room Zack found himself squinting and shading his eyes with his hands. Doctor Wilson anticipated Zack's sensitivity to bright light and produced a pair of smoked glass spectacles. He advised wearing them, along with a hat, when venturing into the bright sunlight.

After the doctor left, Zack and Ann stood facing each other. Her image was slightly blurred, and darkened by the spectacles but Zack could see that she longed to be embraced. He gathered her into his arms and she began to weep. The tension of worrying and the profound sense of relief broke forth in tears of joy. While embracing Zack started to thank her for all the care and attention, "Miss Bell, Thank you for seeing me through all this. I appreciate...."

He was not through with the sentence when she abruptly pushed away from him and in a raised voice said, "Zachary Clayton, if you think I'd do all this for just anyone you are sadly mistaken." Before he could respond to this sudden change of emotion she had her arms around his neck and drew him into a passionate kiss. Then just as suddenly she whirled and ran out the door.

Even with the smoked glass covering his eyes Zack had to shield his eyes to the abrupt effusion of bright light into the room. Ann nearly ran into Seth Thomas as he approached the door to his office and without saying a word brushed on by him. Zack was easing his hand from shielding his eyes as Seth entered the doorway.

Seth glanced at Ann hurrying toward the cafe then turning to Zack asked, "What was that all about?"

Zack was confused and not fully recovered from the kiss and sudden departure. "I'm not sure," he replied, "I was thanking her for all she's done when all of a sudden she stomped out of here."

Seth moved closer to inspect the smoked spectacles and inquired, "Were you thanking her like she was your mother or sister?"

"Well," started Zack when Seth continued, "If you were then you don't know much about women, especially that woman. Like I said before, she has her cap set for you."

Zack was trying to sort out this information while Seth was restraining his amusement to Zack's confusion. With an amused grin he offered, "What she wanted to hear was that you've grown to think of her as special, a woman who you have a great affection for."

Opposing the notion that he would have to be that specific Zack responded, "Well, I figured she'd know all that."

Seth chuckled, patted Zack on the shoulder said, "No Zack, even if they know it they still want to hear it." Seth stepped away and began to search for something on his desk while he asked about the doctor's visit.

Then almost as an after thought said, "Oh, Ned Shiller wants to see you when you're able. He sent in word with Mary Gusterson. She made it sound like it was pretty important." Zack decided to take a ride out to the Gusterson farm in the morning.

Zack moved his belongings back to the hotel and toward evening walked to the cafe. Ann was conspicuously absent and Anthony Bell offered no explanation when Zack paid his bill. He realized his daughter was falling in love with Zack and, although concerned of what could come of it, decided to let her work it out herself. He would only step in if it appeared she was about to do something rash.

*   *   *

The light was late on the gray, cloudy morning that promised rain when Zack mounted the rented horse and turned north. As he rode, he continued his thinking about Ann and the dilemma he felt. He had some unfinished business to attend to in St. Louis, namely confronting his brother about his share of their father's estate. Then there was his agreement with Ben Thompson. He should be buying supplies to take to Ben. He could not imagine taking Ann to Ben's place nor could he imagine himself settling down to a routine life here or anyplace east of the Mississippi River. *Seth was right*, he thought, *I should have told her of my affection for her.* He wanted to have a life with Ann but could not figure what that could be. As he turned through the gate at the Gusterson farm he was no closer to deciding what to do than when he started his journey.

Ned Shiller grimaced as he lowered himself onto the bench, just outside the rear door. Once settled, he produced a letter from his pocket and gestured with it as he told Zack of the contents. Ned's father-in-law wrote the letter telling Ned to buy more horses. Prior to his injuries, Ned purchased almost enough horses and oxen to fill the original order, for which arrangement had been made to have them delivered to the livestock pens at the Cairo wharf. From there they would be shipped to St. Louis.

Knowing he was not going to be able to return to the saddle soon, he asked Zack to take the job. Ned planned to return to St. Louis to continue his recovery.

Ned then outlined a plan that he hoped would appeal to Zack. In a day or two he would have hired a crew to manage the horses Zack would buy during an overland trip to St. Louis. Once the crew and horses were opposite St. Louis, on the east side of Mississippi River, he would have made the arrangement to have them ferried over. Zack liked the plan. The notion of having something to do after being idle so long appealed to him. He would have a little more time in Cairo to decide what to do about Ann and hoped it would be enough. He gently shook the little man's hand sealing the agreement. Ned asked Zack to try and buy a few more horses in the immediate vicinity to complete the order.

Not only did Zack buy a dozen horses that afternoon from the surrounding farms but also found a man who agreed to include Mary Gusterson's horses in the herding to Cairo. During the evening meal Mary greeted this news with delight and appreciation for her good neighbors. She was encouraged by how the men at her table were recovering and the recent improved finances delivered by Zack and Ned. Kenneth's bruises were starting to fade, Zack could see and Ned was hobbling around fairly well. She served a meal in good spirits. As the meal progressed Zack noticed the twins were not mentioned and recalling the adage, *let sleeping dogs lie* did not mention them.

In the morning Ned and the Gustersons waved good-bye to Zack at a crossroads. A cushion of several quilts had been arranged in the rear of the wagon for Ned to sit on. He looked reasonably comfortable as the wagon bumped and the milk cans clanged. Zack decided to work his way west to try and buy more horses before heading to Cairo.

By late afternoon Zack had the pledges of seven more horses to be delivered to Cairo where he promised Ned would pay for them upon delivery. As he worked his way back toward Cairo he noticed a single rider approaching the crossroad intersection he was about to enter. The rider had the horse in a fast trot and appeared to be engaged in a loud conversation. Zack pulled his horse to a stop in a shaded corner of the intersection to satisfy his curiosity about this odd sight. He recognized Ann Bell, dressed more like a man than a woman. Initially he was glad to see her but was puzzled by her attire and strange behavior.

An hour earlier Ann Bell defied her father's protests about her riding attire when she announced her plan of taking a long ride in the countryside. She rented a horse and rode west toward the open farmlands where she could think out loud without being disturbed. She was engaged in a loud, heated debate with herself as she rode, barely paying attention to where she was going. She pulled her horse to a sudden stop when she saw Zack removing his hat in the shade. She was mildly startled by this chance meeting. She had not finished her debate and so was not quite ready to talk to Zack. Similarly, Zack had his own debate going in his head and was not quite ready to talk with Ann.

Zack got all tongue twisted as he tried to include an apology into a greeting, "I'm sorry to see…I mean, I'm glad to see you and sorry to be…. I mean….."

Before he could straighten it out Ann cut him off, "Zachary Clayton, you are just going to have to figure it out and decide what you want!" In the next instant she dug her heels into the horse's flanks and whipped it into a full gallop.

As she sped away Zack called after her, "I WANT YOU!" Ann did not slow down. Zack watched her until she passed out of sight around a tree lined curve in the road.

Ann heard Zack's declaration above the thundering hooves. She, however, was so unprepared to meet him and now so irritated at her response, she was not able to consider any other choice except racing away from the chance meeting. What he called out stuck in her mind and she suddenly realized that her racing off, like she did, would be interpreted as rejection. She slowed her winded horse and got it turned around. The horse could not return to the crossroad at the speed it left it. When Ann got back to the intersection Zack was gone. She tried urging the horse to a faster pace toward town but it refused to go any faster than a resting gait. On the slow ride to town Ann resumed the loud debate with herself. She insightfully added her own willfulness to the dilemma she now faced.

*   *   *

Ned Shiller was pleased with the addition of seven horses to be delivered to the Cairo wharf and asked Zack to get a few more. He reported having bought a used covered wagon and was close to hiring a trail crew for Zack's horse buying trip across Illinois. He invited Zack to join him for supper in his hotel room. Since returning to the hotel Ned was having meals delivered to him while he continued to recuperate. They spent most of the evening going over a map and the details of the trip.

Zack was packed for a three day return to the countryside when he departed early in the morning. He liked being out in the open again, living close to the land while traveling through the thickly forested areas. The insects and creatures of the hard wood forests were different than those of the mountains. At times the foliage could be so dense it dulled sun and sound. He continued to wear the smoked spectacles in bright sunlight except when he was talking to horse owners. He got weary of explaining the reason for them. It was not a successful buying trip. In three days he was only able to buy eight horses with the money Ned gave to him. Zack returned to Cairo leading the horses.

Ned was busy buying supplies and getting the wagon readied while Zack was gone. He reported his progress and announced having hired a three man crew that was subject to Zack's approval. Zack had the option of replacing one or all if he had any disagreement with Ned's selections.

Early the next morning Zack arrived at Bell's Cafe just as Anthony Bell was unlocking the door. Zack decided to try to talk to Ann at least one more time. Anthony Bell greeted Zack and knew by the look on his face that his purpose for being in the cafe was more than just to have a meal.

Ann, carrying a tray of tableware, entered from the kitchen and began to set a table without noticing Zack. She was attending to her task when Zack walked up to her. "I want to talk to you before I leave," Zack interrupted, "I'm leaving tomorrow for St. Louis."

Ann set down the fork, grabbed Zack by the hand and gently ordered, "Follow me." She led him past the kitchen to the rear door of the building where stairs ascended to the second floor. She stopped at the landing. While still holding his hand, she looked into his face and asked, "Will you be coming back?"

"I'd like to but that depends on you." he replied.

She immediately embraced him while saying, "Zachary Clayton, I want you to come back. In fact I don't want you to leave."

Zack realized in that moment that rejection was not contained in those sentences. He folded his arms around her and started to say, "Ann, I have to…"

She cut him off by raising a finger to his lips and saying, "Shh." She followed her finger with her lips.

As much as he wanted to continue the kiss he knew he had to tell her about his immediate plans. He broke off the kiss and started again, "Ann, I've thrown in with Ned Shil…"

Again she stopped his words with a finger and a kiss. This time she withdrew slightly and said with a seductive smile, "Now, you were saying?"

Zack purposely took her by her hands and held them while he told her about his plans to buy horses for Ned. He asked her to wait for him until he returned to Cairo, which would be in a month. Ann stated her willingness to wait in words and another kiss.

"ANN, ANN, We need you out here," called her father's voice down the hall.

Ann broke off the kiss and whispered, "I've got to go. Come back this evening after we're closed." Then she gently pushed Zack out the rear door.

That evening Zack returned to the rear door of the cafe and upon knocking was admitted by Anthony Bell. He soon found himself sitting in the parlor of the family's home above the cafe. Ann orchestrated a conversation that concluded with a plan of Zack returning to Cairo in a month to court her. She cleverly delayed her parent's questions about plans beyond a period of courting. Afterwards Ann escorted Zack back to the rear door and sent him on his way with a kiss.

CHAPTER 10

THE WEDDING

As arranged, Zack walked into the dining room of the Skyles Hotel to meet Ned Shiller. Seated with Ned were three men who were hungrily eating a big breakfast. One of the men was Carl Pettis, the river pirate Zack encountered that night on the Missouri River. Ned introduced the men as the crew for the horse-buying trip.

Eli Diamond was a medium built man with dark curly hair and beard. He was well traveled in Illinois, having worked for a freight hauling company out of the town of Chester. He lost his job when most of the company's assets were destroyed in a fire. He knew about horses and oxen pulling freight wagons. He was thirty-three years old, dressed in well-worn, soiled clothes and had a strong a handshake. He had been looking for steady work in the river towns for a month.

The next man looked more like a boy. Nate Plummer could barely pull himself from the plate of food for the introduction. He said he was twenty years old but Zack figured him for seventeen. Nate arrived in Cairo two days before, having walked from Vincennes, Indiana. He left a family with too many mouths to feed to make it on his own. He told Ned he was an experienced drover.

Carl Pettis was introduced as a man with experience with horses who was working his way home to Kentucky. He had been working at the wharf's live stock pens when he heard about a job that would pay more and sought out Ned to apply for it. Ned knew there were shortcomings in the crew he had assembled but these were the best of the lot he had talked to. Zack decided to talk to each one individually at another table.

Eli Diamond was pretty much what he seemed to be and impressed Zack with an attitude of being willing to give a day's work, every day for as long as he was needed. He planned to look for work in St. Louis when this job was finished.

Nate Plummer quickly confessed to just turning eighteen years old when Zack warned him if he caught onto any lies the liar would be fired on the spot. Nate desperately needed a job and promised to learn and obey on the trail. Aside from his lean and hungry look he had a sincerity about him that Zack liked.

Carl Pettis had only a slight limp remaining when he walked the distance between the two tables. Zack was immediately direct with him, "You give up river pirating?"

Carl was taken aback by the question and at first thought to lie. But the way the question was asked, right at the start, figured Zack to know something of his sordid recent past. "Yes sir, I have," he replied while keeping steady eye contact with Zack, "It be a cruel business Mister Clayton. I lost a brother, a friend and durn near became a cripple because of it. It be no friend of mine." Zack asked about his plans once the trip was done and Carl replied he would resume his journey back to Kentucky with the money he would earn.

Carl did not recognize Zack. The last time he saw Zack he did not get a good look at the grizzled trapper who had bound, gagged and terrified him that night up on the Missouri River. The image of that shadowy figure still occasionally haunted Carl's dreams. More than once he had awakened in a sweat with, "I'll skin ya alive," growling in his ears. He did think there was something vaguely familiar about Zack's voice but he could not place it. Carl got the same warning as Nate and acknowledged he understood.

Zack openly announced to Ned, "These men will do." Then he assigned the men the tasks of completing the loading of the wagon and told them to be ready to depart at first light. Ned and Zack still had a few purchases to make for the trip. When that was done they met in Ned's hotel room. Ned counted out the money Zack would need for the buying of horses and expenses. Ned loaned Zack a money belt to wear under his clothes.

At first light Zack joined Eli Diamond on the seat of the covered wagon. Nate and Carl rode in the rear and would do so until enough horses could be purchased to have them mounted. The wagon moved steadily until late morning. By then they had moved passed the area in which Zack had already covered in his previous horse buying forays. Zack directed Eli to turn into a barnyard of a farm, which had several horses grazing in a pasture. Zack purchased two horses that were saddled from the three saddles in the wagon. Zack sent Carl off in one direction with instructions to have horses and the owner or owners delivered to the wagon. Zack went in another direction. They were to meet the wagon at a designated crossroads ahead.

Two hours later Zack rode in leading a horse and Carl brought in two horses and the owner. Within a few minutes the man departed with his payment. Nate was assigned to herd the horses and chose one to ride. It quickly become obvious to Zack that Nate was having some trouble with getting a horse saddled. Nate revealed his horse riding experience consisted of riding "my Pa's plow plug." Zack quickly went through the basics of saddling, riding and herding with Nate. He rode with Nate for about a mile before he ventured off the main road again to look for more horses to buy. Later Carl returned to the wagon with an owner and two more horses.

At the end of the day they had added only one more horse to the small herd and Nate was catching on to keeping them together. They crossed a short wooden bridge that was surrounded by scattered trees. Zack directed Eli to set up a night camp in the trees and told Carl and Nate to water the horses and secure them to a picket line after they grazed. Zack rode off hoping to add a few more horses before dark. His thoughts drifted to Ann as he rode between farmhouses. Notwithstanding her acceptance of him he was still perplexed about a future with her. He did not relished the thought of spending the winter in Cairo, especially with so much to do in St. Louis. *Perhaps I could send for her to come to St. Louis,* he thought, hoping for a solution to materialize, *But then what?* A plan did not arise.

Darkness had just settled in with the first evening stars appearing when Zack approached the camp leading two horses. As he drew closer he noticed another, smaller wagon parked behind the big wagon. He rode directly to where the horses were picketed. Nate appeared out of the darkness to take the horses as Zack dismounted. He thought he heard Nate chuckling as he led the horses away. Zack had not noticed Nate chuckling or acting strangely before and thought it odd but knew he did not know Nate all that well yet. *He might bare some watching,* Zack thought, with a puzzled shake of his head.

Zack assumed the other wagon belonged to a horse owner waiting to be paid, or another traveler looking for some company. As he entered the light of the fire he noticed two men sitting on the ground, with their backs to him. Eli and Carl looked up as he approached. Rising, Eli said, "Mister Clayton, ya have a visitor." Zack noticed both Eli and Carl were grinning in an unusual manner.

Zack turned toward the sitting men and thought he recognized one of them from Cairo. The other man kept a big hat covering his face. Extending his hand toward the bigger man Zack said, "I'm Zachary Clayton. What can I do for you?" The man started to rise and speak but before he could complete the motion or words the other man whipped off his hat letting long blonde hair fly with it.

Ann Bell fairly leapt at Zack wrapping her hands behind his neck. "Surprise," she exclaimed. Zack was so startled by the sudden movement and the force of her weight that he was staggered backwards. As he regained his balance Nate joined the grinning men watching the scene.

"Ann!" Zack blurted, "What are you doing here?"

Ann withdrew her hands and while placing them on her hips in a mock antagonistic stance challenged, "Well, aren't you glad to see me?"

Still recovering from the shock of her sudden appearance Zack tried to whisper, "Yes, but what are you...?"

Ann stopped his words with a finger to his lips. Zack took her by her hands and while looking over her shoulder toward the grinning men around the campfire said to them, "Don't you fellas have something you ought to be doing?"

In a teasing voice Ann defended them, "Now don't get after them for sharing in my plot."

Just then Eli burned his fingers trying to get the lid off the pot of stew, next to the fire. He forgot to use a cloth to protect himself and said, "Damn it...Ouch...Sorry Miss Bell," as he blew on his fingers. His expletive and apology created a break in the uneasiness and they all laughed.

Ann introduced Thomas Purdy from the Cairo livery stable who she hired to bring her in his wagon to find Zack. Then she led Zack to a plate Eli was filling while saying, "You must be hungry with it being so late and all." While Zack ate the plate of stew the men began finding things to do away from the fire. Ann began to tell Zack what happened after she decided to join him.

*   *   *

Ann Bell did not sleep well and found herself awake in the predawn hours staring into the darkness of her room. She knew Zack and the horse buying crew would be leaving at dawn and contemplated on finding a way to join their departure. She doubted Zack would agree to take her along and her parents would certainly object. She could not do away with a sinking feeling of dread. She dreaded the notion that Zack may not return to Cairo, that something would happen which might prevent him from returning. She decided to go with him to St. Louis. She was sure she could handle the protest her parents would raise but may not be able to overcome Zack's refusal to include her in his immediate horse buying plans. Then it came to her to join him after he was on the road and maybe far enough away from Cairo that he would not insist that she return. At twilight she lit a lamp and began packing. By the time her parents discovered her activities she had two small trunks packed, quilts bundled and a cotton flour sack stuffed with clothes. As predicted her parents raised a storm of protest but nothing they said could dissuade her. Fortunately opening the cafe for the day also demanded her parents' attention and at an opportune moment Ann slipped away to go to the livery stable. She hired Thomas Purdy and his wagon to take her to Zack.

When she returned to the cafe her parents pleaded with her to reconsider. Ann easily asserted, "I'm not going to let him get too far away from me." And with tears in her eyes added, "I love him and I'm not willing to take the chance on him not coming back for me."

Thomas Purdy was loading the trunks into the wagon and was witness to the tension between daughter and parents. He was uncomfortable about being involved in the family strife and thought of somehow disengaging himself. He abandoned that notion when he saw Ann's parents accept that their headstrong daughter was going to leave and they could not stop her short of tying her down. They stood in a departing embrace when he returned to the wagon seat. Anthony Bell extracted a promise from Ann to write as he pressed some money into her hand. Ann climbed onto the wagon seat and Thomas Purdy clacked the horse into motion. Ann turned to wave to her parents as the horse was urged to a pulling pace.

                    *   *   *

Zack was hungry and continued eating through Ann's story. He set down his plate when Ann concluded and invited her to take a walk. A three-quarter moon and the fireflies were rising as they approached the bridge hand in hand. The small hollow sounds of their boots on the planks joined the crickets and other night sounds above the slow moving creek. At the middle of the bridge Zack drew her into his arms and said, "I don't know what I'm going to do with you."

Ann did not speak and drew him into a passionate kiss. His hands roamed her back and buttocks while they kissed. She may be dressed like a man but she felt like a woman, soft and warm. She pressed tighter to him with a grinding of her hips. Gasping in passion Zack whispered, "Ann, I want to lay with you."

Pulling her head back slightly and placing her hands on the sides of his face she responded in a hushed voice, "I know, and I with you." Then after a slight pause said, "But we have to wait until we are married."

"Married?" questioned Zack, "How can we get married out here, in the middle of nowhere?"

Ann had plenty of time to think that question through during her day's ride and was ready with an answer, "Just as soon as we come to a town with a church we can get married. Or if you prefer we can inquire about a Justice of the Peace."

This was all new to Zack and he confessed, "I don't know anything about getting married."

Ann smiled with his confession and while rubbing his face coyly teased, "You want to get married don't you?"

"Yes, I think so," Zack replied, "Anyway it's more of what we'll do after that."

Continuing her tease Ann said, "I know what I want to do with you Zachary Clayton." and engaged him in another passionate kiss.

Zack pulled away a little and declared, "That's not what I mean. I've been thinking about where do we go, where do we live."

Rubbing his face again Ann responded, "I'm willing to go anywhere as long as it's with you, Zachary Clayton. Why don't we use the time it will take us to get to St. Louis to figure it out." Zack agreed and they slowly walked back to the wagons.

Eli Diamond was in the back of the covered wagon arranging the cargo by the light of a lantern when Zack and Ann looked in to see what he was doing. Eli figured Ann would have her way and was making room for her belongings. When he saw Zack's face peering into the wagon he announced, "I cleared some space for her trunks."

Looking around in the wagon Zack directed, "Fix it so she can bed down in there."

Eli then suggested, "If Mister Purdy is to spend the night with us it might be best to just wait to load the trunks in the morning when I have more time to move things around."

Zack agreed and went off to find Thomas Purdy. He noted Carl and Nate had set out their bedrolls and found Thomas Purdy rolling his bedroll out under his wagon.

It had been a tiring, event filled day for all of them. Zack returned to the wagon and found Eli exiting and bidding goodnight to Ann. Zack poked his head into the wagon to check on Ann's comfort. She gave him a lingering kiss before turning out the lantern.

*   *   *

Thomas Purdy waved and hollered, "Good Luck," as his wagon rumbled across the bridge. Eli had the horses hitched to the big wagon and was ready to resume another day of traveling. Ann chose a spirited mare from the small herd to ride and Nate saddled it for her. This left Nate without a saddle so he chose the smallest horse to ride bareback. Carl was assigned to continue his routine of bringing horses and owners to the wagon while Zack and Ann rode off in another direction. Eli clucked his team onto the road.

Horse buying was not as productive as in the previous day and by late afternoon Zack had bought only one horse. Riding with Ann down the side roads and to the many farms was a delight and most informative. Zack learned Ann was an accomplished rider. As a girl she learned to ride on a large horse-breeding farm in Ohio. Her parents managed the kitchen for the wealthy horse breeder who taught his children and the children of his employees to ride. Besides being a generous man he figured the more people who knew how to ride the more people there were to buy horses from him. When he died, the farm was inherited by his son who did not share his father's generosity nor humanity.

Anthony Bell resigned and moved to Cairo to open up a cafe. Over the years Ann continued to ride by joining school friends who had horses or on occasion by renting a horse. Ann was good with people and enjoyed meeting the farm families where they stopped and it was obvious to Zack that the families found her engaging and charming. Zack also learned that Ann enjoyed kissing. When they would stop in the shade or by a creek to get water she would want to include some lingering kisses.

As the days went on and after several such kissing events Zack asked her about it. She answered with a coy tease, "Well, Mister Zachary Clayton, when a girl saves herself for just the right gentleman, she has to make up for all the other ones she didn't kiss." She squealed with a giggle as Zack playfully reached to paddle her for the saucy remark. Then in a mock tussle they were kissing again.

The days rolled into two weeks and Zack could not remember when he had felt so happy. The number of horses he bought steadily grew. It was getting more difficult to find places to camp to accommodate the numbers. At one farm Zack bought a horse and saddle so Nate would be quicker and more efficient at herding.

Eli set a good pace and his choices of the roads to take were proving to be compatible with the purpose of the trip. He also was proving his skill as a camp cook. It was not uncommon for the crew to eat roasted chicken or ham served with fresh vegetables, which Eli bought or bartered for from farm wives. Between Eli and Ann there seemed to be no end to the tasty meals they could prepare. And from time to time Zack would demonstrate his biscuit making skills.

The one to benefit the most from the hardy meals was Nate. He began to fill out and was looking more like a man instead of a skinny boy. Carl also seemed to perk up. At the start of the trip he tended to be morose but that temperament was being replaced with smiling and laughing. Ann had them all charmed and she was proving to be a resourceful and resilient trail mate.

In a night camp Eli announced they would get to Chester tomorrow. He was eager for a reunion with friends and familiar haunts. He described Chester as only slightly smaller than Cairo but growing. It had several new businesses, three churches, a bank, a hotel and a grain mill. It was becoming known as a center for producing and shipping flour and corn meal. Up to then the crew had not passed through any towns of consequence and only one had a church. At the time the church did not have a minister. Later in the evening Ann announced to Zack, "Chester sounds like a good place to get married."

        *   *   *

They established their camp northwest of Chester in a sparsely wooded hollow where they penned the horses by stringing ropes between the trees. Zack, Ann and Eli rode into town with Eli serving as a guide. Once he pointed out the major streets and buildings he departed to look up some old friends.

Zack and Ann checked at a church parsonage and learned that the minister was ill. A minister of another church was conducting his services. They located the minister who seemed beleaguered and denied he could perform a short notice wedding. Ann was somewhat relieved by his refusal in that she was not particularly impressed with the man. She preferred someone who was at least a bit warmer and more friendly.

They were on their way to the third church when a familiar voiced called out to them, "Zack, Ann." It was Seth Thomas who rode up from behind and said, "I've been looking for you two." They all dismounted and held a reunion in the street.

Seth had come up the Mississippi River the day before figuring correctly the place and timing of Zack and Ann arriving in the Chester area. "Every day since you left your parents have been worrying me," Seth reported to Ann, "They figured if anything happened to you I would hear about it. So I thought to take a few days away from them and try to look you up."

Ann told him she was planning to write to her parents from Chester and Seth volunteered to carry the letter. Then she told of their plan to get married. The announcement was received with a hoop and "I declare" to the point of causing people who were passing by to turn to stare at the trio in the street. They told him of their search for a preacher.

Seth said, "If you'll leave everything to me we can have you married proper tomorrow afternoon." Before they could ask for details he escorted them to the hotel, got them checked in and sent the hotel buggy out to their camp to get Ann's trunks.

They were sitting in the hotel dining room when two distinguished looking gentlemen approached the table. Seth introduced them as his brother and uncle. Marshal John Thomas and Judge Walter Thomas were the reasons Seth knew his way around so well and seemed to have so much influence. The congenial men took seats and after a few minutes of discussion had the wedding planned. Judge Thomas reserved the hotel dining room for the ceremony for four-thirty the next day. Marshal John Thomas said he would send a couple of men out to relieve Zack's crew in the afternoon so they could attend the ceremony. A waiter notified Seth that Ann's trunks had arrived and she excused herself. After she departed the men teased Zack about what a lucky man he was for "snaring such a comely filly."

John Thomas rose from the table and as an afterthought said, "Oh Seth, I have some information about those two rogues you asked about." He reported that two men fitting the description of the Gusterson twins were seen on a steamboat heading to St. Louis. Seth said he would write to Ned Shiller to have him post charges against them in St. Louis. Judge Thomas also rose and announced he had some arrangements for the wedding to take care of. After a hardy round of handshakes they departed.

"Seth, how's all this wedding finery going to get paid for?" asked Zack in a dead serious manner, "I may not have enough with me to cover it."

Seth could see that Zack was getting rather nervous and was not fully aware of the extent of the circumstances in play. He was delighted to have found Zack and Ann, enlivened by planning the wedding and amused by Zack's concerns. Hiding his amusement he inquired, "Do you have five dollars?"

Zack studied the question and replied, "Sure, I have five dollars. But I don't reckon five dollars will cover all that's been talked about here."

Seth leaned back with an amused, pondering grin and replied, "Five dollars will cover your share. Can you afford that?" He stuck out his hand while Zack fumbled in the money belt for a five-dollar bill.

Zack handed over the bill while Seth continued, "You see, Anthony Bell gave me some money to spend anyway I see fit to benefit his daughter and from what I've seen so far a wedding is a good cause. And who do you suppose owns this fine hotel where you are staying?" Zack gestured that he did not know. "I'll tell you who, my Uncle Walter. Now you wouldn't want to go and deprive him of having some fun would you? Lord knows he needs some fun with all that's going on in his court these days."

Zack tried to formulate a response, "Well, no... but." Before he could continue Seth patted him on the shoulder and said, "Then it's all settled. You two will have a grand wedding right here tomorrow at this time. There's not much you have to do except show up for it."

Zack started to pose another question when Ann entered the dining room. Seth and Zack rose to her approach. Beaming, she said, "Zachary, you should see the room we'll have." She took Zack by the arm and with a squeezing tease said, "But you'll have to wait until tomorrow." Feeling a bit overwhelmed by the avalanche of information and developing events, Zack responded with a reticent grin.

Seth interrupted, "Well, Misses Clayton to be, that room is yours as long as you want it. I've got it all worked out with the groom." Slightly puzzled by the pronouncement, Ann looked at Zack who nodded to the statement as true. Seth continued, "I'm wondering if you'd like to wait a few days to get married so I can get word to your parents. I'm sure they could get away for your wedding?"

Ann pondered this suggestion carefully. She thought of the need to get back to horse buying and replied, "No, we really do not have time to lollygag here in Chester. What you're hatching now is more time than we can afford. And I want you to know how much I appreciate what you're doing. It's so much more than what I had hoped for."

Seth took her hand in a kind-hearted handshake and said, "Well Miss Bell, I understand. So you get settled in and I'll be sure to deliver the groom to you tomorrow, on time and properly outfitted.

As Seth led Zack to a tailor to get a suit for the wedding he inquired about Zack's plans on where he was going to settle after the horse buying venture. Zack revealed he had not reached a decision but thought he would stay in the fur trade in some way. "In that case," Seth concluded, "You'll probably not need a full time suit, so we'll just rent one."

In a short time they departed the tailor shop with a dark suit, a white shirt with a stiff collar and a dark cravat. They stopped in front of a barber shop where Seth pointed out Zack could get a shave, haircut, bath and boot polishing. When they arrived in front of the hotel John Thomas met them at their horses. He compared wedding progress reports with his brother and concluded the discussion with a warning to Zack. He heard from a country sheriff that "a trio of road agents" had robbed some travelers north of Chester and advised Zack to be alert for them in that direction. The Marshals bid farewell as Zack mounted his horse.

Before he left Chester Zack stopped at a gunsmith shop and bought a small caliber pistol for Ann and a used rifle for Carl. He figured to teach Ann to shoot and arm Carl so that another experienced rifleman was on the crew. He figured Eli could defend himself with a whip or club and did not know if Nate had any skills with weapons.

When Zack got back to camp he assembled the men and announced the wedding plan with an invitation for them to attend. The men immediately began talking about how they would need to clean up and negotiated with one another for hair trimming and clothes washing. Before he turned them loose to attend to these tasks Zack also told them about the report of road agents and his plan for armed vigilance. This news had a sobering effect on the men, especially Carl Pettis. Carl began to worry that his nefarious past was somehow coming back to haunt him. He figured that one day he would have to pay for his misdeeds and becoming the victim of road agents just may be the pay back.

*   *   *

With another transformation having taken place from a dusty horse buyer to a clean and polished groom, Zack stepped from the barbershop into the street. He shifted the bag of clothes and pistols to tug at the tight, uncomfortable collar as he crossed the street. The bright afternoon sun heated the dark suit and he wondered how other men wore such clothing all the time. He entered the hotel and checked his bag at the front desk. When he entered the dining room he saw his crew standing by themselves looking uncomfortable. Seth Thomas had tried his best to ease them but they felt out of place with the finer dressed judge, marshals and other guests. Zack had just joined them when Judge Thomas began to give directions to the assembled group to take the places he assigned to them. Other hotel guests were curious about the private party and stood in the double doorway of the dining room. They were gently parted by the commanding Seth Thomas as he proudly escorted Ann Bell through the doorway.

Ann was wearing a simple white dress, which she had hand sewn. It was among the many items she had packed in her hope chest. Some of the items might be thought unnecessary or frivolous considering she could be heading for a primitive life with Zack. But she had made and collected the items over the years just to be sure she could have some nice things when she got married. One such item was the wedding dress and now she was so happy she brought it along.

Zack had gotten used to seeing Ann in her trail clothes of trousers and shirt and was stunned by her loveliness as she entered the room. Every guest was awed by her radiance as she was escorted to Zack and Judge Thomas. The ceremony proceeded and all hushed to Judge Thomas' authoritative rendering of the wedding vows. When he came to the part of the ceremony where he asked for the ring everyone concerned suddenly realized that they had forgotten the ring. Those who thought of it assumed someone else was taking care of it.

Being a man of some creativity the Judge called for any ring from the guests. Nate Plummer shyly stepped forward with a ring of sorts. When he was making his way to Cairo he happened to get a couple of days work at a blacksmith's shop. There he made a ring out of a horseshoe nail when he tried working the smithy's tools. He did not know much about working metal and made the ring too small for himself. He stuck it in his pocket just to have something in his empty pockets. The time in his pocket had given the ring a certain amount of polishing and he handed it to the Judge. Judge Thomas presented the ring to Zack and Ann.

They viewed the ring as a symbol of their past two weeks together, buying horses. They simultaneously accepted it with knowing smiles. And much to their delight the ring fit perfectly. The rest of the ceremony proceeded without incident and afterwards Zack had his hand shook and back patted by all the male guests.

The dining room was reopened to the public, which created another round of congratulations to the newly wedded couple. Judge Thomas officiated at the wedding dinner that followed and was in very good humor. He presented several toasts to the bride and groom, enjoying every moment of his generous role. At one point Seth embraced Ann and handed her an envelope as he said, "This is from your parents."

She in turn handed him an envelope addressed to them. "Thank you Seth," she whispered, "You'll never know how much having you here means to me and all you've done for us." The big man visibly teared and wiped his eyes with a kerchief.

Other small gifts were presented, including a baby garment from Marshal and Mrs. John Thomas. Ann stood and displayed it to the seated guests and while placing her hand on Zack's shoulder said, "We'll try to fill this soon and you all are invited to the christening." Her remark was greeted with howls of laughter and Zack's embarrassed grin. With that as the high point of the dinner, Seth Thomas, who realized he had consumed too much wine, escorted the couple to the dining room door. He pushed them toward the stairs. "Now you're on your own," he slightly slurred, "I can do no more for you." He returned to the wedding party, which continued on into the evening.

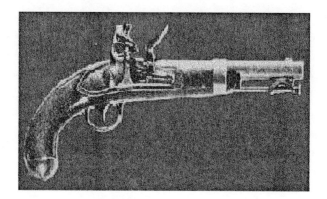

CHAPTER 11

THE ROAD AGENTS

Zack returned the rented suit and as he was returning to the hotel he noticed the hotel buggy was departing with Ann's trunks. Also someone had tied their horses up to the rail. Ann, dressed as she had in the previous days, emerged from the hotel. She greeted Zack with a brief kiss and swung into the saddle. "I'm ready to ride if you are, Zachary," she announced, then with a seductive, mischievous after-thought added, "Unless you'd like to have just a little more time in that fine hotel room."

Zack responded with his shy grin and chuckled, "If we didn't have so much to do I'd take you up on that." He stepped into the stirrup and when seated leaned to Ann for a brief kiss. "Maybe we can get some time to ourselves up the trail some," he suggested.

"I'd like that, Mister Clayton," Ann responded with a bit of a tease in her voice. They turned their horses into the street and had only gone a few steps when the voice of Seth Thomas called out, "Let me hear from you two when you can."

Seth managed to sleep off the wine but one look at him told the couple he was not fully recovered. Zack and Ann waved while saying, "Will do, Seth." "You take care of yourself." Seth waved back as they urged their horses to a trot.

*   *   *

Eli Diamond and Carl Pettis were no worse for wear than Seth Thomas after an evening of celebrating but the same could not be said for Nate Plummer. After the party at the hotel, where he had more than his share of wine, Eli took Nate and Carl to his favorite "bawdy house" at the edge of town. Not only did Nate have his first drink of whiskey but he was also introduced to the pleasures of the flesh by a buxom chippie. On their return trip to the camp, Eli and Carl had to tie Nate in the saddle to prevent him from falling out. All the way back to camp Nate kept saying in a drunken slur, "That were the besss time I ever had in my whooole life." He passed out as they arrived in camp. When Zack and Ann rode into camp he was sitting on the ground with his head between his hands and moaning with a devastating hangover.

Since Nate was in no condition for a shooting lesson Zack took Ann to a ravine near the camp. He blazed a man's chest size in the bark of a big tree with a hand axe and paced off twenty steps. With Ann intently watching, he talked through the loading of the small flintlock pistol. He handed it to her and coached her through aiming before allowing her to bring the pistol to full cock. Zack explained the delay between pulling the trigger and the pistol firing.

Ann aimed the pistol and fired. When the small puff of smoke emitted from the powder pan she flinched, pulling the pistol up causing the ball to strike the tree about four feet above the blaze mark. Zack talked her through loading the pistol and when she was ready she fired again. This time the ball struck high in the blaze mark. Zack drew his pistol and explained each step again as he aimed. He fired and the round struck the blaze mark dead center. They continued the lesson for six more shots from the small pistol and Ann placed the last two rounds close to center. She tucked the pistol in her belt and turned to Zack to give him a hip-grinding embrace. The pistol was an obstruction to the closeness she desired. She smiled in a beguiling manner, "I guess there'll be times when this pistol gets in the way, Mister Clayton."

Getting used to her suggestive remarks and becoming more comfortable with making some of his own, Zack responded, "I guess there will, Misses Clayton." Zack gently removed the pistol from her belt and said, "I'll have to remember not to let a gun come before fun," as he pulled her close.

Ann laughed, patted his face and teased, "Why Zachary, I do believe you've got some poet in you." Turning serious she took his hands and said, "I think I loved you the first time I saw you."

Zack responded to her declaration with a smile and leaned to her for a kiss. Remembering Seth's counsel in Cairo he added, "And I love you." He turned and with a slight indication of hand pressure guided her to where the horses were tied. They exchanged another kiss before climbing into the saddles. During the ride back to camp Ann described an idea of sewing a pouch on a leather vest for the pistol so she could carry it under her left arm. She could not find a comfortable position for the pistol in her belt.

Zack took Carl to the ravine and after pacing off fifty yards Carl proved he knew how to handle a rifle. Eli was offered the same shooting practice and declined saying, "No thanks Mister Clayton. Before a bandit, road agent, or pirate gets close enough to me to do any harm he'll be dodgin' my whip." He demonstrated by rolling out the long black whip from his belt hook and returned the tip with a resounding crack.

Nate was deciding he might survive his terrible hangover when Zack took him to the ravine. Even with his aching head, which throbbed even more with each shot, Nate was a quick study. He mastered loading the pistol in two trials and did well with the Zack's rifle. Zack gave him a warning when handing Nate a pistol to carry on the remaining journey, "I'll want it back in good condition."

"Yes sir," Nate replied as he tucked the pistol in his belt.

        *   *   *

When they were back to the routine of traveling and buying horses Zack and Ann rode together to the potential sources to increase the growing herd. Nate and Carl drove the horses behind the wagon. One day Zack and Ann rode up the lane of a big farm with several horses grazing in a pasture. The owner was willing to sell four horses and pointed them out. One of them was a handsome roan mare with four white stockings. Zack and the farmer had just about agreed upon a price for all four when Ann interrupted by saying to Zack, "You know about a horse with four white stockings don't you?"

"No, I don't think I've ever heard of anything special about them," Zack responded while catching Ann giving him a mischievous wink.

Then in what he knew to be mock seriousness, Ann said, "One white foot buy her. Two white feet try her. Three white feet be on the sly. Four white feet pass her by."

Zack almost laughed when the owner began to defend the horse. Zack hesitated on his last offer for the horses. The owner, who had been dickering to get the price up from Zack's last offer, lowered what he'd been asking. Zack tried to buy only three horses, excluding the mare. In a matter of minutes the owner agreed upon a price for all four horses that was lower than what Zack was willing to pay.

They did not start laughing until they were well out of the farmer's hearing range. "Where did that piece of horse lore come from?" Zack asked between laughs.

"I heard it as a girl in Ohio," Ann responded. "I don't think there's really anything to it."

"Well that fellow thought there was something to it," Zack countered while still chuckling. "I just hope we haven't bought a horse that really has something wrong with it."

They turned at a cross road to head for the wagon. Ann led the way while fording a narrow creek that ran over the road. She turned down stream, away from the road, and signaled Zack to follow. Ann dismounted in a small, tree surrounded glen and led her horse to drink. Zack did the same for his horse and the four horses he was rope leading. Ann tied her horse to a bush and loosened the knots to the blanket she kept behind her saddle. Zack tied up his horses as Ann was spreading the blanket under a tree.

As Zack walked toward her Ann withdrew her pistol from the holster sewn onto her leather vest and tucked it in her belt. Zack drew the pistol from her belt as he pulled her close, "You be the poet and I'll be the horse buyer," he said as he nuzzled her neck. They began to laugh again and it wasn't until their passion rose that they stopped laughing about the white stocking mare.

After they enjoyed their passion on the blanket, they found a deep sun warmed pool in the creek in which to bathe and frolic. They paid no mind to the watching, curious horses as they succumbed to their passions again. Afterwards, while dressing, Zack studied the white stocking mare. He thought he would never be able to look at such a horse again without laughing and remembering this day.

*   *   *

It was said that the whole Titus family did not have enough sense to pour sand out of a boot and that was what Melvin was trying to do. He sat on a log with his boots off striking them in turn on the log then turning them up side down and shaking. A few grains of sand fell out of the wet boots with each shaking. His cousin, Rooster Titus, knelt at the fire tending two skinny rabbits skewered on a green stick for roasting. "Ain't dem harelips cooked yet?" growled Melvin as he continued to shake his boots.

"Hold yer britches, they be close," answered Rooster.

Mobey Bass, also a cousin and the youngest of the group, emerged from the bushes adjusting his trousers after relieving himself. "Cusin Melvin," he stated with a whine, "We gots ta get better vittles. I'm half starvin'."

Melvin looked up from his boot shaking at the gaunt eighteen-year-old boy and noted he was skinny but not any more so than Rooster or himself. "Quite yer bellyachin' or we be eatin' you," Melvin ordered in a gruff manner. Rooster began to laugh, a crowing sound more than a laugh, which had given him his nickname. He announced the rabbits to be cooked enough and tore into one. In a matter of seconds the cousins resembled a pack of dogs fighting over the meager meat with Mobey getting the least amount.

The cousins were the most pathetic trio of aspiring road agents that ever plied their trade on the roads of Illinois. Once they decided to enter a bolder life of crime, which had been preceded by begging, stealing chickens and anything else that wasn't nailed down, their luck had only slightly improved. Between them they had one stolen, rusty pistol, which they were not sure would fire. Their best haul resulted in an incident for which they had become wanted road agents. They just happened to come upon a traveling notions salesman who had parked his peddler's wagon on the side of the road to relieve himself in the bushes. Melvin stuck the rusted pistol in the man's back and helped himself to the man's money pouch. The pouch contained seven dollars in coins. While the peddler was being held at gun point, Rooster and Mobey were going to plunder the wagon.

They took off, yelling and running, when the salesman's wife appeared from within the wagon with a shotgun in her hands. She fired at the cousins who were escaping through the bushes.

Their next attempt at road robbery was also a mixed blessing. In a tree shaded intersection they leapt from concealment to accost a prosperous looking man driving a buggy. Melvin, with a demand of, "Gimme yer purse," pointed the pistol at the man. Rooster got a grip on the horse's halter while Mobey investigated two wicker baskets in the rear of the buggy. He shouted to his cousins, "Hey thar's vittles in here." The man was taking two baskets of food to a wake. Mobey's discovery momentarily distracted Melvin, just as the man was about to hand over his money pouch. While Melvin was reaching for the pouch, the man recognized the rusty pistol as no real threat and kicked Melvin square in the chest with a heavy boot. Then he used his buggy whip on Rooster who released his grip on the halter to protect himself from the stinging leather tip. The man turned his whip to his horse and sped away as Melvin lay in the dust, Rooster licked a rising welt on his hand and Mobey stood holding the baskets.

The ham, loaves of bread and pies from the baskets were gone when the cousins scrapped over the rabbits. Their plan of having horses and pockets full of money had not materialized but they were not detoured. Melvin, who was the self-appointed leader, was confident that it was just a matter of time before they took a big prize. But it really was not the lure of riches that drove them most of the time, it was hunger. They were a ragged, unkempt trio that picked their way through the cover of trees and brush. With their blankets tied up in a roll across their backs they were looking for something to eat.

*   *   *

Horse buying was going very well. Carl and Nate were kept busy with the sizable herd just keeping them together and moving after the wagon. Now and again one or the other had to ride off to round up horses which had strayed. Zack ordered Carl and Nate to mark each horse with a triangle of white wash paint on each haunch in order to easily identify the horses as part of the purchased herd. He also was keeping a ledger book of each horse purchased with a description and cost. It was one of those days when Carl and Nate were having trouble keeping the herd together when the Titus cousins made their appearance. Zack ordered an early camp to let the herd catch up. He found a streamside meadow where the horses could be grazed and watered. Such convenient, good locations were becoming harder to come by as the herd grew. Eli and Ann were setting up camp and Zack was off to assist with the herd when the cousins spotted the big covered wagon parked in the roadside clearing.

To the cousins it looked ideal for their nefarious purposes. There were three horses tied to the rear of the wagon, including the saddled four white stocking mare that Ann had become attached to and had ridden since the day of purchase. As the cousins slipped through the brush to get a closer look a plan was hatching in Melvin's mind. He saw a man at the fire placing a pot for heating. He also saw what he thought was a boy, just a bit smaller than Mobey, dumping chopped meat into the pot. The sight of the early preparations of a stew was enough to increase the gnawing hunger felt by the cousins. They whispered a hurried plan among themselves and moved into position.

The cousins quietly stepped out of the brush in a line with Melvin in the center. Eli and Ann were concentrating on the ingredients for the stew and did not notice them until the cousins were within thirty feet. In a gruff voice, and with as much authority as he could muster, Melvin ordered, "Keep yer paws whar I kin see'um."

Eli and Ann looked up to the voice of a man who was pointing a pistol at them. At that moment Rooster crowed a laugh with recognizing Ann as a woman and announced, "Melvin, he be a girl. We kin get a poke an' thar boodle."

Melvin, who was more interested in keeping a close watch on Eli, glanced at Ann and grunted an acknowledgment. Mobey began to giggle and commenced an excited, stiff legged dance. Melvin turned his head to Mobey, "Shut yer trap boy!" which gave Eli and Ann an opportunity to defend themselves.

In a quick movement Eli loosened the coiled whip on his belt and started a sweeping leather arch aimed at Melvin. The distance was too great to hit him but flying leather would distract his aim if he fired. At the same time Ann pulled her pistol from her vest pouch, cocked it and fired at Melvin. Melvin was turning back toward the movements he saw out of the corner of his eye when the round cut through his matted hair and took off an ear lobe. He reflexively pulled the trigger of his pistol. It did not fire. He dropped the pistol, clamped his hands to his wound and howled, "Ya shot my ear off!" Eli advanced drawing his whip back and aimed another strike, this time at Rooster. Rooster saw it coming, backed up, turned and ran back, into the brush. He quickly disappeared. Seeing the plan disintegrate Mobey also took off, running down the road.

Zack was returning to the camp when he heard the shot. He put his heels to the horse's flanks. Just as his horse was up to a full gallop, he saw a man suddenly enter the road, running at full speed. Mobey saw the rider coming and abruptly turned into the trees. Zack rode past that spot and came to a dust flying halt in the camp to see Ann reloading her pistol and Eli backing up Melvin with his whip.

Ann looked up from her loading and assured, "We're all right." Melvin stumbled, fell down and began to beg for mercy from the flailing whip. Ann completed her loading, cocked the pistol and advanced toward Eli who was standing over Melvin.

Eli glanced in Zack's direction and called out, "Musta been the road agents we heard about. We got this one under control."

Zack turned his horse as he said, "I'll get the other one."

Carl Pettis was taking a break from herding horses to relieve himself. He had dismounted near a large tree to do just that when he heard the shot. He was watering some acorns and looked in the direction from which the shot came. The next thing he heard was running and thought it to be a deer. He wondered if some one had taken a shot at a deer, missed and the deer was running in his direction. Carl quickly buttoned his fly and thought to get to the rifle on his horse. *Maybe I can get us some camp meat*, he thought.

Mobey Bass, who turned his head to look behind him, ran into Carl, who stepped from behind the large Oak tree. The impact knocked Carl down with Mobey landing right on top of him. By this time Mobey was getting winded and struggled to catch his breath while trying to get back on his feet. Zack rode in on the scene and made a running leap off his horse. What he saw was that a man had Carl down and was beating him. Drawing his pistol for a club, Zack reached for the man to roll him off Carl while striking. The heavy pistol hit Mobey through the blanket roll and he grunted to the blow.

Zack rolled Mobey to his back and quickly sat on his chest with the muzzle of the pistol coming to rest on Mobey's nose. "Now you lay real still pilgrim or I'll skin ya alive," growled Zack in a most menacing tone. Carl, who had been momentarily stunned by the collision, thought he was having that dream again as he shook his head to restore his senses. Zack cocked the pistol. Paralyzed with fear, Mobey Bass wet himself.

Carl got himself brushed off, assuring Zack that he was all right. Zack pulled Mobey to his feet and held him at pistol point as Carl tied his hands. Zack ordered Mobey to walk back in the direction of the camp. When they reached the camp Eli had Melvin tied up. Ann was keeping him covered with her pistol. Zack roughly pushed Mobey in the direction of his cousin while saying to Eli, "Here's another one for your collection." Eli grabbed Mobey and sat him down beside Melvin.

Ann carefully lowered the hammer on her pistol as she walked toward Zack. She embraced him while reporting the confrontation with the three men. This was new information to Zack. He had only seen two men and asked about the direction the third man went. Ann pointed out the direction just as Carl rode into the camp. Zack told him not to dismount. Zack mounted his horse and told Carl they were going after the third man.

Zack did not notice that Ann needed more comforting. After the excitement died down she realized that she could have killed Melvin. Up to this point shooting a pistol had only been a challenge, a skill to master. But now the notion of using a pistol to shoot someone had settled in and it frightened her. For the second time she was seeing the hard side of Zack. Her witnessing his besting of the Gusterson twins did not fully prepare her for the hard reality of his rough treatment of the frightened boy. And that was not all of it. She suddenly felt abandoned when she needed to be assured and comforted.

Zack and Carl searched the woods for the better part of an hour without finding Rooster. They stopped and decided to return to camp. Carl was quiet during the search. He was thinking about Zack's warning to the young road agent and while they were stopped decided to reveal his thoughts to Zack. "It were you that hog tied me up on the Missouri," he stated half as a question and half as an allegation.

Zack turned to Carl, made eye contact, nodded his head and said, "Yep."

"I heard what ya said to that fella back there. It was zactly what ya said to me," Carl continued.

Without breaking his gaze, Zack nodded his head again and repeated, "Yep."

"Why did ya let me live back there?" Carl asked.

"You did what I said to do," Zack confidently replied.

"Ya could have left me with no possibles," Carl persisted, wanting to understand the man he had grown to respect.

"That would be the same as killing you," Zack reasoned.

Carl nodded his understanding of the reasoning. He took a deep breath, squared his shoulders and said, "Well, I thank ya fer yer kindness back then and fer now, havin' me on yer crew, knowin' who I was."

Zack extended his hand. Carl shook the hand and thanked Zack again. As they worked their way back to camp both men stayed alert for signs of the third road agent.

Zack was growing to like Carl. He found him to be hard working, responsible and willing to teach Nate.

Carl truly appreciated being hired on as part of the horse buying journey and now that he knew who Zack was he appreciated it even more. Carl knew there was a hardness about Zack, a hardness tempered with fairness. He also knew that Zack killed Jake and with what he knew now, *Jake kilt hisself by not abidin' to a fair warning*, was the only logical conclusion. He bore no grudge for his suffering.

As they were approaching the camp, Zack told Carl to check on Nate and to help with getting the horses secured for the night. Zack rode into the camp to find Eli and Ann continuing with the meal preparations. He reported having found no sign of the third road agent and noted the captured men remained securely bound. "They give you any trouble?" Zack asked Eli.

"Nary a bit, quiet as church mice," Eli replied as he stirred the stew.

Zack moved to Ann who was busy with slicing the loaf of bread Eli had purchased in the morning at a farmhouse. Zack eased his hands around her waist as she worked and as he nuzzled the nape of her neck said, "You doing all right with all this?"

Ann set the big knife down and turned to embrace him. "I'm not sure," she responded, "It all happened so fast." She was worried about what could happen next. She was coming to realize that her new husband was a man with a dark side, a man who could act in a cold, calculated manner and she was struggling to put it into an understandable perspective. "What are you going to do with them?" she whispered, fearing the worst.

Zack had thought this question through while returning to the camp. He had decided to try to teach these road agents a lesson. It seemed to have worked on Carl Pettis. He considered taking the cousins to the closest town to be dealt with by lawful authorities but that would mean having someone guard them while they traveled. *Teach them a lesson and turn them loose*, was the conclusion he reached just before riding into camp. "They need to be taught a lesson and I figure to do it," he replied to Ann.

Carl and Nate tied their horses to a bush. Curiously, they walked to Zack who was cutting hunks of Mobey's matted hair with his knife while Mobey whimpered. Melvin was defiantly telling the boy to stop whining. Nate walked closer to see the road agents he had just heard about from Carl. Finished with Mobey, Zack handed his knife to Nate and said, "I'll hold this one while you do some cutting." Nate did not understand what Zack wanted him to do. Zack repeated his instructions in an icy manner so that Nate would grasp the seriousness of what was about to happen. Zack got a grip on Melvin who began to kick and squirm. Nate hesitated and Zack ordered, "Start cutting!"

Carl stepped in to help restrain Melvin while Nate sawed off huge hunks of matted hair. Melvin screamed and tried to bite the men but in short order he too was roughly shorn. Zack went to the fire where a small bucket of tar was heating and carried it to the cousins. He ordered Nate and Carl to hold them down as he painted the letter T on their foreheads with a stick coated with the hot tar. Melvin was first and began to howl as the hot tar hit his skin. Mobey screamed as the hot T was applied.

When Zack started to cut Mobey's hair, Ann was unable to watch the boy's distress and her husband's seeming indifference. She climbed into the wagon as Carl and Nate joined the hair cutting. She covered her ears when Melvin started to howl. Mobey's screams penetrated through her hands as she pressed them tighter. Then it got quiet. Ann lowered her hands to listen. After a minute of listening she rose and poked her head out from the canvas cover to see the two road agents seated on a log hungrily devouring a plate of stew. Ann descended from the wagon to watch the scene from a distance.

Zack offered them more stew when they finished. They both declined having eaten their fill. Then he ordered them to stand and told them he was giving them a chance to mend their ways. He stretched the truth a bit by saying the tar T would peal off in time and that if they turned to honest work there would not be a permanent mark on their foreheads. If, however, they returned to thievery the T would remain as an everlasting scar. Then he pushed them toward the road. As they made their way down the road he signaled Carl to follow them until they were out of sight.

The evening meal was somber compared to previous times when they enjoyed each other's company. This evening they were occupied with their thoughts about the recent event and picked at their food. The light was fading when Eli built up the fire and lit a lantern to wash the dishes and utensils. Nate was the first to break the uncomfortable silence, "Mister Clayton, I don't know if I cotton to what ya did to those fellas."

Nate's statement reminded Zack of what he said to Gus those many months ago about scalping and torture. "What would you have me do with them, Nate?" Zack asked. Nate did not have a good answer.

Carl was pondering on the striking similarity between his encounter with Zack and how that encounter further contributed to his decision to abandon criminal ways. He defended Zack's actions by saying, "Nate, iffen ya go west, like ya say, there'll be harder lessons than this one."

"How do you know?" Nate countered. Without revealing his past, west of the Mississippi River, Carl merely said, "Believe me, I know."

Ann joined in, "I can't get that man's screaming out of my mind."

Eli agreed with a nod and said, "Yeah, me to. But what was we to do, not being near a town and no lawman to turn them over to."

The discussion continued with everyone having their say and everyone agreeing that if the situation had turned out that they were in the hands of the cousins they probably would have received worse treatment. Zack concluded the discussion with praising everyone for their roles in the event.

When the business of preparing for night in the camp was complete Zack walked out to where the horses were rope corralled. The star lit sky afforded him enough light to make out the dark forms as they settled for the night. He slowly walked around the temporary rope enclosure before returning to camp. The men were already in their bedrolls as Zack stopped to listen to the night sounds. Quietly he slipped through the canvass cover to the bed in the wagon he and Ann had shared since getting married. He sat on a trunk, removed his boots and carefully placed his belt and pistol within easy reach.

The odors of bacon, onions, and coffee beans lingered in spite of Eli having removed the sacks when the wagon was unloaded for the evening. Ann had earlier prepared the wagon for the night by laying out the pad and quilts. Her breathing told Zack she was not yet asleep.

Ann was continuing to think on the hard reality of the encounter with the cousins as she heard Zack preparing for bed. The notion that she could have killed Melvin with her pistol still haunted her but she also knew she had reacted to the danger in an appropriate, self-defending manner and could probably do so again. As Zack got settled beneath the light quilt she curled up to him for reassurance.

"How you doing with all this?" Zack whispered in the darkness. He was glad Ann was able to act calmly in the high-risk situation and had survived the skirmish without being injured. He was also worried. The hardships and risks of being on the trail were new to Ann. He knew he could not fully prepare her for each possible danger. He hoped she had the fortitude for more or even worse perils. He put his arm around her and stroked her hair.

As she snuggled closer Ann whispered, "Better, now that you're here." They fell asleep in the comforting embrace.

*   *   *

Over the next few days they increased the herd to sixty horses and Zack spent the last of Ned Shiller's money. The wagon and herd were only a day away from the spot on the Mississippi River designated as the point from which they would cross to St. Louis. Zack rode ahead to locate the ferry to take the herd across. True to his word Ned Shiller had contracted with a ferryman, which Zack found after inquiring among the docked ferries. Zack returned to the herd to guide them to the ferry.

It wasn't long before the first twenty horses were loaded. Zack and Nate accompanied the first load. Once across Nate was assigned to stay with the horses while Zack went looking for Ned. He had not gone far when he saw Ned driving a buggy. Ned anticipated Zack would be arriving soon and decided to make a daily drive to the ferry landing. This was his second trip. As they approached each other on the road Ned recognized Zack and called out, "Zack! Zack!"

Zack pulled to a stop beside the buggy and extended his hand down to Ned. "Good to see you, Ned. I've got the horses crossing. Want to come down and see what you bought?"

Ned clicked to the buggy mare and said, "Sure do. Lead the way."

Ned tied the buggy mare to the fence of the landing corral while taking a look at the twenty horses. "If the rest look as good as these it'll be a good day for Garrett and Son," Ned remarked as they peered through the wood rails.

"The ones on the other side are as good if not better," Zack responded.

"Well, let's go take a look at them," Ned said with a satisfied grin as he turned to walk toward the ferry. Zack rode his horse in the same direction and noted Nate was waiting on the ferry ready for the return trip. Zack tied up his horse close to Nate as Ned boarded. Ned moved like a man who was pretty much healed from the beating he took and Zack had to look hard at him to see what remained of the bruises on his face.

Ned barely recognized Nate Plummer. Nate was not the skinny kid he hired back at the Skyles Hotel. He was filled out and had the look of an experienced drover. Ned shook his hand in a greeting and said, "Nate, it's good to see you. You're looking fit. You have a good trip?"

Nate grinned and answered, "Yes sir, Mister Shiller. I surely did."

As the ferry pulled away from the landing, Zack began to recount the results of the horse buying trip from the ledger he kept. Ned was very pleased with the accounting. He had thirteen horses more than he was expecting from the money he had given Zack. He also was impressed by the low cost of the expenses Zack had recorded. Ned reported he received a letter from Seth Thomas. He had file charges against the Gusterson twins but so far nothing had come of it.

When the ferry arrived at the east side of the river Carl and Ann had twenty more horses ready to load. Nate joined them while Ned and Zack got out of the way and walked to the wagon. Ned greeted Eli with the same degree of amiability as he watched the horses being loaded.

Nate rode onto the ferry to accompany the horses across while Ann and Carl rode off to gather some horses, which had strayed while they were busy with loading. Ned recognized Carl Pettis from the distance but did not recognize who he thought was another man ride off with him. He turned to Zack and while tapping the ledger said, "I didn't see an entry for the other man you hired."

Zack was puzzled by the remark and responded, "That's because I didn't hire another man."

Ned pointed toward the riders gathering the strays and said, "Well, who's that with Carl Pettis?"

Zack realized he was talking about Ann who from this distance looked like a man. He had gotten used to seeing her dressed in her trail clothes and pitching in with the herding.

He turned to Ned and replied, "That's my wife."

"Wife?" Ned exclaimed, with a look of surprise.

Zack assumed Seth Thomas would have mentioned the wedding in the letter he said he was going to write to Ned but apparently had not. With the strays returned to the herd Ann turned her mare toward the wagon. Ned was about to ask for more details but chose instead to watch the rider approaching. In the easy manner of an experienced rider Ann came to a stop and dismounted. As she walked to the wagon she removed her floppy hat letting her blonde hair fall to her shoulders. She smiled as she approached the men.

Ned exclaimed in recognition, "Ann Bell! Well I'll be damned. Oh, excuse me. I didn't mean to…" Zack and Ann began to laugh at Ned's fumbling which was rare for him. With an embarrassed grin Ned joined the laughter and took Ann's hand as she extended it to him. He recovered quickly and in an excited manner said, "Well, I'm glad to meet you, Misses Clayton. This calls for a celebration." Ned continued to express his surprise in his usual talkative manner.

While he was talking Carl rode up and Ned greeted him. The talk shifted to Carl's experiences with the horse-buying venture and at the conclusion Carl expressed a desire to continue with his plan to return to Kentucky. Zack gave a good report on Carl's work as a drover and Ned offered Carl a job. Carl thanked him and declined, restating his plan to go home. Ned paid Carl what was due him. From the wages Carl bought the horse and saddle he was using and paid Zack for the rifle. He did not have much left but said it would get him to Kentucky. He asked Zack to say good-bye to Nate for him, shook hands and thanked Zack again, and in turn shook hands with Ann, Eli and Ned. He mounted his horse and with a tip to his hat rode off.

"What are your plans, Mister Diamond?" Ned asked Eli.

"Thought I'd try my hand at hauling in St. Louis," Eli replied, "Know of any positions for a teamster?"

"I just may," Ned answered, "I hear Garrett and Son is going to get into the hauling business. I could put a word in for you." Ned went on to instruct Eli on where to deliver the wagon as he paid him his wages.

Eli turned to Zack and asked, "Where do you want me to deliver your and Misses Clayton's things?"

Zack and Ann realized at that moment they had not made a definite plan about where they would live in St. Louis. Before they could address the options Ned said, "Mister Diamond, deliver all those things to my house." Then turning to the surprised couple he announced, "You two are staying at my house for awhile. After all we've got lots to celebrate and to catch up on."

Zack and Ann agreed with nods to one another and with another round of handshakes Zack resolved the problem, at least temporarily, with, "Done."

When the ferry returned Zack and Ann herded the last of the horses aboard and Nate once again accompanied them to the west side of the river. When the ferry returned for the last haul Eli drove the wagon aboard. Zack had also given a good report on Nate before Ned paid him his wages. Nate had never seen so much money at one time, let alone having it in his hand. He asked Ned about how to send some of it home to his family. Ned was impressed with Nate's diligence and offered him a job as a drover. Nate accepted with a smile and a handshake.

During the ride to the western bank Ann tried to buy the four white stocking mare from Ned. Ned would have none of it and insisted she keep it as a wedding gift. Ned was amused by the story about how Zack came to buy the mare and said, "I'll have to remember that poem. I might be able to use it myself." Zack had been riding a tan gelding that reminded him of Hunka and told Ned he bought for himself. He offered the horse he boarded in St. Louis for sale and Ned bought it. Ned settled up with Zack, paying him a bonus for delivering more horses than was expected.

*   *   *

Ned's house was in the same part of town as James Clayton's house and was somewhat similar in construction but that was where the similarity ended. In the Shiller home there was a sincere congeniality and no slaves. Isabelle Shiller was a large, round faced woman who practically dwarfed her husband. Her enthusiasm and sociability matched her husband's. Most would agree that they were perfectly matched. She was also pregnant which added to her size. In the attire of a fashionable, expecting St. Louis lady she greeted the newly wed couple with much warmth. It was clear, by her talk, Ned had informed her of his misadventures in Cairo and of Zack. In a flurry of activity she soon had Zack and Ann moved into the spacious guest room and announced she was going to get to work organizing a dinner party in their honor. In the planning, Zack asked that the McCracken family be included and he would be responsible for inviting his brother.

The next morning Zack borrowed Ned's buggy and drove Ann through the white gate to introduce her to his brother. Toby spotted the buggy from the stable and rushed toward it as fast as a slight limp would allow. "Masta Zachary," he greeted with a wide grin as he grabbed for the halter. When Ann got down from the buggy, Zack introduced her to Toby. With down cast eyes Toby acknowledged the introduction by saying, "Yas sur, Masta Zachary." Zack asked him about the limp. "I'sa got stepped on by a horse," Toby lied. Zack suspected there was more to it than that. Toby had buggy whip welts, which were visible, just under his collar.

Ann had always lived in free states and had not encountered slavery first hand. She was uncomfortable with Toby's obvious subservient behavior. Zack was about to ask if James was beating him again when a big man in dark clothes exited the rear of the house, heading for the stable. He hollered, "Toby," as he placed his black wide brimmed hat over his white hair. Toby turned toward his name being called and knowing he needed to get to the stable to lead the saddle horse out began a fast walk as he said, "I'sa comin'." In less than a minute he led the horse out and the man mounted. Snow Logan urged his horse to a trot as he approached the buggy. Without saying a word he tipped his hat toward Ann and rode through the gate.

Lily answered the door and led Zack and Ann into the parlor. She said, "I'll fetch the Mistress," and left the room. In a few minutes Nancy Clayton descended the stairs. She had a slightly rumpled look about her and it became quickly obvious by her slurred speech, which she attempted to conceal that she had been drinking. She greeted Zack with a stiff, pretentious embrace and coolly acknowledged Ann. Zack invited her and James to the dinner party being organized by Isabelle Shiller. Nancy declined saying that James was off on a business trip and she would not think of attending unescorted. Nancy abruptly ended the social call by excusing herself and saying, "I'm sure you can find your way out."

While driving back to the Shiller house Zack told Ann what he knew about his brother, Nancy and Snow Logan. To his surprise Ann expressed sympathy for James and Nancy. "It must be awful for them to have sickness come between them," she explained, "Granted they are not dealing well with it but I feel sorry for them just the same." Zack reflected on her perspective. Still he knew that no matter how much sympathy he had for his brother, he was going to have to confront him in the matter of their father's estate. Snow Logan was another matter for Ann. Her recent experience with the road agents had taught her to be less forgiving to those who ply a criminal trade. "You be careful of him, Zachary," she urged with a worried tone.

Zack patted her knee and replied, "I'm always careful, you should know that by now." Ann smiled at him and threaded her arm around his as the buggy proceeded down the street.

*   *   *

The dinner party at the Shiller house was a pleasant, congenial affair. It was attended by the aged widower, Miles Garrett, Ned's father-in -law. He knew Zack's father from the early days of St. Louis and was polite enough not to say much about James. He was turning over the family business to his son, Henry Garrett, and to Ned Shiller.

Henry Garrett and his wife, Mary, were a little late to the dinner with Henry saying he was attending to some business. He was adding freight hauling to the business as a natural off shoot of buying and selling draft animals. His father did not completely agree with expanding the business but figured he needed to let his son make his own decisions. Henry Garrett was a big man with a striking resemblance to his father and was as equally forceful. He thanked Ned and Zack for sending two good men his way.

Also attending were Patrick, Lucy and Robert McCracken. Zack's reunion with the McCrackens was full of getting caught up with each other's activities. After some initial shyness Robert warmed up to Ann. Lucy mentioned Robert's remembering Zack's promise to take him on another horse ride, which prompted Robert to start begging for a ride. Zack reassured him a ride would be forthcoming. Isabelle Shiller found time between her duties as the hostess to fuss over Robert.

Patrick told of having signed on with a steamboat company with his goal of becoming a river pilot or captain. He liked that he was able to be at home more than when he operated his own boat. The conversations continued through dinner with everyone enjoying the meal and the good company.

After the dessert Ned rose with his glass of wine and proposed a toast to Zack and Ann. The guests sipped the wine in their honor. Then Ned, having had just a bit too much wine, proposed a toast to Ann, "To the best lady pistol shooter it's ever been my pleasure to be acquainted with." Ann blushed to Ned's exaggerated version of her shooting a road agent. His comments did, however, raise everyone's curiosity and Ann satisfied them by telling a factual account of the event.

CHAPTER 12

THE TWINS

Frank and Billy Gusterson were growing restless after a week of being cooped up in a small cabin. When they returned from a successful river pirating job on the Missouri River with Snow Logan they heard they were wanted men. According to the story they heard that fellow they beat up in Cairo was a horse buyer who lived in St. Louis and had pressed charges with the local law. They were cursing their bad luck and found guarding the warehouse where the stolen furs were stored very boring. There did not seem much point in guarding the warehouse, no one but Snow Logan came around. They almost wished someone would snoop around, at least that would be a break in the monotonous routine.

James Clayton chose well in placing the warehouse and two cabins in the center of a thickly wooded hollow north of St. Louis. The mouth of the Missouri River was only a few miles away. There was good access to the Mississippi River on a short path through the trees. Another path linked with the road leading to St. Louis. He recently had it widened to accommodate a wagon, making it much easier to haul furs out and supplies in. Snow Logan lived in one of the cabins when he wasn't on a pirating trip. The other cabin could be occupied by any of the pirating crew and Snow chose to hole up the Gusterson twins there until they went out on another job. They had performed better than most of the men he had recruited and certainly a lot better than his last crew that included the Pettis brothers. On occasion he lamented to James Clayton on how hard it was to find reliable men. He was encouraged about Frank and Billy. When he heard they were wanted by the law, he told them to stay put and he would keep them supplied in food and whiskey until the next pirating trip. He underestimated their whiskey consumption.

*   *   *

While Ann was shopping with Isabelle Shiller, Zack was looking for a house to rent. His search took him by his brother's house and he decided to stop in for a brief visit. Perhaps he could save Ann the discomfort of another cool reception by visiting alone and he might be able to be more direct with James with fewer distractions. As Zack rode up to the stable Toby was washing a shiny back carriage from a bucket of water. Toby looked up at the approaching rider before recognizing Zack and looked indecisive on how to dispose of the wet cloth and grab the halter of a guest's horse.

As he dismounted Zack said, "How you doing, Toby? Don't bother with the horse. I'll tend to him."

Toby let the cloth fall into the bucket and said, "I'sa good Masta Zachary."

Zack stepped toward Toby with his hand extended saying, "Most folks call me Zack." Toby was not accustomed to this simple man-to-man approach and was fearful of taking the hand extended to him. Besides, his hands were wet. Since he knew that neither James nor Nancy Clayton were home and there was no chance of them seeing him break from his assigned social station he dried his hinds on his trousers and shook Zack's hand. It was a strange, embracing feeling to shake hands with another man and Toby liked it. But there was also a degree of discomfort knowing his owner would disapprove of such behavior. "And how are you, Zack?" Toby responded with barely a trace of his subservient accent.

"I'm well." Zack replied and was about to inquire about his brother when Lilly exited the rear door of the house and hollered, "Time to fetch the Mistress, Toby!" She then saw Zack standing with Toby and quickly cupped her hand over her mouth in chagrin. Zack waved to her as she rushed back into the house. Toby reached for the bright blue coachman's coat and black top hat lying on the carriage's front seat. Earlier he delivered Nancy Clayton to a friend's house for afternoon tea and was instructed to return for her after he had washed the road dust from the carriage.

Zack inquired, "Is my brother at home?"

Toby was fumbling with the buttons as he looked up to reply. A rider coming through the gate diverted his attention. He immediately dropped his eyes and whispered, "Yas sur, he be ridin' in now." Zack turned to see James riding through the gate. Toby finished with the buttons and stepped into position to receive his master's horse. He held the horse tightly while James dismounted.

James greeted his brother in a pleased manner, "Zachary, It's good to see you. Nancy told me you were by with your new wife. Sorry I wasn't here to meet her. What's her name? Nancy couldn't remember for sure."

"Ann," responded Zack.

"Ann," James repeated as he glanced at Toby leading the horse away, "Well you'll have to bring her back. Perhaps Nancy can put together an evening when we can all get together." Zack was about to respond when Toby returned to the carriage and climbed into the driver's seat. James asked him, "Where you off to, Toby?"

"Ta fetch Miss Nancy," Toby replied, "She be over to Miss Clara's."

James backed from the team of carriage mares and with a go ahead gesture said, "Well, be off with you. No need to dawdle."

"Yas sur, Masta James," Toby complied as he clicked the mares forward.

James watched the carriage rolling toward the gate before turning back to Zack, "Come on in the house," he invited, "We can talk some."

James led the way toward the office he kept in a rear room. While they passed through the kitchen he instructed Aunt Milly to prepare some coffee.

She said, "Have half a pot from this mornin', Masta James. You want it or fresh."

James looked to Zack to see if he had a preference. Zack said, "Warmed up will do."

James turned back to Aunt Milly and said, "Heat it up and bring two cups to my study."

"Yas sur, Masta James," she complied as she took the coffee pot from the warming shelf and placed it on the stove.

Zack and James were just getting seated in the small study when Lilly delivered the coffee. She was quietly in and out of the room as if she was some transient silent spirit. "Did you get my letter?" James asked. Before Zack could respond, James went on to say the position of guide for the spring supply train to the Green River had been filled. Zack did not indicate that he would have turned the offer down. James went on to describe the plan of putting together an annual supply train to carry the needed goods to a rendezvous and to return with the collected furs. He was very optimistic about the plan and described it as a sound business venture.

Zack heard that other companies had the same idea and figured his brother was a bit over confident considering the competition. Zack noticed that James was not coughing as much but still had a sickly pallor about him. James was having one of his better days. James inquired about where Zack was staying and remarked he knew of Ned Shiller when Zack told him of staying temporarily at Ned's house. "Well you know you and Ann, that's right isn't it? Ann?" James invited, "have a place here if you want."

Zack responded yes to the name. Then Zack told James he was looking for a house to rent and thanked him for the invitation. As the pleasantries drew to a close Zack was about to ask James for an accounting of their father's estate. James, however, beat him to it, "You must have been in Cairo when I completed the sale of the livery. I have a full accounting here in my ledger that you're welcome to go over. I can write a draft for the full amount due you or if you'd like I can invest all or part for you. There's a couple of things I'm working on that could pay a handsome profit."

James' directness and willingness for a full disclosure left Zack some-what disarmed. He was prepared for a confrontation with his brother, which did not seem necessary. "I'd prefer a draft for my share," Zack responded, "I have some ideas of my own for investments."

Without further inquires James wrote a draft and as he was handing it to Zack there came a quiet knocking on the door.

Lilly poked her head into the room and said, "Masta James, Masta Logan be here to see…"

James abruptly cut her off, "I'll be right there. Now get." Turning to Zack, James said, "I have something to tend to. Shouldn't be but just a minute. If you don't mind I'd like to ride to the bank with you. I have some business to tend to." Zack nodded his willingness to wait. James closed the door as he left the room. From down the hall Zack could hear James' raised voice say, "I told you I do not want us seen together…" In a few minutes James returned as if nothing had happened but Zack noticed the increase in tension and coughing.

*   *   *

The twins were aware of their being more easily recognized if they were seen together so they planned to buy whiskey at different saloons. They figured it was just a matter of time for them to be arrested if they spent too much time in St. Louis and had begun to talk about leaving for other pastures. Snow Logan promised them one more pirating trip, then it would be a simple matter of getting on a boat to New Orleans.

Snow Logan walked into a saloon after his tense meeting with James Clayton and was not in a good mood. He wanted to expand his pirating operation by adding more men to his crew and to include the Mississippi River, which would be closer to comforts versus the cold camps on the Missouri River. He knew there was a ready market for most any goods in the new settlements west of St. Louis and wanted to capitalize on the needs. James refused to put up the capital to expand the fur pirating venture and Snow figured to drown his frustration with whiskey. He hired the Gusterson twins, to replace the Pettis brothers, after seeing them come out on top in a saloon brawl, and they had since proven themselves during recent pirating forays. Snow knew he could find other men of criminal intent to join his band but that would have to wait until he could figure out how to pay for it.

As he stepped up to the bar, he saw Frank Gusterson at the end of the bar downing a drink while a bartender was filling a bag with bottles of whiskey. Snow casually joined Frank and whispered gruffly, "I thought I told you not to come to town!"

After only a slight glance toward Snow, and a pause to sip his second whiskey, Frank replied in an equally gruff whisper, "I don't cotton to be talked to like that!" Frank did not feel any particular loyalty to Snow Logan and saw him only as a means to wintering in New Orleans. He was confident that if it ever came to fighting it out with Snow he was at least equally matched. With Billy at his side Snow would not stand a chance. Neither men wanted to draw any special attention to themselves and began to back away from the feeling of wanting to escalate the confrontation.

Snow moved several feet away to take a new position on the bar. Frank paid the bartender and quietly slung the bottle filled sack across his shoulder. It was obvious to Snow that Frank was going to leave and he made a subtle gesture for Frank to hesitate. When he saw Frank comply he stepped nonchalantly toward the door. Once outside he scanned up and down the street. When he was satisfied that no lawmen were on the street he signaled Frank with a head gesture to proceed.

Just as Frank stepped out the door Zack and James were turning from around a corner, riding their horse to the bank. Frank stepped back into the doorway, using Snow as a shield, and in a whisper asked, "Ya know that fella pullin' up to the bank?"

Snow immediately recognized James Clayton and guarding his association with him replied, "I hear tell he's James Clayton."

The name of Clayton lit a memory spark in Frank but the name James did not seem to fit. "Which one?" he inquired.

"The thin fella in the beaver hat," Snow answered.

When Zack dismounted in front of the bank Frank fully recognized him as the man who broke Billy's arm. "Who's the other fella?" he continued.

Snow turned slightly toward Frank to try to discern the reason for all the questions. Frank's face was set in a glower and revealed no hint of what he was thinking.

"I hear he's a brother to James. Zachary is his name, so I'm told," Snow responded.

The initial spark of recognition became a flame in Frank's mind. *Zachary Clayton,* he thought, *That's the name of the fella who gave that gold to Ma.*

"Why all the questions?" Snow asked as he watched Frank step out from the doorway and turn toward the alley where his horse was tied. The clinking of bottles, from Frank's quickened pace, muffled the reply. Before Snow could ask him to repeat it Frank disappeared into the alley.

Billy Gusterson also had a sack of bottled whiskey, which he acquired at a saloon a few blocks away. Pulling at the wide brim of his hat to cover more of his face he stepped to his horse tied up to the rail in front of the saloon. Billy was tying the sack to the pommel when he saw a buggy approaching. He heard a man from across the street call out a name, "Hey Ned, Ned Shiller," and the buggy stopped right behind Billy's horse. Soon he was aware of the man standing in the street, on the opposite side of the buggy, carrying on a conversation with the driver. Billy was figuring on how to get his horse backed out, from between the horses on either side, while the buggy blocked his path to the rear. He peeked at the buggy from under his hat brim and immediately recognized Ann Bell as one of the three people in the buggy. She was turned toward the man in the street and Billy distinctly heard her being introduced as "Misses Zachary Clayton" by the man driving the buggy.

Upon hearing the name Billy stole another glance in Ann's direction and saw her acknowledge the introduction to the standing man while the other woman sat with her hands resting in her lap. As with his brother, a few minutes earlier, a flame of recognition lit within Billy's brain. Keeping his face concealed Billy pretended to adjust the knot on the sack while he tried to tune in on the conversation. The man in the street was talking about buying some horses from the driver. The driver agreed to meet with him after returning his wife and friend home from a shopping trip. The standing man accepted the appointment and the buggy pulled away. Billy was relieved that Ann had not turned in his direction, she surely would have recognized him.

Back in their cabin the twins were well within their second bottle of whiskey when they came to at least one accurate conclusion. Zachary Clayton, the man who broke Billy's arm and had given the gold to their mother, was married to Ann Bell. While getting caught up on their drinking, they exchanged their separate observations of Zack and Ann. Frank expressed their mutually held distain for Ann, "That's the snooty bitch of a café girl who would hardly give us a howdy."

"That's the one," his brother agreed. Their final and most foreboding conclusion was not accurate. They concluded that Zack knew the location of a gold mine that their older brother discovered.

"We gots to find a way to get it from 'em," Frank slurred.

"I agree," Billy drunkenly responded. "But how?" they both said in close unison. They argued through several schemes and the last of the second bottle before the whiskey completely did in their sinister planning for the night.

*   *   *

In the privacy of the Shiller guest room, Zack told Ann about the newly acquired bank balance. She reacted with delight and during the following embrace said, "Oh Zachary, now we can buy a house. Isabelle was telling me just today about a house for sale. She said her friend who was recently widowed wants to sell her house and move back east."

Zack paused and carefully chose his words so as not to dampen Ann's enthusiasm while working on getting the conversation to go in another direction. "Yes, we could look at it. We can also look into investing in a venture my brother put me on to." He revealed the idea of buying a variety of supplies to be delivered to the mountains. He also described his existing agreement with Ben Thompson.

His description gave Ann the impression that any day now he would be departing for the trading post on the upper North Platte River. She reacted, with a degree of urgency in her voice, "You're not going anywhere without me!"

Zack was a bit surprised with the suddenness of her reaction but it fit with the topic he planned on introducing next, namely what she wanted to do while he put together a plan of returning to the mountains. He was aware she was quickly making friends in St. Louis and might want to remain while he made a trip west. He drew her close and said, "Are you sure you want to go? It will be a long and wearing trip."

Ann pushed away slightly and answered, "Zachary Clayton, you should know me well enough by now. I said you're not going without me."

Zack wanted her to know more about such a journey and said, "It will not be an easy trip, like the one from Cairo. We'll be out there where there are no roads, no farms and…" Ann stopped his words with a fingertip to his lips and whispered as she drew close for a kiss, "Zachary, I'm going." They did not stop with one kiss.

Early the next morning, Zack and Ann went hunting for a house to rent. They appreciated staying with the Shillers but wanted to be in a place they could call home even if it would only be for a few months. The second house they looked at was owned by an elderly widower who knew Zack's father from the old days. He was preparing to move to Natchez to live with his son for at least the winter. The house was old but comfortable, had a small stable and an attached wood shed. It was in a neighborhood of similar small houses and practically across the street from the McCrackens. The owner planned to leave it partially furnished. Mutual agreement about the comfort of the house was easily reached and Zack paid the rent in advance, to the end of March, the earliest they could start west.

Initially, Ned and Isabelle Shiller greeted the news of the rented house with protests. They liked having the charming couple as houseguests. As Isabelle's pregnancy advanced she was in need of having someone around while Ned was attending to business. Promises of frequent visits soon had Isabelle reassured. Later she told Ann that the widow who had her house for sale also was selling some of her furniture. They made plans to go to look at the furniture.

*　　　　*　　　　*

Billy Gusterson was dressed to make himself look inconspicuous. He and Frank finally came up with a plan after almost a week of heavy drinking and arguing. They decided Billy would ride around town and make discrete inquiries about Zachary Clayton. They were convinced that if they had more information they could devise a plan to get him to reveal the location of the gold mine.

On Billy's second day of scouting he happened upon Ann and Isabelle. Ann was driving Ned Shiller's buggy with the four white stockinged mare tied to the rear. Billy watched them stop in front of a small house. He pretended to examine the hooves of his horse from a safe distance while he watched the women enter the house. In a short time they had the windows and doors open as they dusted and aired the house.

Billy rode around the neighborhood and noted the lay of the neighboring houses and the accesses to the house in question. In a bolder pass he rode directly in front of the house to get a closer look. He even tipped his hat to Lucy McCracken as she led Robert across the road.

Lucy McCracken watched Billy ride down the road and thought there was something suspicious about him. While she was waiting for Robert to awaken from his nap she looked out her window to see if she could tell what Ann and Isabelle were doing. She was planning to help them prepare the house for occupancy. She noticed Billy who appeared to take more than just a passing interest in the little house. When she greeted Ann she remarked on her observations and pointed at the rider who was just turning the corner at the crossroad. Billy had his back to the house and was just far enough away that Ann did not recognize him.

Ann and Lucy were back in the house when Billy found a vantage point in some bushes just off the crossroad. His patience was beginning to pay off with useful information and it was about to get better. A large wagon pulled up in front of the house and two men began to unload furniture. Minutes later Zack and Ned rode up. They tied their horses to the fence and began to help move the furniture into the house. When the wagon was emptied, the men who came with it drove away with a wave. A short time later Zack appeared at the door carrying Robert. He mounted his horse and while holding Robert turned into the road. He rode toward the cross road where Billy was concealed. Billy saw him coming and stepped deeper into the bushes. Zack turned the horse in the crossroad to return to the house. Billy heard Robert plead, "Faster, faster," while Zack guided a slow turn.

Billy watched for the next hour. He saw Ned Shiller help his pregnant wife into the buggy and tie his horse to the rear. He saw Lucy McCracken lead her son back across the street. He saw Zack and Ann wave goodbye to their visitors. When he saw Zack leading the two remaining horses to the small rear stable he had seen enough.

*   *   *

Eli Diamond considered it a fortunate assignment to be delivering furniture for Zack and Ann. He had not seen them since they all arrived in St. Louis. He was happy with his decision to relocate to St. Louis and liked his job with Garrett Hauling. Hauling goods in and around St. Louis was more desirable than being on a long haul where the creature comforts could be few and far between. While getting unloaded, he visited and got caught up on the news with Zack and Ann. He told them he was courting a widow woman and if it came to announcing a wedding date he would be sure to send an invitation to his friends. When the job was complete, he stated it was necessary to get back on the road because he had another load to pick up and deliver before dark. He turned to wave back to Zack and Ann as he urged his horses toward the crossroad. Eli saw Billy Gusterson in the bushes as he passed but figured him to be just curious about the moving activities. Eli had gotten used to the curiosity of neighbors and passer bys as he made his deliveries.

When Zack and Ned entered the house Robert immediately began begging for a horse ride. Zack stalled him long enough to get the bed reassembled. On the inside of a side rail he saw written in black ink **GUSTERSON & SONS**. He was about to point it out to Ann but saw she was busy and he decided to show it to her later. With all the strenuous activity Isabelle became fatigued and asked Ned to take her home. They departed with a wave and promises of returning for a visit in a few days.

Robert was becoming impatient with being put off and as soon as the Shillers left began anew with begging for a horse ride. Lucy tried to intervene knowing Zack and Ann still had much to do with moving in but Zack stepped in, swept the boy up in his arms and said, "A horse ride, huh? You want to go for a horse ride?"

Robert squealed and laughed with being swept up. As he clapped his chubby little hands he reiterated, "Yeah, yeah, yeah!"

Ann and Lucy followed as Zack carried the boy out the door. They smiled while watching the happy boy get his horse ride and heard him saying, "Faster, faster," as Zack urged the horse down the street.

When Lucy left with Robert the little rented house looked almost as neat as hers. She and Ann had unpacked the trunks, made the bed, hung curtains and put everything in its place. Since Patrick was working on a steamboat, and had been gone for a week, Lucy was glad for the diversion. She accepted an invitation for dinner the next evening before she departed.

Zack and Ann embraced in the kitchen and Ann said, "I'm famished. Let's see what Isabelle packed in that basket for us to eat." She broke from the embrace to uncover the large split wood basket.

Zack took her by the hand, led her toward the bedroom and said, "First there is something I want to show you."

When Ann realized where he was leading she pulled him to a stop and gracefully stepped into a hip grinding embrace. "So you want to try this goose down mattress before supper, do you Mister Clayton?" she seductively whispered.

"That's not a bad idea Misses Clayton," Zack responded with his shy grin, "but that's not why I brought you in here."

Ann loved teasing him and as she drew her fingers through his hair said, "Why else would you drag me into the bedroom, Mister Clayton?"

Zack knew he was being teased and seduced. And he might have been further seduced into climbing into the bed with her had he not wanted to show her the writing on the bed rail. He pulled the soft, thick mattress aside to expose the rail and pointed to the lettering. "Did you see this when you bought the bed?" he asked.

Ann leaned closer for a better look and replied, "No, I didn't. The bed was made up when I bought it. It looked sturdy and the price was right, so I bought it."

Zack took her into his arms in a loving embrace. He stood holding her for a long minute.

Ann sensed his thoughts drifting and whispered, "What are you thinking, Zachary?"

Zack pulled her closer and replied, "Gus." After a long pause he inhaled deeply and said, "If we ever have a son I want to name him John Gusterson Clayton."

Ann leaned back slightly, cupped a hand lightly to the side of his face and said, "After seeing you with Robert today I thought about how nice it will be to see you with our son someday." The moment of serious disclosure lingered as they resumed the embrace. Then in her coy, teasing, manner Ann whispered, "We can get started on making that son right now, if you'd like."

Zack started to quietly laugh and taking her face in his hands said, "Maybe later, Misses Clayton. Let's eat, I'm hungry too."

*   *   *

The Gusterson twins took turns secretly spying on Zack and Ann. After two weeks of spying they had not uncovered any discernible pattern nor information they could use to their advantage. Between their frustration, boredom and consuming copious amounts of whiskey, they dwelt on the fantasy of gold. The fantasy was bordering on being delusional as they grew to believe that Zack was withholding a great fortune from them.

Over time they had so reinforced ideas of a gold mine with each other that they now believed in a mine where all one had to do was to walk around and pick up nuggets. Any exaggerated idea of such a scene, once shared with the other, became reality in their minds. As the delusion grew so did their desperation.

Snow Logan began to see the change in the twins. He never knew what mood he would find them in when he approached them about completing a task around the warehouse. The pirated furs had long since been shipped and he had them shifting stores around in the warehouse just to keep them busy. At times he found them to be morose and lethargic. At other times they would be short tempered and surly. The one thing he could count on is that they would be drunk every evening. They refused to explain their singular departures from the warehouse and when asked they would respond, "Mind yer own business." After awhile he just pretty much left them alone.

Snow Logan had other things to think about. He was having troubles that far exceeded being concerned about what the twins were up to. Snow was becoming bored with the first signs of winter setting in and longed to be back on the river. Being on the river would at least get him away from Nancy Clayton. What he thought was only going to be a brief dalliance with her was getting out of hand. She was demanding that he take greater and greater risks to be with her, and on two occasions was almost found out by James. He barely slipped out the back door, boots in hand, as James entered through the front of the house.

Also Nancy was drinking more and Snow feared it was only a matter of time before she revealed their sordid relationship to her husband. When drunk she would revile her husband and on one occasion told him that she wanted James "dead and buried".

Snow's comings and goings were evident to the house slaves and he knew that if something ever happened to James they would surely implicate him. More that once he knowingly intimidated them with glowers and threatening gestures as a warning to maintain their silence about what they were seeing. It was all getting out of hand and Snow Logan was beginning to think about where to relocate, in a hurry.

*　　　　　*　　　　　*

In early November Zack and Ann were beginning to develop a routine. Zack would head to the Berthold Mercantile Company to place orders for his planned trip or go to the warehouse where his goods were stored to sort and inventory. He also worked on the three wagons he bought from Henry Garrett which he kept parked in the Garrett barns. While he was gone, Ann would shop for the house, work at home and regularly visit Isabelle and Lucy.

One crisp fall afternoon, Zack saw Toby sitting in the carriage parked in front of a store while cases of wine were being loaded in the back. Zack walked up to him and greeted, "How you doing, Toby?"

With a grin and a wink Toby replied, "I'sa good, Masta Zack."

Zack returned the wink to communicate his acknowledgement of Toby addressing him as Zack instead of "Masta Zachary". Zack was about to ask Toby about the purpose of his trip into town when Nancy Clayton exited the store. She appeared as if she was not going to speak. Zack tipped his hat to her and greeted, "Hello Nancy."

Nancy feigned surprise and replied, "Zachary, I didn't see you there. How are you?"

Zack removed his hat and was about to answer when Nancy signaled one of the workmen to assist her with getting into the carriage. The man extended his hand to her for balance and she stepped up into the rear seat. Once seated she turned to Zack and said, "Oh, we are having a dinner party for General William Ashley next week. I'll send an invitation to you and…uh, Misses Clayton. I hope you can attend." Without waiting for a reply Nancy tapped Toby on the shoulder with her parasol and tersely said, "Toby!" Immediately Toby flicked the reins and clicked in his teeth.

The horse and carriage pulled away leaving Zack standing with his hat in his hands. With a subtle shake of his head in response to his thoughts of not being willing to subject Ann to Nancy's discourtesies, Zack replaced his hat and turned toward the bank.

Zack was not aware that Frank Gusterson was watching him from a doorway down the crowded street. Frank watched him enter the bank and paid particular attention to the paper money that Zack folded and stuffed in his pocket as he exited the bank. He continued to watch as Zack entered the offices of the Berthold Mercantile Company to pay his bill for the latest shipment of goods, which were now in the company's warehouse. Then Zack returned to his horse and rode in the direction of the doorway where Frank was standing. Frank turned his back to Zack as he rode by. Frank continued the surveillance until Zack turned a corner and rode out of sight.

Zack was on his way to the Shiller home. He promised Ann he would meet her there when he was done with his business. Ann told him earlier that Isabelle was overdue for child birthing and she planned to spend the day with her.

Arriving at the Shiller house, Zack noticed several horses and buggies tied up around the house. He knocked on the door and Henry Garrett answered. At first Zack thought he might be intruding on a private business affair, which Ned hosted at times. Ned burst forth from among the gather people and excitedly announced to Zack, "Zachary, I have a son!"

Zack extended his hand to Ned, "Congratulations, Ned," and before he could say more Ned was off shaking everybody's hand again and saying, "I have a son."

After a few minutes and a congratulatory drink Zack found Ann in the kitchen helping with food for the well-wishing family members and friends. Ann told him that the boy was born just before noon and that mother and son were doing well. As she handed Zack a piece of bread she was slicing she purposely bumped him with her hip and said, "Now it's your turn, Mister Clayton. I hope you're up for it."

As usual Zack grinned at her antics and replied, "How about right now?" He reached around her waist and pulled her close. Ann giggled and the other women in the kitchen turned to see what the giggling was about. While carefully positioning the slice of bread and the bread knife she had in her hands Ann stretched to place a kiss on Zack's cheek. And while she did she whispered, "We might not get invited back here again, so let's make it later."

*   *   *

Frank Gusterson added another brick to the wall of delusions he and Billy were building by reporting, "He's spending our money! He takes our gold in the bank and walks out with foldin' money. Then he buys what ever he wants with our money!" As evening descended they began their usual pattern of arguing and drinking. In a whiskey haze Billy started the line of thinking that would finally lead to a plan. "Ya don't s'pose that Bell bitch knows where it is?" he wondered.

"Naw," Frank replied, expressing a mutually held sentiment that neither would share such a secret with a woman.

But Billy persisted with the speculation, "What if he did tell her or gave her a map? Or she knows where he keeps the map?"

Frank argued that even if she knew they were still stuck with figuring out how to get the information. Billy was not ready to give up and said, "What if we was'ta just ask her if she knows?"

While slow shaking his head no Frank replied, "More'n likely she'd sic the law on us iffen we was…"

Billy cut him off, "What if we was'ta grab her and make her tell. If she don't know we could trade her fer the map."

Like a piece of lumber set in a lathe the idea of abducting Ann began to take shape. When Billy and Frank Gusterson geared up for the tasks of a mutually accepted goal they had an uncommon sense of what each would do toward reaching that goal. It was well after midnight when they con-cluded the plan to abduct Ann Clayton.

CHAPTER 13

THE ABDUCTION

Zack studied the announcement in the newspaper that lay before him on the kitchen table:

FOR THE ROCKY MOUNTAINS
The subscriber wishes to engage 50 men
To ascend the Missouri River to the
ROCKY MOUNTAINS
To be employed to transport goods.

To each man fit for such business
$100.00
Apply to J. Clayton or Wm. Ashley
At St. Louis.
The brigade will set out on or before
The last day of March next.

Zack figured he might be hard pressed to find suitable manpower for the trip he was planning with this kind of advertising becoming widely known. He discussed the other implications with Ann. The price for good horses, mules and oxen was sure to rise with the increased demand. Also the price of trade goods could be affected. He was fairly secure with the quantities of trade good he had already purchased but still had some items yet to buy. In light of the potential manpower shortage and a possible shortage of draft animals they decided to begin recruiting men for the trip and to make another livestock buying trip into Illinois.

It was mid morning when Zack put on his heavy blanket coat to go and seek out Nate Plummer and Eli Diamond. They may not want to make a long trip west but they may know men who will. The road had turned to cold, sticky mud when he turned his horse toward town. The first November snow had been heavy and wet. Most of it melted during the last few warmer days but the moisture left the roads soft and gummy, leaving stiff wagon ruts and hoof prints in the road. The late morning sun would soften the soil to be rutted anew with each passing wheel and hoof. That is if the sun came out from behind the overcast sky. Patches of darker clouds hinted that more snow was on the way.

Zack caught up with Eli Diamond as Eli was returning from making a delivery. Zack rode beside the lumbering wagon and presented his notions. Eli was interested in make the trip to Illinois but doubted he would go on the westward trip in the spring. "I'm still courtin' that widow," he reported, "and can't be doin' any long trips jest yet." He also said the hauling business was slowing down some as winter set in, and thought he should be able to get away for a short trip into Illinois. He introduced his assistant for the day. Jeb Smith was a carpenter from Ohio who recently arrived in St. Louis. He was working as an assistant teamster until he could get himself established as a carpenter.

As Zack turned from the wagon he said, "Now you let me know if you happen across anyone who'd like to make either trip."

With a wave Eli called to the departing rider, "I'll do that."

Jeb Smith had several questions about Zack's offer of a westward journey. Eli deferred the questions by advising, "He's a good man. A fella can't do no better by signing on with him but I reckon you'd best put your questions to him direct."

Zack rode out to the Garrett corrals and found Nate Plummer cutting out a horse for a buyer. Zack watched him for a few minutes, noting how easy he worked in the saddle compared to the awkward boy he was just a few months ago. Nate had turned into a first rate horseman. When his task was finished, Nate rode to the high rail fence and greeted Zack. While still mounted they talked over the fence. Nate was interested in returning to Illinois to buy livestock. With the colder weather he was less busy and was looking for something to do that was more adventuresome than the routine feeding. Also he was interested in going west in the spring and was considering responding to the announcement in the newspaper. Zack told him that he could not pay as much as the announced one hundred dollars but he could offer the position of head drover. "Ya mean I'd be the boss of my own crew?" Nate asked.

"Yep," Zack replied, "probably need two more drovers. Know anyone who might be interested?"

Nate thought on it for pause and responded, "Could be. There's a couple fellas who just signed on here. They be a little green but I can learn 'em."

Zack smiled at Nate's confidence and his success at recruiting the first man for the spring venture. They sealed the bargain with a handshake over the fence. Nate inquired about Ann and Zack invited him to stop in for supper to visit with her. Nate agreed but said he'd have to check in with the corral foreman before he could get away.

A few minutes later he rode out the gate, which was opened by a skinny boy no older than himself. Leaning toward Zack he nodded in the direction of the boy and said in a slightly muffled tone, "That be one of the fellas I was telling you 'bout." Zack looked in that direction and noted the boy reminded him of Nate's gaunt features as he gorged himself in the Skyles Hotel dining room. As they turned their horses toward the road Zack noticed Nate had a pistol tucked in his belt and remarked on it. Nate patted the handle and said, "It's used but shoots good. Bought it with what I earned on that trip with you."

           *   *   *

The snow started with big, heavy, wet flakes when the twins set their plan in motion. They took the road to the small house with Frank leading the way by one hundred yards. He would come up to the house from the rear, through the stable. Billy would follow, and taking a signal from Frank to proceed, would walk to the front of the house. Their plan was to enter the house at the same time, from the opposite doors, which would not give Ann a chance to escape. They would be able to tell from their first pass if Ann was home alone.

Although the snow reduced visibility, Lucy McCracken thought she recognized Frank Gusterson as the man she had seen before, watching the Clayton house, the day they moved in. She thought to run across the road to tell Ann but knew the man would be long gone before Ann could get a look at him. She went to get a shawl to warm herself from standing in the draft from the window. When she returned to the window she saw Billy Gusterson riding by. She shook her head in disbelief. *How can that be?* she thought, *How did that man get around so fast and come by again?* She did not notice the subtle differences in the riders' clothing nor in the horses they rode. Just then Robert let out a screech. He had been playing quietly with a carved wooden horse on the floor in front of the fireplace and got to close to the big water filled iron pot. Lucy had earlier filled the pot in preparation for giving Robert a bath and once heated swung it out from the flames for dipping the water into a washtub. While playing a horse race Robert lost his balance and placed his hand on the hot metal to right himself. Lucy hurried to pick him up.

Finding only the four white stocking mare in the stable Frank felt assured the scheme was unfolding as desired. Had he found two horses in the stable he would have kept on riding, which also was a signal to Billy to keep on riding. Frank dismounted and as he entered the stable he talked softly to the mare. The snow was falling heavier and visibility was diminishing. Billy first appeared only as a dark shape coming through the snow. As he got closer, Frank was able to clearly identify him. Frank waved a signal indicating their plan was in motion. As he continued to talk to the mare he placed the saddle on her back and cinched it up. He led the mare out of the stable and tied her close to where his and Billy's horse were tied. Frank loosened the saddle ties holding the large burlap bag and Billy checked the position of the rope and big kerchief in his coat pockets. They were ready for the next step in their plan.

Ann was sitting at the kitchen table writing a letter when the twins arrived at the stable. She was writing to her parents and periodically would stare into the fireplace as she formulated a sentence or thought through an event she wanted to describe to them. Her writing had consumed most of an hour and she had not noticed the change in the weather. Once finished with what she wanted to write, she decided to leave the letter for later. She rose, looked out the window at the thick snowfall and realized she had not brought in the clothes she washed and hung out. She slipped into the coat that hung next to the rear door and stepped out into an inch of snow on the ground. She put her head down to keep the snow out of her eyes as she walked to the clothesline. She turned her back to the wind and reached for a shirt.

Billy was about to step out from behind the stable, to head for the front door, when Ann opened the rear door. He saw her soon enough that he was able to step back without being seen by her and to signal his brother to hesitate. Carefully, he peeked around the side of the stable and saw Ann turn her back to him. In the wink of an eye the twins sized up this unforeseen opportunity and quickly stepped through the boot muting snow toward the figure shaking the snow off a shirt.

Ann felt two powerful arms grab her from behind and before she had a chance to scream a kerchief was stuffed in her mouth. She struggled as coils of rope were wound around her. She had the presence of mind to use the only weapon she had and stomped on the foot of the attacker. She heard a groan and felt his arms slacken enough that she struggled free. She tried to run but slipped in the snow and fell. With her arms pinned to her side by the rope she tried to rise but was quickly prevented from doing so by a man holding her down. She managed to roll away and flailed with her feet at the pursuing attacker. She got in a kick to the man's arm but that did not slow him down. She felt the rope tighten and extended to restrain her feet. Then a burlap bag was placed over her head and quickly slid down her body. She continued to struggle and make muffled yells. During all the frantic struggle Ann did not get a good look at her abductors. All she saw was dark forms in heavy coats who acted swiftly and efficiently.

When the bag was secured Frank stood up and looked around for any sign that their abduction was witnessed. Seeing none, he signaled Billy who was already in position to lift and carry their bagged quarry. They quickly moved toward the horses and Ann was placed over the mare's saddle and tied in place. The twins mounted their horses and turned back the way they came. While leading the mare they rode at a steady pace so as not to draw attention to themselves.

Lucy McCracken stepped out on her front porch while holding her sobbing son. She reached down for a scoop of snow to place in his burned hand. Robert resisted anything coming toward his hand and Lucy had to put him down in order to coax him into opening his hand. Robert felt almost instant relief in his burning palm from the cold, wet snow. Lucy looked toward the Clayton house and through the thick snowfall saw the dark forms of three horses moving away from the stable. Robert's diminishing sobs drew her attention back to him and she scooped up more snow for his burn. When she looked back to where the horses had been they were gone. Lucy was worried. About what she was not quite sure. She just felt something was not right at the Clayton house. She decided to dress for the weather and cross the road to see for herself.

Lucy carried Robert across the road, and although she tried stepping across the slushy ruts, she got her shoes muddy and wet. She knocked at the front door and got no answer. She opened the door and called, "Ann, Ann. It's Lucy." Still with no answer she stepped in and put Robert down. Leading Robert by a hand, she checked the rooms and saw nothing out of order. She stuck her head out the rear door and called, "Ann, Ann." She was reluctant to walk out to the stable and leave Robert unattended in the house. She also knew that as soon as he saw a horse he would start begging for a ride. The falling snow began to lighten as she stepped back into the kitchen.

Zack and Nate stopped at the Berthold Mercantile Company as they rode through town. Nate wanted to check on a heavy coat he had ordered. A clerk carried the thick blanket capote to Nate and he tried it on. It was a handsomely colored coat with wide horizontal dark green stripes separated by thin golden stripes. It had a wide hood, in the same pattern, attached to the shoulders. Zack told Nate about having a similar capote and how at times, in the cold wind in the mountains, he tied a scarf over his hat then pulled the hood over both. Nate pulled the hood over his hat to feel the effect. Zack asked the clerk if he had the same coat in a smaller size and the clerk volunteered to show some to him. Zack declined saying he would bring his wife in later to choose the colors she wanted.

Patrick McCracken was glad to be back in St. Louis. He arrived very early in the morning and for the past several hours had supervised the unloading of the steamboat's cargo. With that done, he was on his way home to his wife and son. This trip had been longer than usual. When the steamboat got to the mouth of the Ohio River it encountered large chunks of ice in the current and slowed in order to avoid them. If the cold continued, the great waterways would freeze over and it was possible he would not make another trip until spring. He was cold, tired and hungry when he left the docks. As he walked he tried to avoid the sticky mud ruts in the road. When he turned onto the road to his house he heard horses coming up behind him and stepped more to the side of the road. He turned to his name being called, "Cap'n Mac." He immediately recognized Zack as the one who called and paused to set down the heavy bag he was carrying.

"It's good to see you, Cap'n," Zack said as he pulled his horse to halt.

"It's good to be home," Patrick replied.

Zack introduced Nate Plummer and volunteered to carry the bag. After the bag was hoisted up to ride across the pommel they continued down the road, talking as they went.

Lucy returned to her house and was watching out the window again, looking for Zack or Ann to return. She saw her husband approaching. Quickly she picked up Robert, wrapped her shawl around the both of them and stepped out on the porch. After embracing her husband she called out to the road, "Zachary, I was hoping Ann was with you. I was over there earlier and she is not at home."

Zack paused from turning his horse and replied, "She probably went off to visit Isabelle or maybe shopping."

Lucy reported she had not seen Ann leave and was a bit worried about the man she thought was watching the house. Zack was momentarily puzzled by her report and knowing Lucy was a worrier he assured her he would check it out.

Zack was about to step out the rear door when he heard the McCrackens knock on the front door. He called out, "Come in." Robert was talking about a horse ride as they entered. While searching the house, the only thing Zack found to be a little unusual was the letter Ann had been writing lying on the kitchen table. Her habit was to return an unfinished letter to her correspondence and writing supplies box to finish later.

The snow was falling lighter as Zack stepped out the rear door to check the stable for Ann's horse. A ray of sunshine poured through a small break in the clouds causing a bright shimmering effect in the air. Zack only walked a few feet and froze in his tracks. He signaled Nate, who was following, to stop. In quick steps Zack walked around the disturbed snow under the clothesline. He read the sign of two sets of boots coming from the stable and the struggle that followed. He also saw the same set of tracks return to the stable. He followed the tracks and saw the prints of three horses departing. He had a dreadful sinking feeling when he came to the only possible, logical conclusion for the tracks. Ann had been abducted!

Returning to the house, Zack urgently questioned Lucy. When he shared his conclusion of Ann having been abducted Lucy became very distraught and began crying. Robert began crying at the same time and Patrick tried to comfort them. Zack did not want to take any more time to try to get more information from Lucy. She had not provided any useful information up to this point. He was more concerned about getting on the trail of the three horses and readied himself for the task. While he gathered his rifle and tomahawk he asked Nate to go for the Marshal.

Nate responded, "You may need a hand on the trail and I'm willin' and ready." Zack quickly studied on the response and turned toward Patrick.

Before he could ask, Patrick volunteered, "I'll go for the Marshal. You two get after them pirates."

Zack picked up a red kitchen towel and tore it in half. He handed half to Nate and said, "Tear this in strips." As he tore his half of the towel into strips he displayed it to Patrick and said, "We'll tie these strips so as to mark our trail. You be sure to tell the Marshal that." Patrick acknowledged the instruction. Zack called over his shoulder as he exited the front door in a fast walk, "Com'on Nate. Let's get goin'!"

For the first one hundred yards the horse tracks were easy to follow. They had only slightly filled with snow. When the tracks turned onto the road they were mixed with the tracks of other horses and wagons. Zack rode slowly studying the tracks on the road. Periodically he instructed Nate to tie a strip of the red towel to a bush or on an over hanging branch. As they traveled north, the number of tracks in the road diminished and the trail of the three horses was easier to follow. Zack stopped to study the tracks as they left the road onto a narrow lane through a thick stand of trees. The lane also contained the tracks of narrow wheels. Before heading down the lane Zack and Nate tied a red strip on each side of the juncture.

Earlier, the twins saw the narrow wheel tracks and cursed its meaning. The tracks indicated that since they left the warehouse the carriage that delivered *that woman* to Snow Logan's cabin had entered the lane. This was not a time in which they wanted any extra eyes about. They discussed the potential problem and decided to leave the lane and cut through the trees so they could scout the warehouse area from hiding.

What they saw gave them reason to make a change in their plan. Toby, dressed in his bright blue coat, was dutifully wiping snow and mud from the carriage with a cloth. There was no way the twins could get to their cabin without being seen by him. Ann heard them talking in urgent, hushed tones. There was something familiar about their voices but she could not quite place them. The twins decided to stay in the trees and come up behind the warehouse out of Toby's sight. They were not completely successful with that strategy. Toby saw the horses and riders moving through the trees. Toby kept to his task when he made that observation. He had long since learned that when it came to *white folks* it was best not to indicate, in any way, what he saw or heard. He was already uncomfortable enough with having to drive *Miss Nancy* out to this remote cabin. He worried that *Masta James* would discover these trips and in his wrath blame the carriage driver for his part in the illicit rendezvous.

The twins were only slightly distressed by Toby's presence. Their primary plan was to take Ann to their cabin where they could coerce her into revealing the location of the gold mine, much in the manner they coerced their mother to reveal all she knew about Zachary Clayton. Taking Ann into the warehouse, instead of the cabin, was an acceptable alternative. The warehouse was a rough-cut lumber building without windows. On one end it had big double doors in which a wagon could be backed through in order to load or discharge cargo. On the side, opposite the cabins, it had a single door and that was where they would enter; out of sight from any prying eyes on the other side of the warehouse.

They tied the horses up, out of sight as much as possible, where the leafless trees were thickest. Then Frank hoisted the bag over his shoulder and followed his brother toward the warehouse. Billy entered through the side door and went directly to the two oil lanterns. Frank followed through the door and dumped the bag on a stack of recently acquired buffalo hides. Billy got the lanterns lit and Frank closed the door. After knowing nods to one another, they left the warehouse, in opposite directions, to assure that their presence was unnoticed. From their individual vantage points they observed *that Nigra* was still wiping down the carriage and there was no sign of *Snow Logan and that woman.*

In hushed tones, they compared observations when they returned to the warehouse door. They decided they could start their interrogation. The carriage was far enough away that only something unusually loud would carry that far. And the walls of Snow's cabin were thick enough that neither occupant within should be able to hear what was about to happen in the warehouse.

Ann felt hands roll her over. She blindly tried to get in a kick with her bound legs. Frank restrained her legs and growled, "No more kickin' or I'll beat ya to a pulp! You understand?" He held strong pressure on her legs until he saw the head of the bag nod yes. Billy scooted a wooden keg of gunpowder to the stack of hides. Frank slipped the bag up to Ann's shoulders. Together the twins lifted Ann up and sat her on the keg. Just to make sure she would not try to kick again Billy tied her legs to the keg with a nearby loose coil of rope. Billy removed the bag with a swift jerk. Frank was in position with his fist poised in front of Ann's face as the bag flew away. He meant to terrorize her from the first moment she saw him.

Ann's eyes widened in recognition and terror when she focused beyond the fist. She never liked the Gusterson twins and abhorred their crude attempts to flirt with her when they came into the café in Cairo. She also feared them from having twice witnessed their brawling.

Frank touched his fist to the point of her nose and said in a menacing growl, "No screamin'! No raisin' yer voice! You understand?" Ann nodded yes to his threat. Frank let the threat fully soak in before he spoke again, "You got something that belongs to us and we want it! You understand?"

Ann did not know what he was referring to but reflexively nodded yes. Opening his fist Frank put his fingers on the gagging cloth. He put his face up close to Ann's and whispered, "I'm gonna take this out. No screams!" When Ann did not respond with a nod he grabbed her hair and hissed in her ear, "You understand?" Ann could barely nod yes against the strain on her hair but she managed just enough of a nod that Frank loosened his grip.

Billy stepped behind Ann and placed his hands on her shoulders while Frank removed the gag. Instinctively Ann moved her jaw, tongue and lips with the new freedom. Frank kept the gag close to her mouth in case she attempted to scream. When it appeared she was not going to try to scream he said, "Now you tell us where our brother's gold mine is!"

Ann was at a loss. The first image that came to her mind was the big, simple-minded boy, Kenneth Gusterson. She had not ever heard of him having a mine and thought with a puzzled expression, *Kenny has a mine? A gold mine?* She tried to speak her thought but her mouth was still very dry from the gag and from the fear. Her voice trembled and cracked, "Mine?…I don't know of… Kenny… having a mine."

Frank assumed she was being evasive and signaled to Billy with a nod. Billy ran his hands down inside Ann's coat and roughly grabbed her breasts. Frank was prepared for her to scream, and when she tried, he quickly stuffed the gag back into her mouth. Billy became more aggressive with his hands and licentiously reported, "She's as much of a woman as I always thought."

Frank did not want his brother getting too distracted from their main purpose and reminded him, "Billy, Billy. Maybe later. We got other things to do." Billy nodded an acknowledgement and returned his hands to Ann's breasts. Taking advantage of her increased fear Frank grabbed her hair again and growled, "Not Kenny! John! John Junior!" Again Frank removed the gag. Ann could scarcely turn her attention from the rough fondling and in an anguished tone responded, "I didn't know John....Never met him."

The interrogation continued in this manner for several minutes with finally Ann understanding that her husband had given gold nuggets to Mary Gusterson. She tried to explain that she was aware of him giving money to her but denied she knew anything about gold. The twins believed her. Her answers were consistent with their thinking that a man would never trust a woman with such a secret. They had anticipated this possibility and planned to have Ann write a ransom note to Zack. Frank tied the kerchief to gag Ann again. Then he and Billy discussed how to retrieve the pen, ink and paper from their cabin. Billy left the warehouse to check on the activity in front of the cabins and returned with a report that Toby was sitting in the carriage. They decided to wait until the carriage left in order to go to their cabin.

Zack rode slowly through the trees staying on the tracks of the horses he was following. He paused periodically to peer as far through the trees as possible. With each pause he signaled to Nate, with a raise of his hand, to also pause. Suddenly he signaled a halt. He dismounted and waved for Nate to do the same. Quietly he handed the reins of his horse to Nate. He pointed to the dark form of a building through the trees and whispered, "You wait here. I'll slip up on that building and scout it out. If you hear shootin' come a runnin'." Nate quietly acknowledged the instruction.

Zack stalked through the trees until the forms of three buildings became clear; two cabins and a larger barn like structure. He scanned the open area and was drawn toward some moving, something blue. The color appeared faint through the falling snow. Then he caught the smell of wood smoke. He continued his stalking until he could see he was approaching the edge of the trees. The snow flakes had gradually increased in size and rate to the point that he knew he would have to get much closer to see anything clearly. He circled the clearing, staying in the trees, with his goal of getting closer to the blue movement. As he got closer he was able to make out the horse and carriage. They were almost white with a mantle of snow. Then he saw Toby, who had been standing on the opposite side of the carriage stamping his feet for warmth, shake the snow off his hat and a cloak he was wearing over his blue coat. Toby climbed into the front seat of the carriage and drew the cloak tightly around himself.

What's Toby doing here? Zack thought to himself. He did not linger on the question and thought, *Well, he is here and I'd better check him out!* Backing a few steps back into the trees Zack walked a wide arc so he would come up to a brush pile that sat just inside the tree line. The carriage was parked parallel to the brush pile. He walked in a crouch for the last few yards and slowly raised his head to look over the brush pile. Toby was occupied with rubbing his hands together under the cloak and had not heard Zack's snow muffled steps through the trees. With a hand cupped beside his mouth Zack called to Toby in a forced whisper, "Toby, Don't look around!" Hearing his name and the order Toby stiffened. "It's Zack. Have you seen two men?"

The source of the voice was just out of Toby's peripheral vision as he sat very still and nodded yes to the question. "Where?" came the next question. Toby slipped his hand out from under the cloak and pointed at the wooded hillside beyond the warehouse.

"What are you doing here?" Zack asked.

Toby changed the direction of his pointing finger to the cabin and replied, "Miss Nancy. In there."

Zack slowly lowered himself to hunkering behind the brush pile to think. He could not come up with any reason that Nancy Clayton would be involved in Ann's abduction; therefore it was unlikely Ann was in that cabin. He decided to continue scouting the area for signs that would lead to Ann. He rose and directed a warning to Toby, "There may be shooting. If so, just take cover."

Toby nodded an acknowledgement to the warning and thought, *Oh Lord, Masta James knows it all and has sent his brother to shoot them.* But that did not make sense to Toby. He tried to reject this thought by coming up with another explanation. His puzzlement was only partly relieved when he saw Zack's form, through the thick falling snow, look through the windows of the two cabins and move on. What ever he was looking for it did not seem to be in the cabin where Nancy Clayton entered nor in the smaller adjacent cabin.

There was no sign of activity in the dark smaller cabin and when Zack looked through the window of the other cabin he saw the fireplace was burning low. There was not enough light in the cabin to make out details and he saw no movement. The only set of tracks he found were the mostly filled in tracks of Nancy Clayton. He did not linger to wonder why she was in the cabin. He briefly followed a depression in the snow he assumed to be a path through the trees to the river. He stopped at a skiff covered with a tarp. He pulled the tarp away enough to allow his arm through and separated a calked seam in the bottom of the boat with his tomahawk. He figured the skiff to be a possible means of escape by who ever the abductors were, and he wanted them to have one less means of a get away. Then he circled the backside of the warehouse and found the three horses tied up in the trees. He immediately recognized Ann's mare and noted the two sets of boot prints leading to the warehouse. His next stop was back to Nate. Zack had completely circled the warehouse and cabins. All the signs lead him to believe that Ann was in the warehouse with two men. He could not explain Nancy's presence in the cabin but that would have to wait. Rescuing Ann came first.

Zack led Nate to a large tree that stood on the side of the hill, which provided a view of the single door in the side of the warehouse. After he told Nate he figured Ann to be in the warehouse with two men, he instructed, "If either of those two come out that door shoot them." He handed Nate one of his pistols and continued, "Be careful to make sure it is not me or Ann comin' out that door!"

Then in a few steps Zack was out of sight in search of a way to see into the warehouse. He examined the big double doors for cracks and found where the doors met in the middle there was enough of a space to peer in. His view of the interior was limited but he could see light coming from a lantern. Then he saw the dark form of a man stand, stretch his arms above his head and yawn. Zack moved to the side door and listened for any sound from within. He found a small crack in the door and tried to peer through it. The crack was not big enough to see anything other than light. From his vantage point Nate watched Zack's scouting but the snowfall was thick enough that Nate could barely make him out.

Toby was getting colder while he sat still and worried. He was wishing he was dressed in heavier clothes and dreaded the possible gunfire. He started to shiver and was considering turning in his seat to reach for Nancy Clayton's lap blanket, which lay in the rear seat. Then from behind he heard a cough, a familiar cough. He turned slowly to see James Clayton dismounting from a horse. James appeared almost apparition like with a layer of snow covering his heavy coat and hat. Without saying a word, James glared at Toby then turned toward the cabin. As he walked he pulled a pistol from inside his coat.

When James was about twenty feet from the cabin door Snow Logan opened the door with the intention of calling to Toby to bring the carriage closer to the cabin. James cocked the flintlock pistol and brought it up to aim just as Snow was opening his mouth to yell. His eyes widened with recognizing James but before he could react further James fired. The round struck Snow in the chest and pushed him back into the cabin. While continuing to advance James dropped the pistol and pulled another from under his coat. Nancy was screaming when he stepped through the doorway. Once inside the cabin James fired the second pistol. Nancy Clayton continued to scream.

Toby leapt from the carriage, taking the lap blanket with him, and squatted down behind a carriage wheel. He did not know if this was the shooting Zack warned him of. It didn't matter. He pulled the blanket tight and tried to make himself as small and as inconspicuous as possible.

The twins jumped to their feet to the shots and screaming. Drawing their pistols from their belts they looked in the direction of Snow Logan's cabin then at each other. "What do ya spose that fool Snow is up to?" Frank wondered for the both of them.

"Hard to say," Billy replied, "I'll sneak a look."

Zack also startled to the shots and screams. The sounds did not come from within the warehouse, of that he was sure. He had his ear up to the door and heard Billy's voice coming his way. He decided to make his move by leaning back and kicking the door with the bottom of his boot. The door violently flew open striking Billy who was just reaching for the latch. Billy staggered backwards and fell in a pile of loosely coiled rope. He dropped his pistol in the process. Frank turned toward the disturbance and cocked his pistol. Zack's rushed him before he was able to aim. Zack parried Frank's gun hand with his rifle barrel. During the upward motion the pistol fired harmlessly into the roof. Zack continued his charge and drove Frank backwards against a wooden crate. One of the lanterns was sitting on that crate. The lantern was knocked off spilling the oil and a flame quickly followed the spill. Zack saw Ann sitting on the keg as he rushed Frank. While he temporarily had Frank pinned against the crate he yelled, "RUN, ANN. TRY TO RUN!"

Desperately Ann rocked the keg and managed to tip it. She fell over and immediately began to squirm against the ropes that bound her. By this time Billy was trying to get to his feet. In his haste to rise from the coils of rope he got a coil tangled in his boots. Rather than stop to free himself he strained against the tangle and moved toward Zack. Ann managed to free one leg by rolling with the keg. Her motion put her right in Billy's path. She got a glancing kick in on his lower leg as he tried to get by her. Billy fell again, swearing loudly as he went down.

Zack could not turn around to see what the noise behind him was about. He was defending himself against Frank's blows, who was using the pistol as a club. The struggle was in close quarters and Zack had to use his rifle to block the blows.

Billy struggled to his feet to Frank's call, "Billy! Billy! Get him!" Pulling the coils with him Billy again moved toward the struggle.

With another roll Ann was free of the rope around her legs but her arms were still bound to her sides. She stood just as Zack yelled again, "RUN, ANN! RUN!" Ann moved toward the open door but tripped on the wad of rope Billy was dragging. She fell against a crate, knocking her breath out and lay there momentarily stunned.

Billy got free from the rope and rushed Zack from behind. He got in a good solid punch to Zack's back. Frank took advantage of the distraction and delivered a clubbing blow to Zack's head. Zack went down in a heap. Billy delivered a kick to Zack's shoulder and was about to deliver another when Frank stopped him. "We got our gold man," Frank announced, "Let's get 'em tied before he comes to." Billy reached for the long tangle of rope he had been dragging and quickly cut enough to tie Zack's hands behind his back. Frank took the rope and ordered, "Get the horses! This place is gonna burn quick."

The flames were licking up the side of a crate and reaching for the dry lumber wall. Billy stopped long enough to find his pistol then headed for the door. He noted Ann was lying on her side gasping for breath through the gag. She helplessly watched Billy go through the door. The flames were producing enough light that Ann could make out Frank as he tied Zack's hands. The flames were also producing smoke, which distorted the surroundings for her. She had studied the interior of the building while tied to the keg and knew the only other route of escape beside the door Billy went out was the big double doors. With the echo of "RUN ANN, RUN!" in her mind she got to her feet and stumbled toward the doors. She managed to push the handle on the sliding door latch with her head, releasing the catch. Then with her shoulder she pushed. The big door creaked and resisted opening. The heavy iron hinges and the snow accumulation hampered her effort. She pushed harder until a gap appeared, which was big enough for her to squeeze through. She stumbled out into the snow and fell.

Nate concentrated on the dark form moving in his direction and it did not look like Zack. When he heard the two shots and screams he cocked his pistol. He was not sure where the shots and screams came from. Almost immediately after that he thought he saw and heard Zack kick in the side door. It was hard to tell with the heavy snowfall inhibiting vision and hearing. The next shot he was sure came from within the warehouse. When he was absolutely sure the dark form of a man was not Zack he yelled, "Throw up yer hands or I'll shoot!"

Billy did not heed the warning. He raised his pistol and fired at the voice. The round struck the large tree from behind which Nate was peering. Nate aimed and fired. With a loud groan Billy went down and rolled in the snow. Clutching his side he got to his feet and stumbled back toward the warehouse. Nate cocked Zack's pistol and aimed at the retreating figure. He pulled the trigger, click, misfire. He hurriedly cocked the hammer again, click, another misfire. Then his target disappeared in the curtain of white. Nate stepped back behind the tree and went to his knees. Using his body as a shield from the falling snow he examined the pistol and quickly surmised the powder in the pan was damp. He knocked it out and replaced it with fresh powder from his powder flask. He looked around the tree, no movement was visible. He tucked Zack's pistol in his belt and loaded his own.

Frank was dragging Zack toward the doorway. With his effort and the sounds of the crackling, growing flames he did not take special notice of a faint gunshot. With his back in the doorway, he turned to look up the hill from which he expected his brother to appear leading the horses.

Billy staggered into him and painfully groaned, "I've been shot."

Frank dropped his grip from the shoulders of Zack's coat and reached to grab Billy who was losing his balance. "Ya hit bad?" Frank asked.

Billy was holding both hands over a spot on his right side. "Winged me purty good. He's up the hill apiece." Billy replied. Just then a section of burning cedar shingles collapsed into the warehouse.

Frank knew there were enough gunpowder kegs in the warehouse to blow it apart. "Can ya walk?" Frank asked wanting to get some distance from the impending blast. Billy painfully nodded yes. "Then make fer the boat. I'll carry our prize." Frank ordered. He was about to reach for Zack when Nate fired at them.

Nate had followed Billy's tracks in the snow. When he saw the forms of two people he fired, this time without warning. He was not completely sure that the forms were not Zack and Ann so he fired to miss. The round smacked the side of the warehouse.

Frank changed his mind about trying to tote Zack. He grabbed Billy by an arm for support said, "Let's get out of here!"

Nate exchanged pistols and cautiously advanced. He could see the dark forms moving away from him. Keeping his hand over the flintlock to keep it dry he tried to aim. The dark forms disappeared around the end of the building.

Looking between the spokes of the carriage wheel Toby saw the smoke and flames come through the warehouse roof. He also heard the shooting and realized there was something happening in the warehouse that was independent of the shooting in Snow Logan's cabin. While he was wondering about what was happening Ann appeared as a dark form clumsily running from the warehouse. When she fell down Toby decided to go and see who it was. Holding the snow covered lap blanket tightly around himself he cautiously approached the struggling figure in the snow. At first all he saw was a person who was bound with coils of rope and gagged with a dark cloth. Upon closer inspection he recognized Ann.

He removed the gag and after a deep breath Ann frantically blurted, "Zachary's in there!" Toby tried to loosen the knot in the rope but his hands were too cold and stiff. With a sob Ann pleaded, "Never mind that. Go get Zachary." Toby raced to the double doors and pulled the door open enough for him to squeeze through. As he entered the heat from the flaming roof quickly melted the snow on the blanket.

Shielding his face from the heat, Nate stepped through the side door and found Zack lying on the floor. Nate was getting a grip on Zack's coat to start dragging when Toby suddenly appeared through the smoke and flames. Nate did not know who he was but Toby's quick action of joining in to drag Zack out of the burning building confirmed he was a friend. They grabbed Zack under his arms, lifted and exited through the door. The lap blanket snagged on the doorframe and Toby left it behind.

The roof of the warehouse was completely engulfed in flames and more of it was collapsing. "This way!" Nate yelled as he guided up the hill toward the large tree where he had earlier kept a vigil. They did not stop until they reached the base of the tree. Both men were near collapse but they paused only briefly to catch some breath. In a few more steps they were behind the tree and laid Zack on his side. Breathing hard, Toby tried to work at the rope knot that bound Zack's hands. At that moment the flames reached the gunpowder kegs and the warehouse went up in a rapid series of deafening explosions. A mass of flaming debris arched into the snow filled air.

With her eyes fixed on the double doors Ann rose to her feet and strained against the rope, trying to free her arms. She was barely conscious of saying, "Zachary... Zachary... Zachary," hoping to see him come out the doors. The force of the explosion knocked her off her feet and flaming debris rained on and about her. She screamed and rolled in the snow.

Patrick McCracken, Marshal Dufrane and two deputies were riding down the lane when they saw the bright flames through the trees and snowfall. They urged their horses faster and were about to break out of the trees when the explosion occurred. Horses and men startled to the roar and flying debris. When the horses were back under control the men rode to the edge of the clearing and dismounted. The Marshal directed a quick search of the area. Patrick found Ann who was lying too close to a large piece of smoldering wood. He scooped it away from her, burning his hands in the process. She also had small embers burning on her clothes and in her hair, which he extinguished with scoops of snow.

James Clayton had stepped across Snow Logan's body and fully intended to shoot his wife who was sitting on a bunk bed. Her screams of terror jolted him. His rage, however, would not permit him to let her go unpunished and he fired to miss her. Nancy collapsed to the floor and curled up in a fetal position. James was immobilized by a fit of coughing when the explosion shook the cabin. He tripped over Snow's body and fell, striking his head on the door. The rear wall and the shingle roof were on fire when the Marshall and deputy dragged James from the cabin. The Marshal returned through the smoke to carry Nancy out. When they were ready to go back for Snow Logan the flaming roof fell in. They could do no more.

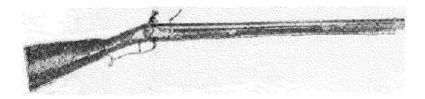

CHAPTER 14

THE AFTERMATH

The deputy assigned to check out the smaller cabin retreated from the flames after a quick search of the interior. The team of carriage horses bolted when the explosion occurred and got the carriage hung up on a stump at the edge of the clearing. After a few minutes the deputy was able to calm the terrorized horses, extricate the carriage and direct them to where James and Nancy were being attended. The lawmen loaded the helpless couple in the carriage and a deputy drove it to the lane to get the still nervous horses farther away from the fires. James' frightened horse was in the trees and permitted the Marshal to mount in order to also be moved to safety.

Ann was sobbing uncontrollably when Patrick McCracken picked her up and carried her to the carriage. He sat with her in the front seat and held her in his arms. Marshal Dufrane knew James and Nancy Clayton. He had seen Ann with Isabelle Shiller but did not know her. From what he knew so far, the abduction described by Patrick McCracken was more complex than he originally understood it. Four men were missing from the original report of the abduction; Zachary Clayton, Nate Plummer, and the two abductors were yet to be discovered. He saw Snow Logan's body in the burning cabin and he assumed James Clayton's Negro carriage driver must also be about. He made sure the people in the carriage were safe and directed the deputies to continue a search.

When the explosion ripped the warehouse apart Zack and Toby were behind the tree enough that they were protected from the blast. Nate was almost there except for a leg. A flying inch wide wood splinter drove into his calf. He instinctively moved to get behind the tree. Just then the flaming debris began to rain around them. Toby crawled onto Zack to protect him. A chunk of burning rafter came tumbling through the bare branches and landed square on Toby's back. It quickly burned a hole through the blue wool coat. Toby howled in pain and rolled off Zack, which dislodged the burning wood into the snow. Toby tried to get up to run from the searing pain but Nate forced him back down and scooped snow onto the smoldering coat.

When Nate was sure the smoldering was extinguished and that Zack was safe, he attended to himself. He took a folding knife from his pocket and gingerly cut loose the trouser material around the splinter. Then while sitting in the snow he closed his eyes, clamped his teeth, held his breath and jerked the splinter out. He recoiled in pain and laid back. The sweat from the exertion of dragging Zack and the sweat of pain chilled on his back and forehead. *I got to keep goin'*, Nate thought, *I'm the only one that ain't hurt bad.* He reached into his coat pocket and took out the last piece of red towel. He grimaced as he poked a portion into his puncture wound. Then he remembered why he was carrying the strips and looked in the direction of the blown out warehouse. *Oh no*, he thought with a sinking dread, *Misses Clayton was in there.*

Toby was lying, belly down, in the snow softly groaning. There wasn't anything more Nate could do for him. Nate crawled to Zack, who was moaning and moving his head. Nate cut the ropes, which bound Zack's wrists, and carefully rolled Zack to his back. Zack appeared to be coming around and moved a hand toward the crown of his head. Nate guided his hand away to examine Zack's scalp. He did not see blood. "Zack, Zack. Can you hear me?" Nate probed. Zack appeared to try to open his eyes but otherwise did not seem able to respond.

James Clayton sat in stunned silence, in the rear seat of the carriage, stroking his wife's hair who had resumed a fetal position with her head in his lap.

Ann's sobbing slowed. She took a deep breath and said, "Did you see Zachary?"

Patrick replied, "No. Where did you see him last?"

After another sob Ann said, "In the warehouse. He was fighting with those awful Gusterson brothers. He told me to run." The thought of Zack being killed in the explosion filled Patrick's mind. Ann sensed his shift in attention and suddenly pulled away from him. She looked into his face, which bore the expression of anguish. In a quick turn she slid from the carriage seat, planting her feet in the snow. Her hands came up to her mouth in shock as she gazed through the snowfall toward the warehouse. The cabins were fully engulfed in flames, providing a stark contrast to the blown out pieces of warehouse lying about. Patrick followed Ann and stood beside her as they viewed the scene of destruction before them.

Continuing their search, Marshal Dufrane and the deputies found where the skiff had been sitting. The area where the boat sat was almost bare of snow. There were tracks indicating the boat had been pushed into the river. The snowfall continued to limit visibility and they could not see a boat on the river. They turned from the river and followed Zack's tracks through the trees. They came upon the three horses tied in the thicket and continued following boot tracks that were rapidly filling with snow. The lead deputy saw men lying at the base of a big tree and called out, "This way Marshal! I see 'em, this a way." The Marshal hurriedly pushed through the snow to see the three injured men. He quickly determined he would need horses to get them all out at once and sent a deputy back to get the three horses in the thicket.

They got Zack positioned in a saddle but it soon became obvious that he had not come around enough to hang on. Nate volunteered to ride behind Zack to keep him in the saddle. Then Toby was loaded and said he could hold on for the trip to the carriage. The Marshal mounted Ann's mare to break trail through the accumulating snow toward the two horses that Nate told him were further up the hill. They found the horses, brushed the snow off the saddles, and all got mounted to head for the lane.

After the shock of seeing the destroyed warehouse began to wane, Ann and Patrick returned to the carriage to get out of the snowfall. They were absorbed in their individual grief when they saw a rider slowly appear through the thick white air, riding slowly toward them. They recognized Marshal Dufrane with his dark eyes and great drooping mustache peering out from under his snow covered hat. He rode past them and dismounted at the rear of the carriage. Then one by one the other riders appeared. When Zack and Nate came into view Ann jumped down from the carriage and ran up to the horse. When the horse came to a halt, Zack was holding to the pommel with his head resting on the horse's neck. Nate had a tight grip on the sides of Zack's coat. With tears of joy streaming down her face Ann brushed the snow from Zack's hair. "Oh Zachary, Oh Zachary," she repeated. Zack opened his eyes slightly and mouthed, "Ann." His eyes were closing when the Marshal arrived to get his charges off the horses.

Marshal Dufrane was a thorough man and not willing to leave anyone behind in this rescue if he could help it. With quick additional questions to those who could talk he determined, with reasonable certainty, he had found all the people he was going to find. Now his task was to get them out of the weather. The snow was getting close to a foot deep and coming down even thicker. With the experience of a man who was used to taking charge he organized the group for traveling. Zack was placed in the front seat of the carriage and Patrick was assigned to drive. Toby said he could continue to ride. Nate and a deputy were assigned to ride close to him. The other deputy was assigned to lead the remaining horses to break trail in front of the carriage. Ann mounted her mare to ride beside the carriage.

The closest large house that could accommodate this many injured people was that of James Clayton so Marshal Dufrane decided to head there. The property also had a sizeable stable in which he could confine and care for the horses, which were bound to be exhausted. Riding to place himself between the trail breaking horses and the carriage he gave the order to move out. When they turned from the lane onto the road to St. Louis, the landmarks were obliterated by the thick blanket of snow. Visibility was very limited and the tracks they left were filling in almost as fast as they were made. They had not gone far when Toby passed out and fell from his horse. Nate and the deputy called out in unison, "MAN DOWN!" The Marshal called a halt to the lead horses and rode back to the carriage. He directed James out of the carriage and got Nancy to sit up. Then Toby was placed sitting in the seat with his head on his knees. James got back into the seat with instructions to hold Toby in place. In mute cooperation James did what he was told to do.

*   *   *

Lilly and Aunt Milly were not prepared for the group that pulled up to the porch but as soon as they understood what was needed they became a whirl of activity to that purpose. Most everyone was covered with snow and they all looked beaten down, cold and wet. In a short time, Marshal Dufrane had everyone inside. Zack and Toby were carefully laid on quilts on the parlor floor. Ann and Patrick were quick to shed their wet coats and direct what energy they had left to concentrate on Zack and Toby. Lilly directed a deputy to carry Nancy to the upstairs bedroom. Nate and James were seated at the dining room table and Aunt Milly poured mugs of hot coffee for them. James sat vacantly staring out the window. He allowed Nate to assist him with getting his wet coat off and sipped on the coffee with encouragement.

Once he was sure that everyone was being attended to, Marshal Dufrane and the deputies got warmed up with hot coffee. They discussed the next step, getting the horses out of the weather. The deputies wanted to try to get home rather than stay overnight in the Clayton house. When they were ready to go back into the snow, Patrick went with them to help with the horses. He also wanted to leave. He knew his wife would be sick with worry and wanted to tell her that Ann was safe.

Marshal Dufrane's last instruction to a deputy was to get the word to a doctor to come to the house as soon as possible. He decided to stay the night in hopes he could more thoroughly sort out the events of the past hours. He still had unanswered questions.

                    *   *   *

Only the most hardy of St. Louis' citizens ventured out during the next two days. The winter storm with its deep snowdrifts brought the city to a standstill. The able bodied occupants of the Clayton house established a routine for caring for the injured. Initially Ann agreed to sleep only after exacting a promise to be awakened if there were any changes in her husband. Once that was promised she rolled up in a blanket only a few feet away. Both Zack and Toby were in and out of consciousness during the first twenty-four hours.

When the blue coat was removed from Toby, tuffs of wool stuck to the edges of the large weeping burn wound. With each change of a wet towel dressing Lilly carefully picked off the tuffs. Toby was able to drink broth between short, fitful periods of sleep. James began to participate in the management of his snow bound guests and uncharacteristically carried in firewood and snow to melt for water. Aunt Milly was Nancy's exclusive caretaker. Nancy did not leave her bedroom and was reported to be moving about very little. She was not physically injured but still seemed to be in a state of shock. Nate helped out where he could by limping to where he was needed. He was encouraged that his puncture wound was not showing any signs of infection.

Marshal Dufrane took advantage of the confinement to get his questions answered. James Clayton confessed to shooting Snow Logan in a fit of rage. Nancy Clayton did not seem able to clearly answer questions. The Marshal figured she probably could not add to what he already knew. Ann Clayton easily identified her abductors as Frank and Billy Gusterson.

Marshal Dufrane was familiar with the names. He was the man who took the report from Ned Shiller about being assaulted in Cairo. He also received a letter from Marshal Seth Thomas detailing the twin's assault on their mother and brother; with additional information about his suspicions of other assaults and robberies. By the end of his questioning Marshal Dufrane had all the information he needed to piece together the separate but simultaneous incidents at the warehouse and cabin. The only remaining unanswered question would have to wait. Did Frank and Billy Gusterson escape? The condition of the river at the time, with chunks of floating ice and poor visibility, would have made for perilous boating but it was certainly possible that they made it down river. He planned to have a handbill printed, which would be distributed to the towns down river, describing the Gusterson twins and their crimes.

*   *   *

When the winter storm abated, the citizens of St. Louis began to dig through the thick white blanket of snow. A day later Doctor Norton paid his first visit to the Clayton house. He found Zack to be sitting up for short periods and complaining of dizziness, headache and wandering concentration. Doctor Norton also noted the characteristic flatness in his emotions and voice, indicative of a concussion. He could not add to the care Zack was receiving and remarked to Ann's queries, "Slow and easy…he'll get better in little steps."

He was not as optimistic about Toby. The large burn was showing signs of infection and Toby was in considerable pain. He instructed Lilly, who had become Toby's primary caretaker, to lay a boiled, damp cheese cloth on the wound and to let it dry. Once dried she was to pull it off, bringing with it the infected pieces of skin. Then do it again several times a day. He also prescribed laudanum prior to each cloth removal and instructed Lily on the dosage. After examining Nate's wound he patted him on the shoulder and said, "I wish I was as young and healthy."

Doctor Norton spent a long time with Nancy Clayton and when he came down the stairs James was waiting and asked, "How is she? Is there something you can do for her?" Doctor Norton spoke privately with James for several minutes and concluded his report with, "Maybe she'll come out of it and maybe she won't. I've seen it go both ways with women who have suffered similar misfortune. I'll look in on her from time to time. You should encourage her to do more, little by little."

Marshal Dufrane departed with Doctor Norton with both saying to send word if anything more was needed. Nate left the next day. He was worried about his long unexplained absence possibly jeopardizing his job. He waved to Ann who came out on the porch to see him off. Two days later Zack was able to ride so he and Ann got their horses saddled and went home. That afternoon Toby was moved to the slave quarters.

The reunion between Lucy and Ann was joyful and tearful. Lucy kept apologizing. She felt she should have done something. Only after Ann insisted that Lucy could have done no more was Lucy able to relinquish some of her feelings of guilt. Every day during Ann's absence Lucy waded through the snow to tend to her friend's house. She kept a low fire going, stocked the woodbox, swept, dusted and generally made things tidy. It became part of her routine for those few days, just as caring for her husband, son and her house was her routine. Only after many assurances by Ann that she was fully capable of resuming the management of the household was Lucy able to go home.

In the quiet and privacy of their home Zack told Ann about the gold, the circumstances by which he came by it and its delivery to Mary Gusterson. Ann expressed an understanding about how Frank and Billy could have come to believe, perverted as it may be, that Zack knew of a gold mine discovered by their brother.

"I wish now I had never brought that gold back with me. Look at all the trouble it caused. Who knows how many others could come looking for a mine. Gold has a way of affecting some men that way," Zack said. Taking Ann in his arms he continued, "I don't ever want to go through something like that again. I don't think I was ever so scared as I was worrying for you."

Ann pulled him tightly to her and replied, "And I was scared for you, Zachary." After a pause Ann suggested, "Maybe we should never mention the gold to anyone from this time forth."

Zack agreed but cautioned, "Marshal Dufrane will probably want to know more about their motives. He said he wanted to talk to me about that."

Ann, knowing she had reported some of the conversation between herself and the twins, offered a way out, "Tell the Marshal about the money you took to Mary and we'll say Frank and Billy just came up with a notion of gold on their own."

Zack revealed the damage he caused to the twins' hidden skiff, which lessened their chances of another successful escape. They decided to relay the pertinent facts to Seth Thomas in Cairo. In a carefully composed letter they asked Seth to use his discretion in what he reported to Mary Gusterson about the probable fate of her twin sons. They asked Seth to deny, and to ask Mary Gusterson to do the same, any knowledge of gold.

Ann added a post script; *"Say hello to my parents for us. Tell them I'll write to them later. With fond regards, Ann & Zachary"*

*   *   *

Marshal Dufrane left the little house disappointed. He was sure there was more to the story about gold than "the imagination of whiskey sodden scoundrels" but that is all Zack would tell him. And Ann said she was playing along with them about gold in order to gain some time or to gain some advantage. There had been no evidence for the drowning of nor the appearance of the Gusterson twins since the incident. He still considered Ann's abduction an open case. The Justice of Peace convened a coroner's inquest into the death of Snow Logan and from the evidence ruled the incident to be justifiable homicide. Again Marshal Dufrane was sure there was more to the relationship between James Clayton and Snow Logan than what came out in the proceedings. Nancy Clayton was excused from testifying because of her *delicate condition*. Toby was not called as a witness and was only briefly mentioned in the inquest record; *A male negra slave was found not fit to offer testimony.*

While his recuperation progressed, Zack had several visitors. The McCrackens visited daily. Patrick reported the Mississippi River to be frozen over and he was only working a few hours a day on boat maintenance. He figured it would be spring before he made another river trip. During each visit, Lucy busied herself with some small project to help Ann. Robert entertained Zack with his accounts of where he was riding his carved wood horse.

Ned Shiller, his wife and newborn son visited once. The Shillers named the boy Miles after his grandfather. Ned confirmed Zack's speculation that good draft and pack animals were going to be in short supply come spring. Zack spoke of considering another buying trip into Illinois and Ned stated he would buy any of the animals over what Zack could use. He offered a prepaid bonus, which Zack accepted.

Nate Plummer and Eli Diamond visited twice. Zack thanked Nate again for dragging him out of the burning warehouse. Nate wanting to set the record straight said, "Could'na done it without Toby."

Later Nate said, "I reckon Mister Pettis was right."

"How's that?" Zack asked.

"Remember how he said there would be some hard lessons to come fer me?" Nate inquired.

Zack replied, "I remember. How's that apply?"

Nate scratched his youthful attempt at a beard and said, "Well I didn't shoot that fella good enough, like ya asked me to. Might have come out different."

Zack nodded sympathetically and said, "Yep, I reckon Mister Pettis knows something about hard lessons."

During their second visit Zack talked to them about his plan for a trip to Illinois. Eli reported the Mississippi River was frozen over and a few daring travelers were crossing it by horse and wagon. The cold was a blessing on one hand. They would be able to cross the river at no extra expense. The cold, however, would make a buying trip more difficult. Just staying warm would be a problem. Ann started a list during the planning session from the items the men said they would need. As before, they planned to ride in the wagon until enough horses were purchased to have everyone mounted. Ann objected saying she wanted to start the trip on her mare. She like the horse and wanted a familiar mount. Eli volunteered to rent a team of horses and ready them for the trip. He would hitch them to one of Zack's wagons on the morning they would depart. The tasks were easily divided among themselves and they set the first of January as the day of departure.

Over the next few days Zack and Ann shopped for the supplies and equipment they would need. With each day Zack felt stronger and more able to do the things he needed to do. One cold, dreary afternoon he rode out to the warehouse. All that was left of the warehouse and cabins was the charred remains of fallen walls. He made his way across the floor of the warehouse with a stout limb he snapped from a tree at the edge of the clearing. Using the stick like a broom he swept back and forth in the snow in the area where he fought Frank Gusterson. After several sweeps he found what he was looking for, his rifle. Bringing it up, he brushed off the snow and ashes. The stock was mostly burned away and patches of rust dotted the barrel. With a cloth he carefully wiped the flint and frizzen. He cocked the hammer and squeezed the trigger. The hammer sprang forward and a shower of sparks was directed into the powder pan. Zack nodded with satisfaction. The mechanics of his rifle were in working order.

The next day Zack stopped at the Hawken Brothers shop. While examining the charred stock Jacob Hawken asked, "What happened to it?"

Zack replied, "Got left in a fire awhile back."

Then Jacob Hawken's full attention focused on the man before him and he exclaimed, "Zachary Clayton? Is it you boy? Why I haven't seen you since you bought this here gun. What has it been, two, three years?"

Zack extend his hand to the talkative gunsmith and during a shake said, "It's been some time, Mister Hawken."

Jacob Hawken grimaced at the damage to the rifle. "Bad business that doings out at that warehouse." Looking up he continued, "You and your wife come through it all right?" Ann's abduction and Snow Logan's death were common knowledge in St. Louis. Accounts of the incidents had been printed in the newspaper with follow-up stories about the coroner's inquest.

"We're doing well," Zack replied.

"And your brother?" Jacob inquired. Zack's intent was to go visit his brother after getting his rifle examined but before he could answer Jacob continued, "I haven't seen him for a spell. He used to be a decent sort. I hope he gets himself squared away. You say hello for me when you see him next, you hear."

"I'll do that, Mister Hawken," Zack replied.

Setting the rifle down on the counter Jacob said, "It appears to work but I'll have to check the temper on the springs and maybe replace them.

If they are still good all you'll need is a stock and a good cleaning. You want anything special in a stock?" He pointed to a rack of stocks ready to be fitted.

Without really looking, Zack replied, "Nothing fancy. I'm more interested in it shooting true again."

With confidence in his trade, Jacob guaranteed, "Oh, it'll do that. Plain or fancy stock." He estimated it would take him two days to restore the rifle and then test fire it.

When Zack rode through the gate at his brother's house he saw four horses tied up at the hitching rail and there were several men standing on the porch. Zack figured them to be responding to the newspaper announcement and decided to visit Toby prior to interrupting James. He tied his horse to the stable fence and walked to the little house to the rear of the main house. Toby answered the door to Zack's knock and invited him in. In the privacy of the little house they shook hands. "How's your back?" Zack inquired.

"I'sa healing," Toby responded, "It pains me less and Lilly says there be only one little hole left. She stuffs gauze in every day."

Zack nodded an understanding. While he patted Toby on the shoulder and said, "Glad to hear that Toby. Is there anything I can do for you?"

Toby declined the offer saying he was well taken care of. Zack thanked him again for pulling him out of the warehouse. And like Nate, Toby responded, "I could'na done it without Nate."

They talked awhile about each other's recovery. Then Zack asked, "How's my brother and Nancy doing?"

Toby went from smiling to a frown and said, "Masta James been busy with General Ashley. They be hiring them fellas on the porch. Masta James be coughin' a bunch and he ain't lookin' so good. Miss Nancy ain't hardly left her room and Lilly says she talks to herself." Then Toby asked about Zack's plan to go west in the spring saying he overheard James talking about it. Zack told Toby about the three wagons he bought and the goal of hauling supplies to Ben Thompson's place.

With a sudden expression of desperation Toby said, "Take us with you, me and Lilly!" Toby saw the look of surprise on Zack's face and without waiting for an answer he presented his case by saying, "I be good with animals and hard work. Lilly be good with cookin' and the likes. We needs to be free."

With a sinking feeling of knowing he must turn Toby down Zack said, "I can't do it Toby. I don't approve of your bondage but it would be like stealing from my brother. You know that."

With down cast eyes Toby nodded a sad understanding but decided to give it one more try and said, "Just think on it some, Masta Zack. Me and Lilly gonna be free. If we ain't goin' with you we find a way to go in the spring.

Taking Toby's hand in a departing handshake Zack said, "I'll think on it."

While Zack waited on the porch to see James he thought on Toby's request. He was aware of a growing number of hard, cruel men who were hiring themselves out as slave chasers. More than once he saw slaves who had run away being led into town with ropes or chains around their necks. It was not hard to envision Toby and Lilly, in a battered condition, being lead through town after being captured. He did not fault their desire to be free but he worried their plan could lead to grave consequences. James' appearance on the porch interrupted Zack's thoughts. James was calling in the next applicant when he saw Zack. He made the excuse of being busy with hiring and promised to send word for a more convenient time for a visit.

*   *   *

The Christmas season was a flurry of social activity in St. Louis and it found Zack and Ann trying to balance their time between preparing for their trip into Illinois and visiting with friends. A few days before Christmas, they were sitting in a café warming up and having a meal. Ann began reminiscing about her parents and her time as a waitress in their café. She was missing her parents during this first holiday season away from them, which was only slightly lessened by the long letters they exchanged. Since the rivers had frozen over, the mail was much slower. She had not heard from them recently and sorely missed the letters. It had become her habit to read their letters to Zack in the evening. "Do you think we can get to Cairo on our trip?" she asked.

"Not likely the best way to go if we're intent on getting the job done as quick as possible in this cold. I figure to go east a ways then turn north," Zack replied. He reached for her hand across the table and in a sympathetic squeeze said, "Let's look for something to send to them today."

On Christmas day Zack and Ann joined the McCrackens along with other friends and family of the Shillers for a Christmas dinner. Ann wore the bright red and yellow blanket capote Zack bought for her. She thought it was a bit gaudy but understood that was the purpose. Zack wanted to be able to see her from afar during the up coming trips. He wore a new wide brimmed gray felt hat. Ann bought the hat and sewed on a colorful hatband. She saw similar colors in the hatbands, serapes and wool belts on the men who had traveled the Santa Fe Trail. She liked the colorful Mexican influence in their clothing.

*   *   *

The first of January dawned cold and clear. The horses' breath streamed from their nostrils as they labored, pulling the canvas covered wagon over the frozen roads toward the river. Eli Diamond steered them down the bank in the path of previous travelers who had made the crossing in the days before. The heavy ridged iron horseshoes tore at the clumps of snow and ice as they rolled toward the east bank. Zack sat in the seat beside Eli. Ann, Nate, and Tom Miller rode in the back, huddled together for warmth. Tom was one of the two Garrett employees that Nate recruited for this trip. Ed Elliott also wanted to go but reluctantly stayed behind to feed the stock in the Garrett corals. Ann's mare was tied to the rear of the wagon. The ice groaned and popped at irregular intervals as they crossed, raising everyone's anxiety. Everyone that is except Eli Diamond. He assured them he had made similar crossings on frozen rivers and the sounds from the ice had no relationship to the heavily laden wagon. Despite Eli's assurances there was a collective sigh of relief when they reached the east bank.

The first two days were disappointing in that Zack was able to buy only one horse. It was becoming obvious that other buyers had preceded them and they would have to travel farther than originally planned. They were pleased, however, with the accommodations Zack and Eli designed and commissioned. When parked for the night, a large canvas tent, supported by poles, extended from the rear of the wagon. Set within the tent was a small iron box stove sitting on detachable legs. The stove had large handles on each side, which fit onto metal hooks mounted underneath the wagon for safe transporting, despite being hot. A detachable stovepipe extended through a riveted metal ring in the tent roof. A warm area for eating and sleeping was provided when the tent and stove were in place. In the morning, after a breakfast of coffee and porridge, the stove was capped and placed on the hooks. The tent was taken down, folded, and loaded in the wagon. Setting up and striking camp quickly became an efficient, cooperative effort.

On the third day Zack bought enough horses to have his crew mounted and the journey began to take on a routine similar to that of the buying trip from Cairo. There was an important difference however. Zack was mainly interested in buying oxen and mules that had not been shod. He was too uncertain about acquiring the services of a blacksmith for the planned spring journey and wanted draft and pack animals that would be less likely to have problems in that circumstance. When they came across horses that would be good pack animals he bought them. There would be plenty of buyers in St. Louis, beside Ned Shiller, who would take them off his hands.

The planned ten day, wide circle trip was in its fourteenth day when Zack decided to close the circle to the area where they originally crossed the river. Nate and Tom were herding twenty-two oxen, ten mules, and nineteen horses. Tom Miller had proven himself to be a hardy, reliable drover on the cold January trail. It was mid morning when they crossed the frozen Mississippi River.

CHAPTER 15

SPRING

Winter slowly loosened its freezing grip on St. Louis during the fourth week of March. The first signs of spring gradually emerged bringing the city to a renewed level of activity. The streets and roads became quagmires of mud as horses and wagons mixed and remixed the sticky goo with their passing. Men and animals labored in the mud to ready for the upcoming ventures to the Rocky Mountains. Within the warming air the sense of competition quickened. The urgency of the competing fur companies to be the first to start the new season percolated into all the related businesses. The wharfs of St. Louis were again a beehive of activity when the great rivers were released from the covers of ice. Goods and people from distant river towns poured in to add to the level of bustle on the streets and in the business establishments.

With each passing day the steamboat pilots reported the ice floes to be rapidly softening, however there were new hazards appearing in the currents as the early spring melt and rains caused the rivers to rise. Large trees were uprooted in the spring erosion and floated down stream. Most of the time they were easily spotted by the river pilots aboard the steamboats but dangerous submerged tangles also resulted during this annual rite. The river pilots had to maintain a constant vigil for the hazardous debris and changing currents as they navigated the mighty rivers.

Patrick McCracken was a happy man as he sloshed through the mud on his way home. His months of diligence on the job had paid off with a promotion to second pilot on a new steamboat. The *Alice* was a newly designed shallow draft stern wheeler capable of carrying three hundred and fifty tons up the Missouri River. Commissioned by the St. Louis Fur Company the *Alice* would carry men, horses and supplies to Fort Kiowa at the mouth of the White River. This trip would not be like the previous long trip for Patrick where he had to winter over at Ben Thompson's trading post. After unloading, the *Alice* would return to St. Louis for another load. In just a day or two he would be on the river again.

Zachary Clayton was also a happy man with the coming of spring. Idleness had made him restless and irritable since returning from Illinois. The severe winter weather of late January and all of February kept him inside with not much to do. The buying of trail and trade goods was completed in January. Now it was just a matter of time and true spring before he could start moving them. He sold the horses he could not use to Ned Shiller at a handsome profit and, as predicted, the demand for good livestock was increasing. He rode out to the corrals he leased to check on his livestock and found them well tended. The corral owner had wisely anticipated a western movement with the growth of the fur trade and built livestock pens northwest of St. Louis. Along with Zack's animals, he was managing the animals of other western bound groups.

Zack and Ann were excited to be moving the first of several loads of goods from the Berthold Mercantile Company warehouse to the leased corrals. Zack hired Jeb Smith to live at and stand guard at their base camp located within a stone's throw of the corral. He helped drive the oxen on the first trip. Jeb had not found carpentry work and left the Garrett Hauling Company. The money was the same working for Zack but within the bargain was a prospect of working for Ben Thompson at the end of the trip or signing on with a flat boat crew to return to St. Louis in the fall. Either prospect appealed to him. Eli Diamond gave him a good recommendation, "A reliable man who learned to handle a team and wagon. If he's as good a carpenter, you'll not do better."

Zack chose a six oxen team to pull the wagon through the muddy streets to the road for the base camp. Their riding horses were tied to the tailgate. He and Jeb used sticks to guide the team as they walked beside the plodding lead animals. Ann rode in the seat usually reserved for a driver managing the reins for a team of horses or mules. Since there were no reins to manage, she sat back to watch the scenery and occasionally pointed out the growing signs of spring. It was evening before they reached the corrals. They set up the stove and tent to live in while they got the base camp organized.

Zack and Ann would make four more similar trips, hauling goods to the base camp. They established the routine of getting loaded in the early morning, traveling the day on the road, spending the night at the camp and returning to their house the next day. On the second trip they left the second wagon and used the third wagon for the subsequent trips. Between trips they began packing their household articles for the last trip to the corrals. Most of the items fit into crates and barrels. The only piece of furniture they decided to take with them was the bed made by Gusterson & Sons.

On the evening before Patrick McCracken's departure for the upper Missouri River, the friends gathered for a farewell dinner. Silas Cooper, from Patrick's last flatboat crew, attended. He had joined Zack's crew for the trip to Ben's place with the expressed purpose of building a flatboat and returning to St. Louis with Ben's furs. Patrick endorsed him for the enterprise and Zack was glad to have him and the other rivermen. Silas did not like steamboats and warned Patrick about a recent incident involving a steamboat blowing up near Memphis. "I don't trust them smokin', belchin' machines," he said, "Give me a flatboat or keelboat any ole time."

Lucy McCracken had a hard time getting through the meal. She became tearful with any mention of Zack and Ann departing. "I don't know what I'm going to do without you two," she blubbered on more that one occasion. Robert was confused by his mother's tears. Previous visits with Zack and Ann were fun and sometimes resulted in a horse ride with Zack. He began to tear with his mother, which would momentarily distract her from her anticipated loss. At one point Patrick reminded her, "It's me that's leaving tomorrow. Not them."

"I know," Lucy responded, "But you'll be back. I may not ever see Ann and Zachary again." She and Robert became tearful again.

*   *   *

One evening, between hauling trips, Zack talked to Ann about Toby and Lilly. He described his last conversation with Toby and what he knew of the fate of runaway slaves.

"We should try to help them in some way if we can," concluded Ann, echoing Zack's thoughts. "I feel like we owe them something. Toby pulled you out of that awful fire and Lilly helped us all," she continued.

"I agree," responded Zack, "But short of helping them run away I don't know what we can do."

After a thoughtful pause Ann suggested, "Maybe your brother will be willing to give them their freedom. We could ask him."

Zack countered, "That's not likely. He's too caught up in the idea of slavery. He gets power from it."

"Then perhaps he'd consider selling them to us. Once we owned them we could do what we want," Ann said, contributing another suggestion.

"I don't know if we have enough money left for that. I've pretty much spent it all on what we need for this venture," Zack pointed out.

Ann rose and returned with her stationary box. She withdrew an envelope from the box and said, "I have a little left from what my parents gave to me."

Zack looked at the paper money and replied, "Well it won't hurt to try. Besides I wanted to say goodbye to James. We'll call on him tomorrow."

*   *   *

Lilly answered the door and greeted Zack and Ann with a smile. After hearing the request to see James she responded, "I'll tell Masta James." In a short time she returned and escorted them to James' office door where she knocked softly.

"Come on in Zachary," James called out. James rose from his desk chair as the door opened and with a sweeping gesture of his arm signaled Zack and Ann to sit in chairs across the desk from him. James was coughing softly into a handkerchief during the gesture and when he returned to his chair he took a deep breath and lowered the handkerchief. Looking at Ann, James said, "How are you Ann?"

Ann returned his greeting with a smile and replied, "I'm well, James. And how are you?"

James leaned back in his chair to cover another cough. When he recovered he replied, "I've had better days. He then looked at his brother and said, "Well Zachary, I expect you'll be back on the trail soon. Do you know when that will be?"

"It'll be a few days yet," Zack replied, "Still have some sorting and packing to do."

With a smile of a winner in a competition James bragged, "Well, I guess my brigade will beat you out of here. They should be on the trail tomorrow."

Deciding not to engage in James' perceived rivalry, and to get to the main point of the visit Zack said, "I want to talk to you about Toby and Lilly."

James reacted with a look of consternation and said, "What are those two Negras up to now? It's been awhile since I've had to teach them some manners."

"It's nothing like that," Zack quickly replied, "I want you to set them free."

James reacted with a look of surprise and before he could say something he began a series of shallow coughs. When he recovered, he made eye contact with Zack and with a wheeze in his voice he said, "You want me to do what?"

With determined seriousness, Zack replied, "Set them free."

James leaned back and with equal seriousness said, "I won't do that! They're mine, my property. I own them."

"Then sell them to me," responded Zack, "Name a fair price."

"And what would you do with them, brother?" James countered angrily, "Set them free I suppose." Gesturing to include Ann he continued, "You two haven't turned into godless abolitionist have you?"

"No we have not," responded Zack, "It just isn't decent for one man to own another."

James paused and eyed the couple, "You two know, of course, that it's a crime to preach abolition in this state."

Ann started to respond but Zack, placing his hand on hers, signaled her to not engage his brother in a political argument. Zack knew it was futile to argue with James. He also knew he wanted to be on the offensive and countered, "And you know, of course, that it's a crime to do business with river pirates."

James' eyes widened and his face reddened, in dramatic contrast to his paleness. "You don't know what you're talking about!" James almost shouted.

Zack knew he was back on the offensive and continued, "There's at least three fellows I'm sure I could persuade to tell their stories to Marshal Dufrane. And I'm sure Marshal Dufrane would be very interested in what Pettis, Potter and Black Dog know about stolen furs. Who do you think put those rifle splinters in Snow Logan?"

James quickly surmised Zack apparently knew enough about the business with Snow Logan to be real trouble. James, however, was not trapped and rapidly calculated his next move. He rose from his chair and while shaking his finger at Zack said, "That is something that should be discussed in private, between gentlemen, not in front of a woman."

Zack quickly rose to meet the feigned physical challenge. "She stays," he countered using his dominate size to set a limit of how far James could go.

The paleness returned to James face as he put the handkerchief to his lips and he slowly returned to his chair. Then with a steely calmness he said, "You do what you may, Zachary. You know how the coroner's inquest treated the matter with Snow Logan. They know what to do for a prominent citizen, such as myself. If you think you can change that, go for it." After a pause, then with a wave of his hand James said, "Now I want you to leave and don't come back."

Zack extended his hand to Ann who rose to join him. Zack knew James had successfully dismantled his brief advantage and there wasn't anything left to do but leave. He did not have the time to go hunting for Snow Logan's former gang and James was probably right about being given preferential treatment according to his status in the community. To continue to try to work something out with James would be useless.

Zack and Ann briskly exited the house onto the porch. As Zack was turning to shut the door, he heard James shouting, "Lilly, Lilly, you get that no account Toby and bring him to me. Now!"

Zack and Ann were just reaching their horses at the hitching rail when they saw Lilly exit the rear of the house in a run. By the time they got mounted, Lilly and Toby were hurrying toward the rear door. Zack watched them disappear into the house. He handed the reins of his horse to Ann and said, "Wait here. I'm going to scout this out."

Zack reentered the front door without knocking and proceeded to retrace his steps to the office. When he entered the hall he heard James' voice shouting, "Don't you ever think of running off!" As he reached the open door he heard the sound of a blow and Toby's pleading voice, "Please Masta, please."

Stepping into the room Zack saw James swinging a leather belt toward Toby's back. Lilly was hunched over on the floor sobbing with Toby kneeling over her trying to protect her from the belt. The belt struck Toby and James drew back for another blow. Out of the corner of his eye James saw Zack rushing toward him but did not have enough time to prepare for the clash. Zack grabbed James by the swinging arm and immediately wrenched away the belt. With a quick movement Zack turned James and reached for his coat collar. He pulled down the coat, instantly restraining James' arms. "You two get out of here!" Zack ordered to the terrified slaves. Toby and Lilly scurried from the room.

Guiding James by the grip on his coat, Zack maneuvered him into a chair. Then changing his grip to the front of James' shirt Zack menacingly threatened, "I don't abide by the beating of people or critters for no good reason. If you continue with this you just may be the one to get a beating."

James was startled and completely taken aback by his brother's swift, unexpected attack and felt a sudden rush of fear. Zack continued his threat, "I may not be able to get you to set them free but I swear if I ever hear of you beating them again I'll thrash you to an inch of your life. Do you understand me?"

Aunt Milly, who had been upstairs tending to Nancy, heard the commotion in the office, and quickly, but quietly descended the stairs. She heard the back door slam as Toby and Lilly beat a hasty retreat. Cautiously she eased up to the office door and peeked around the doorframe. She saw James nodding his head yes to his brother who had her master pinned in a chair.

Zack saw the movement of Aunt Milly's head and ordered her to step into the room. "Your master here has just agreed to never beat Toby and Lilly again," Zack announced, "If for some reason he changes his mind I want you to send word to me. Can you do that?"

With her eyes widened from bewilderment of what she was seeing, and from the authoritative manner in which she was instructed Aunt Milly replied, "Yas sur, Masta Zachary."

Zack loosened his grip on James's shirt and stepped away considering if he wanted to add anything to the harsh encounter. He decided he had said enough. James looked sufficiently intimidated. He backed toward the door.

Choking on some phlegm James gagged and then spit into his handkerchief. Rising slowly from the chair he pointed a finger at Zack and said, "Marshal Dufrane will hear about this."

Zack paused in the doorway and in a voice that communicated a deadly seriousness responded, "That won't save you from a beating."

Zack realized he just may have put Toby and Lilly in more danger by his rough handling of James. His brother was not all that forgiving and was certainly capable of taking out his frustration on his slaves. By the time he got to the front porch, Zack decided he was going to have to help Toby and Lilly run away. He was surprised that Ann was not where he left her and stepped away from the house to look around. He spotted the horses tied up in front of the slave quarters. Ann must have seen Toby and Lilly leave the house and followed them.

Ann was examining the welts across Toby's shirtless back when Zack entered the small house. "Is he hurt bad?" Zack asked.

"Skin's not broken," Ann replied, "Lilly's pretty shaken up by it all."

Zack glanced over at Lilly who continued to sob while she sat in the corner with her knees drawn up to her chest. Turning back to Toby he announced, "We had not better stay here long. My brother will get suspicious and probably take it out on you. Toby, you and Lilly get together what you'll need and meet me tonight, just after dark, down by that big Oak tree in the corner. Do it all quiet like. I'll get you out of here to some place safe."

Toby tried to grin through a grimace of pain and nodded his head in understanding. In a wounded whisper he said, "Thank you, Masta Za..." and hesitated to complete the sentence. He knew that at least part of what this whole affair was about was his not having to call another man "Masta" and figured that now was as good as time as any to get started. He stood up from the stool to face Zack and repeated, "Thank you. We'll be there."

James sat at his desk for a long time after his brother left. The exertion and fear left him feeling drained. He poured a drink for himself from the brandy decanter sitting on his desk. After the first big gulp he sipped slowly and thought about what had occurred in his office. He knew Zack must have considerable information about the river pirating operation by the names he used and knowing the details about Snow Logan's wounds. James wondered, *But how will he use that information?* He correctly surmised that Zack probably had not reported that information up until now out of some regard for the family honor. And he probably would not use it just to obtain the freedom of slaves. He might, however, use it to counter any charges or complaints rendered against him with the law. So the threat about going to Marshal Dufrane, about being pushed around, was out. James decided to wait it out. *After all,* he thought, *Zachary will be leaving for the mountains in a few days and things will get back to normal.*

With most of the livestock having been picked up by the new owners Nate Plummer did not have much to do around the corrals. He was waiting for word from Zack to report to the base camp and thought it must be soon when he saw Zack and Ann ride into the barnyard. After a few minutes of getting caught up with each other and some discussion about a date to depart, Zack revealed his main purpose for the visit. He asked Nate to accompany him to collect Toby and Lilly. Nate agreed to the plan.

This would give him the chance to do something for Toby and Lilly. He felt a kinship with Toby for his role in the warehouse fire and appreciated the care Lilly had provided in their snowbound confinement. They agreed upon a meeting place. Nate would bring two borrowed horses from the Garrett corral for the journey. During the discussion, Ann was not hearing a role for herself and insisted on being included. Zack tried to talk her out of it but she prevailed.

                    *   *   *

That evening a warm spring rain was wetting the landscape when Nate, leading two saddled horses, arrived at the rendezvous point. He had just pulled up under a heavily budding Black Gum tree to await Zack and Ann when he saw them turn a corner and ride his way. Nate dismounted to check the cinches on the horses. Dark would be coming a bit earlier with the cloud filled skies and he wanted to use the remaining light to insure the readiness of the horses. Zack and Ann dismounted to join Nate. There was no real reason for them to whisper but because of the nature of their mission they went over their plan in hushed tones. "Can them two ride good enough iffen we have to run fer it?" Nate asked.

"I'm not sure," Zack responded, "If they can't, we'll just have to teach them in a hurry." Then as an afterthought Zack added. " Might be best just to tell them to hold on with us leading the horses."

In the growing darkness, Zack led the way with Ann riding behind him and Nate bringing up the rear. He planned to ride right by James' house so he could see if there was any suspicious activity that might cause a change of plan. There was none. The house was dimly lit and no movement was detected.

Zack proceeded to the corner of the property where Toby and Lilly were supposed to be waiting. A flock of squabbling birds had chosen the big Oak to roost in for the night. They were only beginning to settle down when Zack called out in a forced whisper, "Toby…Toby." The sound and the movement below distressed the birds and they began to squabble and rustle anew. The noise of the birds seemed deafening when quiet secrecy was desired. Zack looked around cautiously and called again, "Toby...Toby."

Ann was the first to see movement emerging from the bushes behind the tree. "There they are," she whispered.

Toby and Lilly were also nervous about the noisy birds and unsure about the dark shapes they could barely make out in the gloomy night. Toby recognized Zack voice with the second calling, and taking Lilly by the hand, made his way to the Oak. Zack and Nate dismounted to assist the now fugitive slaves into the saddles. They handed the bundles of clothes and scant person possessions to Ann who was prepared to secure them with a short length of rope to her pommel. When Toby and Lilly were safely in the saddles Zack whispered, "Can you two ride?"

"Pretty good," Toby replied in a whisper as he gripped both hands on the pommel. Zack could not see Lilly shake her head no. She was frightened to the point of being mute. Zack and Nate remounted, keeping the reins of the horses in their hands.

""Let's move out," Zack whispered.

The rain softened road muted the horses' hooves as the short string of riders made their way through the darkness. Zack chose a route that would lead them directly out of town. For a short while they would be going out of their way in order to avoid potential discovery on the more traveled thoroughfares. The clouds began to break up permitting narrow beams of moonlight to reach the ground as they rode in silence.

It was after midnight when they approached the base camp. Zack rode ahead to alert Jeb Smith. He was pleased to find Jeb to be a light sleeper and found himself challenged as he dismounted near the tent. They had a lantern lit when the others rode in. Jeb wasn't all that happy about having run away slaves in the camp. It wasn't that he approved of slavery. He was aware of the kind of men who chased run away slaves and the potential for trouble by having Toby and Lilly in camp. But he agreed to help and set about making space for two more people in the tent.

*   *   *

Eli Diamond pulled up in front of the house when Zack and Ann were loading the household belongings into their wagon. With his assistance they loaded the last of the crates and trunks. Eli announced he was getting married in May to the widow woman he had been courting. He knew Zack and Ann were not going to be able to attend the wedding but he wanted to invite them anyway.

"Oh, I wish we had time to meet her," Ann exclaimed as she gave him a congratulatory hug. Zack offered his congratulations in a hardy handshake.

Turning back to Ann while putting his hat in his hands Eli said, "I'll never forget you Misses Clayton. I don't know when I ever felt so warmed and welcomed by someone as I have by you. Except, of course, by the future Misses Diamond." Then with a devilish, teasing grin he added, "If I ever have to face down road agents again I'd want you and your pistol by my side."

Ann chuckled at his reference to the incident on the road from Cairo. "And I, Mister Diamond, would want you there with your whip," she graciously replied.

Turning back to Zack and extending his hand again, Eli said, "Mister Clayton, I don't think I've ever had so much adventure and made money doing it before I met you. I thank you for it."

Zack shook the stocky teamster's hand and replied, "You are very welcome Mister Diamond." Then with a teasing grin added, "And if I ever run onto road agents again I'll turn them over to you two."

A minute later Eli Diamond was back in his wagon, tongue clicking his team into motion.

After a final tearful goodbye in the road, Lucy and Robert McCracken waved again at the wagon as it turned out of sight. Robert carefully held a letter Ann had given to him to mail for her. It was the last letter she would write to her parents from St. Louis, knowing it may be a very long time before she could post another one.

*   *   *

When the lumbering wagon drew to a halt at the Garrett corrals Nate Plummer, Tom Miller and Ed Elliott were ready. Zack introduced Ann to the new man and described them as Nate's drover crew. Ed shyly acknowledged the introduction. Zack pointed to a space in the wagon for their belongings. As the men loaded their bedrolls and bundles of clothes into the back of the wagon, Zack noted that all were carrying a rifle and had a pistol tucked in a belt.

Taking notice of Zack's scrutiny, Nate said, "My crew balked at spendin' their hard earned wages on these here used guns but I tole 'em there ain't no place to spend money where we're goin'.

Zack inwardly smiled at Nate's brashness. "Nate's right boys, and if we didn't have our guns we just might not be around to spend money ever again," Zack said reinforcing Nate's claim to leadership over the two younger men. Zack made a superficial examination of the firearms and nodded with approval.

"I ain't had time to get in much shootin' practice with 'em," Nate announced.

"Well, I think as part of getting organized for the trail you'll just have to set up a place to shoot. Everyone in the crew could probably use some practice," responded Zack. He wanted to put Nate in charge of more and more details over time. Checking out everyone's proficiency with firearms certainly was within Nate's capability. "And there'll be some who need the practice more than others. You'll have to sort them out," Zack added.

Nate was especially pleased with the degree of confidence Zack
expressed in front of Tom and Ed. "Iffen you're ready Mister Clayton, me
and my men will get this team movin'?" Nate offered.

Zack gestured to Ann to climb into the seat and he followed. Once
seated he signaled to Nate, who had walked up to the lead oxen. Nate in
turn called to his men, "Move 'em out."

　　　　　　　*　　　　　　　*　　　　　　　*

For two days Zack directed the organizing and loading in preparation
for the trail. The mounds of goods were reduced to bags and crates that
would be carried by pack mules. Silas Cooper and his two boatmen
arrived with the tools they would need for building another flatboat. Jeb
Smith began spending time with them. He was curious about flatboat
construction. Early on, Zack was pleased with the compatibility of the
men he had gathered. If they could work as a team on the trail, the tasks
and perils of the long journey would be easier to surmount.

Zack was also pleased with the response he got when he told the crew
about Toby and Lilly. Some of the men were concerned with breaking the
law in Missouri and were assured by Zack that he would take full respon-
sibility for any consequences. Besides they were not going to be in
Missouri very long. Those with doubts agreed that they could look the
other way in regards to the runaway slaves being in camp.

In parties of two and three, Nate took the men to the shooting range he
set up and gave Zack a report on the levels of proficiency each man displayed. At the end of one such report, Zack instructed, "Be sure to get my
wife out there for some practice. It's been awhile since she shot her pistol."

Late in the afternoon Zack saw Nate leading Tom Miller and Ann
toward the gully where shooting practice occurred. He followed with his
rifle and arrived just as Tom fired at a target. He watched as Nate set up
some bottles for pistol shooting. Both Ann and Tom missed with their
first shots. Nate had them talk through the steps of reloading. They fired

again and both hit their targets. Then Zack took a turn with a pistol and shattered a bottle. As he was reloading, Nate and Tom returned to camp.

Ann was looking off to the west as if to imagine the miles ahead. "Zachary," she said, "I hope we don't have to use our guns except for hunting."

Placing his arms around her from behind Zack drew her close and replied, "Me too, but if we must, I think we're ready."

*   *   *

In the morning everyone was up early. The camp was noisy and some-what confused as the oxen were being hitched to the wagons and the pack mules were being loaded. Zack knew this first morning of getting started on the trail would take longer. After a few days, men and animals would develop a routine and it would go much faster. Toby and Lilly were help-ing where they could. When Zack saw them he ordered them into a wagon. "I'll find work enough for you two," he told them, "when we are further down the trail. Don't worry, you'll earn your keep."

When it looked like all was in readiness to roll one of the mules broke loose while protesting its load. The mule brayed and bucked until the packs were shaken off, then it ran off. Nate pursued the mule over a rise while Tom and Ed gathered the packs. When Zack saw Nate returning, leading the mule, he noticed Nate had his horse up to a full gallop. When Nate got closer to the camp he called out, "WE GOT BAD COMPANY ACOMIN'!" Nate had recognized James Clayton's carriage from afar, trav-eling in the direction of the camp, and thought it best to give an early warning to Zack. Riding up to Zack, Nate reported what he had seen.

Zack quickly gave orders to Ann and the men who gathered around, "Ann, you make sure Toby and Lilly are well hidden. And tell them to stay hidden!" Ann rushed off toward the lead wagon. "Now the rest of you get back into position to roll. I'll handle this," he continued to the gathered men. They returned to their assigned wagons. Nate led the errant mule back to where its load had been dumped.

Zack rode out past the stringed mules and pulled to a halt just as the carriage topped the rise. He dismounted to await his brother. As the carriage drew closer he saw an accompanying rider and someone other than James was driving the team of black carriage horses.

The carriage driver slowed the horses and received instructions from someone in the rear seat to halt when coming to within a few feet of Zack. The rider and driver were not familiar to Zack. Both had a lean, cruel look about them. Zack guessed them to be runaway slave chasers that James had hired.

James stepped down from the carriage, and while gesturing to the rider said, "Search the wagons."

Zack moved his rifle from the cradle of his arm and pointed it in the direction of the rider. "There'll be no searching!" Zack spoke, countermanding the order.

As James approached he said, "Toby and Lilly ran off and I think you're behind it. I think they're here, with you."

Keeping his eyes and rifle on the rider Zack repeated, "There'll be no searching!"

James was livid with his order being overturned and rushed at Zack, drawing a pistol from under his coat. Zack saw the pistol coming up and countered by swinging his rifle barrel to block its path. With a snap of the muzzle on the pistol barrel, he knocked it from James' hand. Then Zack stepped forward and pushed James to the ground. The slave chasers moved their hands toward their pistols. Zack heard a pistol cock from behind him and out of the corner of his eye saw Ann bringing her pistol up toward the slave chasers. Then Zack heard the cocking of other firearms and with a quick glance to the rear saw several of the men raising rifles toward the slave chasers. Moving their hands slowly the slave chasers raised their arms.

While keeping a watch on his brother, Zack ordered the slave chasers to dismount. James was winded by the exertion and being pushed to the ground had him fighting for breath. He sat up and was extracting a handkerchief from his coat sleeve when Zack reached down to pick up James' pistol. Zack cocked the pistol, aimed and fired between James' boots. Wide-eyed with fear James scooted back. The black carriage team began to prance nervously and James scooted again, away from the hooves. At the same time he began coughing.

"Keep a watch on James," Zack directed to Nate, who had stepped up closer. He handed James' pistol to Nate. Then Zack walked toward the slave chaser who had been driving the carriage. With intimidating, steely eye contact Zack extracted the pistol from the man's belt. Stepping back he cocked the pistol then slowly aimed it at the man's chest. With deliberate intent he gradually lowered the pistol, pausing at the belly, groin, and a knee. He fired into the ground between the man's feet. With his hands in the air the slave chaser danced backward in alarm. Again the horses pranced nervously. Tucking the pistol in his belt Zack approached the second slave chaser and in the same intimidating manner fired his pistol at his feet.

Zack noticed some links of chain dangling from a bulging saddlebag. He lifted the flap and extracted a hinged iron collar, which had a lock and a length of chain attached. Handing it to a slave chaser he ordered the collar to be placed on James. He pushed both men in that direction. James tried to struggle against the placement of the collar but was easily subdued by the bigger men. "Now, put him in the carriage," Zack directed. The slave chasers did as they were told.

"If you two ever come after me again, you'll not leave where you found me. You understand me?" Zack threatened the slave chasers.

"Yes sir," they responded.

"Get mounted!" Zack ordered.

Stepping in the direction of the rear seat of the carriage Zack removed the flints from the slave chasers' pistols. He signaled Nate to do the same with James' pistol. Then he placed the pistols on the floorboard. Looking up to James, who was coughing and tugging on the iron collar, Zack said, "James, I'm sorry it had to come to this but don't you ever come at me with a pistol again. I do not want to shoot you but I will." James was so preoccupied with the collar and coughing Zack was not sure James heard what was said. Instead of repeating himself Zack simply ordered, "Get out of here!"

The carriage and rider turned to follow the trail from which they came. After going a few yards the trail crew's firearms were lowered and the hammers were carefully returned to safety. Turning to Nate, Zack said, "Mister Plummer, follow them past that rise just to be safe." Nate mounted his horse and turned toward the moving carriage. "Now for the rest of you," he continued, "I thank you. Let's get that mule loaded. We're burning daylight."

The men moved toward their respective assignments digesting what they had just witnessed. It was obvious to them Zack had the capacity for decisive leadership and by that they felt assured. Some worried, however, that this small, bloodless skirmish was an omen for things to come.

From the back of his horse, Zack surveyed the length of the caravan. The mules were ready and all the bullwhackers were in place. Looking to the rear he saw Nate topping the rise at a steady, undisturbed pace. Raising his arm in a sweeping forward gesture Zack called out, "Move 'em out."

The wagons lurched to a start as the walking bullwhackers cracked their whips and called to the oxen. The string of mules, tied to the last wagon, responded to the tension on the leads by stepping to follow. Zack rode up to the rear of the first wagon where Ann had gone to comfort Toby and Lilly. When he called her name Ann poked her head out of the canvass cover. "Ride with me for a spell," Zack invited as he patted the rear haunch of his horse, signaling where he wanted her to sit. Ann carefully stepped up on the tailgate and when Zack was in position placed her hand on his shoulder. She stepped out and while grabbing both his shoulders slid into position behind him. She wrapped her arms around his waist.

Zack guided his horse to ride parallel with the wagon, "Well, we're on our way, Misses Clayton."

Placing her cheek to his back and squeezing with her arms Ann replied, "That we are, Mister Clayton."

ABOUT THE AUTHOR

DUANE HOWARD is a member of the WESTERN WRITERS OF AMERICA and the WEST ROCKIES WRITERS' CLUB. His short stories and articles have appeared in COWBOY MAGAZINE and NEWCOMERS MAGAZINE. He lives with his wife on the western slope of the Rocky Mountains. He divides his time between gardening, hunting, fishing and writing.

Printed in the United States
52336LVS00004B/1-30

9 780595 187515